Rules We're Meant to Break

RULES WE'RE MEANT TO BREAK

NATALIE WILLIAMSON

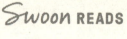

Swoon READS

NEW YORK

A Swoon Reads Book

An imprint of Feiwel and Friends and Macmillan Publishing Group, LLC

Rules We're Meant to Break. Copyright © 2019 by Natalie Williamson. All rights reserved.

Printed in the United States of America. For information, address Swoon Reads,

175 Fifth Avenue, New York, NY 10010.

Our books may be purchased in bulk for promotional, educational, or business use.
Please contact your local bookseller or the Macmillan Corporate and Premium Sales
Department at (800) 221-7945 ext. 5442 or by email at
MacmillanSpecialMarkets@macmillan.com.

Library of Congress Cataloging-in-Publication Data

Names: Williamson, Natalie, author.

Title: Rules we're meant to break / Natalie Williamson.

Other titles: Rules we are meant to break

Description: First edition. | New York: Swoon Reads, 2019. | Summary: High
school senior Amber falls for star basketball player Jordan despite the
strict anti-attachment rules she has long followed that stem from her
mother's dating track record.

Identifiers: LCCN 2018039218 | ISBN 9781250313263 (hardcover)

Subjects: | CYAC: Love—Fiction. | Dating (Social customs)—Fiction. | High
schools—Fiction. | Schools—Fiction. | Mothers and daughters—Fiction.

Classification: LCC PZ7.1 W563 Rul 2019 | DDC [Fic]—dc23

LC record available at https://lccn.loc.gov/2018039218

BOOK DESIGN BY KATIE KLIMOWICZ

First edition, 2019

10 9 8 7 6 5 4 3 2 1

swoonreads.com

For Danny, my partner in everything
I couldn't have done any of this without you

And for Gracie, the Buffy to my Amber
I'll see you on the other side of the rainbow bridge

prologue

I stare at the clock all through last period, willing time to speed up so the final bell will hurry up and ring. Today is Friday and also my birthday, and my best friend Hannah and I are going shopping for something to wear to dinner tonight. My mom and her boyfriend, Howard, are taking us to this fancy French place across town, so I want to look extra nice. Partly because of the restaurant, and partly because some of Howard's extended family will be there, including his nephew, Tyler.

Tyler, who came to watch his school play football against mine two weeks ago and made sure to sit next to me in the bleachers. Tyler, who slipped his hand into mine somewhere around halftime and didn't let go for the rest of the game. Tyler, who pulled me aside before I left and kissed me until I was breathless. Tyler, who I've seen three times since then, all of which involved more excellent kissing and hands in interesting places.

So, yeah. I'm a little excited about tonight. I haven't been able to keep the stupid grin off my face all day.

Finally, finally, the bell rings and I snatch my books off my desk and scramble toward the door. I'm moving so fast that I knock into someone on my way out of the room.

"Sorry!" I yelp, jumping back.

"It's okay," the guy says easily, and I look over and see that the person I almost knocked into is Jordan Baugh, possibly the hottest guy in all of ninth grade. He was my number-one crush this year before I realized Tyler liked me back, and I'm still not totally immune to him. I blink at him like an idiot, but he grins at me. "I was looking at my phone, anyway. Go ahead."

"Thanks." I stare at him a second longer before I duck my head and rush away.

I make a quick stop at my locker to grab my backpack and then go find Hannah at hers.

"Hey, birthday girl," she says when she sees me coming. "I have to get one more thing and then I'm ready. Matt said he'd meet us at the car."

"Cool." Matt is Hannah's older brother and our most frequent chauffeur since he got his license this summer. Luckily he's pretty cool as far as older brothers go, and he doesn't seem to mind driving us around most of the time. "Do you care if he drops us off at my place first? I don't want to have to carry our backpacks around the whole time."

"I figured," Hannah says, slamming her locker door closed.

We find Matt in the parking lot and he lets me ride shotgun and insists that I pick the music again, like he did this morning. I go with Taylor Swift to see how he'll react, and Hannah and I both crack up laughing when he lets out a defeated sigh, rolls down the window, and blasts the music.

"Only on your birthday, Richter," he says, pointing a finger at me when he drops us off in front of my mom's apartment building.

"Noted." I grin at him as Hannah and I get out of the car.

We take the stairs to the third floor, still giggling about Matt as we come out into the hallway and head for number 304.

"And when he hit that high note!" I'm saying to her as I turn my key in the lock and push open the door.

"Right?" Hannah asks, following me into the apartment. But then she stops short and frowns at something over my shoulder. "Whoa. Where did your couch go?"

I whip around to look and freeze when I see my living room. The leather couch that used to be against the left wall is gone, the dents in the carpet the only sign that anything was ever there at all. I stare at it for a second, not understanding what this means. But then hot awareness creeps up my spine and I take a deep breath and blow it out as I drop my backpack on the floor and step further into the room.

Hannah stays frozen on the welcome mat as I move into the kitchen and open the pantry cupboard.

"Amber?" she asks, as I slam the cabinet closed again and start toward the bedrooms. "What's going on?"

I don't answer her. Instead I keep moving, stepping into my room to verify that yes, everything is the way I left it this morning. My bathroom is close to normal, but the scale in the corner is gone, and so are the guest hand towels. In my mother's room, I find more dents in the carpet. One of the mismatched nightstands and the dresser are gone. Mom's bras and underwear and workout clothes are stacked on the bed in neat piles, and a pair of her shoes is tucked against the far wall.

I close my eyes for a second and then head back out to the

main living space, ignoring Hannah's worried gaze. I go over to my backpack, pull out my phone, and call my mom's cell. She's at work this afternoon, and normally that means calls to her cell will go to voice mail. But she answers on the first ring, and that's how I know what she's going to say before I even ask the question. I still ask it though. Because there's a routine to these things by this point.

"Mom," I say, listening to her breathing on the other end of the line. "Why is all of Howard's stuff gone?"

❋

Half an hour later Hannah and I are sitting on one of the benches in New Market, outside of the little boutique where I wanted to buy a dress to wear to dinner tonight. There's no point in buying the dress now, because dinner obviously isn't happening. But I wanted to walk, and New Market is the closest place to my apartment that made sense. So here we are.

"Did she say why?" Hannah asks me now, breaking the silence for the first time in a while. "I mean, I thought things between them were fine."

"I heard them fighting a few weeks ago. But only that one time, so I thought . . ." I stop and shake my head. "It doesn't matter what I thought. She always does this. She always ruins everything. Which is why I should've known. I should've seen this coming. I've had enough practice by now."

Howard is the third guy who's lived with us since my dad left when I was five, and none of them have ever lasted long. Mom didn't say much on the phone, but she said enough for me to know that while Howard's move-out day wasn't her choice, him leaving definitely was.

"Amber," Hannah says, reaching out to put a hand on my shoulder. "No. Ugh, God. This sucks."

"Tell me about it." I shrug off her hand and get to my feet, my face hot. "But we're here and I have Mom's credit card to buy myself a dress. So we should still go shopping, right?"

"I don't know if that's—" Hannah starts, but I give her a look that shuts her up.

I try on a ton of shirts and dresses in the boutique, but nothing fits right and I can't stand to look at myself in the mirror right now because my face is blotchy and red and my mouth is a thin line. So we leave without buying anything and go to the bookstore, where I buy myself a hundred dollars' worth of horror novels. Normally romance is more my thing, but blood and guts sound a lot better to me right now.

"Where to next?" Hannah asks, shading her eyes and looking around. "We could go get something to eat. Or maybe look at the record store?"

"Let's go to The Pet Shop," I say, my gaze catching on the sign across the parking lot.

"Okay," Hannah agrees, linking her arm through mine and marching us in that direction.

I had a hamster named Neville in middle school who died before Howard moved in with us last year, but Mom wouldn't let me get another one since Howard is allergic to pet dander. Today seems like the perfect day to fix that problem. It is my birthday, after all.

I'm thinking about small mammals as we approach the store, trying to decide what to do. Should I get another hamster, since I loved Neville so much? Or a rat since they're supposed to be sweet but would probably freak Mom out more?

"Is there a puppy tied up to that tree, or am I imagining things?" Hannah asks.

I look where she's pointing and see she's right: There's a black and tan puppy tied up to the tree in the little planter in front of The Pet Shop. It's warm today, in the high eighties, but the puppy doesn't have a water bowl or anything nearby. Its little tongue is hanging out as it pants rapidly in an attempt to cool itself down.

Hannah and I exchange looks and rush over to the dog. It sees us coming and gets to its feet, straining at the leash tying it to the tree, tail wagging furiously. But then it chokes, and I realize the leash is one of those noose kinds that you loop around the dog's neck, not clip to a collar. "Hold on, baby," I say to the puppy, closing the rest of the distance between us and holding out a hand for it to sniff. Hannah goes for the leash on the tree while I pick the puppy up and carefully loosen the makeshift collar so that I can take it off.

"What kind of asshole would leave their puppy outside a freaking *pet store*?" Hannah says, untangling the leash from the tree.

I look into the little puppy's face and feel tears pricking the backs of my eyes as it licks me. "The kind of asshole who isn't coming back."

Hannah's face falls. "You think so?"

"If I had to guess, yeah. But let's go in and check."

We meet the owner of The Pet Shop, who introduces herself as Stephanie, and after checking with her employees and customers over the intercom, she confirms our suspicions that the puppy was dumped.

"It happens more often than you'd think," Stephanie says, sighing and reaching out to scratch the puppy's head as it laps up water. "People think it's better to leave them here than at the shelter because they'll be found quickly. They assume we can adopt them out. But most of the time, we have to call the shelter too."

"You do?" I ask, looking from her to the puppy, who abandons the water bowl to come lick my legs.

"Yeah," Stephanie says. "But don't worry. This little lady won't stay in a shelter long. Puppies find homes really quickly. It's the older dogs I worry more about."

I bite my lip and look down at the puppy's sweet face, then reach down to pick her up. She looks like a shepherd of some kind, though it's hard to tell for sure, and her big brown eyes suck me in as she snuggles into my lap.

"Oh no," Hannah says, and I look over at her.

"What?"

She shakes her head and looks at Stephanie. "Don't worry about calling the shelter. What all do we need to get so we can take this pup home?"

❋

We have to call Matt to pick us up because we can't carry the bed, toys, and twenty-pound bag of dog food back to my place. His eyes widen when he pulls up to the curb in front of the store, but he gets out and helps us load everything without a word. I get shotgun again, and the puppy stays in my lap.

"Who's this?" Matt asks, looking over at me as he starts the car back up.

"Buffy," I say.

He reaches over to stroke a hand down Buffy's back, then puts the car in gear. "Okay then," he says, and he drives us home.

By the time my mom gets back from work at five thirty, Buffy is asleep on her new dog bed, which I set up along the blank wall where Howard's couch used to be. Hannah and I are on the floor on either side of her in spite of the love seat and chair Howard left behind, and we've got season six of *Buffy the Vampire Slayer* playing on the TV.

"Amber?" Mom says, looking at all of us, and I can hear the bite in her tone. She knew I'd be upset, but she obviously wasn't expecting me to bring home a dog.

"Mom," I say evenly, and we stare at each other for a long moment. I dare her with my eyes to ask me about the dog, to try telling me I have to let Buffy go.

Finally, Mom sighs. "Do you still want to go to dinner, or would you rather I order in pizza?"

"Pizza is fine."

Mom blows out a breath and heads back to her bedroom to change. Her footsteps falter around what I'd guess is the doorway to her room, and for a second my heart squeezes in my chest. But I push that feeling aside, because I'm still angry right now and being angry is a lot easier than crying.

We eat pizza on the floor and then Hannah and I take Buffy for a walk around the apartment complex. My phone buzzes in my pocket as we're walking, and I pull it out to find a text from Tyler.

Hey. Uncle Howie told me what went down with your mom. I'm so sorry.

Hope surges in my chest and I hurriedly hand Buffy's leash to Hannah so I can text him back.

Thanks. Since we had to miss out on dinner tonight, do you maybe want to hang out tomorrow? We could go see a movie or something.

The little bubble showing he's typing pops up almost immediately, but it takes him a long time to reply.

I don't think that's a great idea. It'd be weird, you know?
Happy birthday though.

I suck in a breath, and Hannah holds out her hand.
"Show me." I pass over my phone. "Shit."
And that's when I start to cry.
Hannah guides me to one of the picnic tables by the pool and wraps an arm around my shoulders, waiting without saying a word until I've gotten everything out.

"This is the worst birthday ever," I say finally, with a huge sniff.

"Yeah," Hannah says. But then she leans down and scoops Buffy up, depositing her in my lap. "It hasn't *all* been bad though. Right?"

I rub Buffy's ears between my fingers and lean in so her little face is right next to mine. "No. It hasn't all been bad. But I can't keep doing this, Han."

"Doing what?"

"Getting my hopes up. Letting myself believe that the next guy will be different. I was starting to really like Howard, you know?"

"I know," Hannah says quietly.

"And Tyler . . ."

She sighs. "I know."

We sit in silence for a while, long enough that the sky starts getting dark, and then suddenly I sit up straight.

"What?" Hannah asks.

"Maybe what I need," I say, looking over at her, "is to start preparing for the next guy right now."

She frowns at me. "What do you mean?"

"Well there's always a next guy, right?" Hannah gives me a look like she's not sure how to respond to that without sounding like a jerk, so I keep going. "And since I know that already, I should have known better than to get involved with Tyler, or even to start liking Howard in the first place."

"I don't know," Hannah says. "It wasn't all bad with them, right? There was some good stuff too."

I shake my head. "Yeah, but they're still gone, and today still sucked. If I make sure I don't get attached to anyone next time, it'll be better for me when things end. For everyone, really."

Hannah doesn't look totally convinced, but she doesn't disagree with me out loud, so I'm calling that a win. I get to my feet and set Buffy down gently, taking her leash in hand.

"Come on," I say to Hannah. "I want to do this now, before I forget."

"Do what now?" Hannah asks, her brow furrowing as she gets to her feet.

"Write down the rules for next time," I say.

"Rules? What did you have in mind?"

When everything is said and done, I end up with nine rules to follow for the next time one of Mom's boyfriends moves in.

1. *Always keep your eyes on the horizon.*

2. *Children of Mom's boyfriends are roommates to be tolerated, not friends.*

3. *Get used to introducing yourself to strangers. It's going to happen a lot. (Of course, if said stranger looks like a creeper, throw this rule out the window and run.)*

4. *Related, get used to spending holidays with strangers too, because that's pretty much the norm.*

5. Protect your plate at all large meal gatherings, holidays or otherwise.

6. Never ask Mom's boyfriends for help, unless it's a legitimate emergency.

7. Never get romantically involved with anyone connected to Mom's boyfriends or their families.

8. Don't get involved in any "family" drama, even if it's juicy and hard to resist.

9. Keep your real life separate from Mom's life with her current boyfriend.

Just reading through the list relaxes me, and I feel totally calm for the first time since Hannah and I got back to my apartment. I tuck the finished rules into my favorite book and hide it behind some of my new horror novels on the bottom shelf, and then I go out to watch another movie with Hannah and Buffy before we all go to bed.

The next morning I pull out the list to check that it's still there, and I find that Hannah has made a last-minute addition.

10. Remember you love your mom. I know it's hard sometimes. But do it anyway.

I debate scratching it out, but decide against it and tuck the list back into its hiding spot. Hannah meant well, and she's probably right. Knowing my luck and Mom's track record with guys, I'm going to need the reminder.

one

OCTOBER, SENIOR YEAR

Rule number one for surviving my mother's love life? Always keep your eyes on the horizon. That's why instead of putting my things away in my new bedroom, I'm alternating between writing an English essay that's not due for two weeks and obsessively refreshing the admission status page on KU's website. Good grades and a college two and a half hours away from here. That's what's on my horizon right now.

"Amber," a voice says, and I look up to see my mom standing in the doorway. She raises an eyebrow and looks from me to Buffy, my German shepherd, who is stretched out next to me on the bed.

"What?"

"You know what."

I sigh. Kevin, Mom's new boyfriend and the owner of this house and this bed, is not a pet person. He doesn't want Buffy on the furniture. Mom had to know I'd break this rule, but I don't think she expected me to do it on the first day. "Buffy, off."

Buffy shoots me a hurt look and slinks off the bed.

"Thank you," Mom says, her gaze flickering between me and Buffy and all the unopened boxes of my things. "Are you taking a break?"

"Uh, yeah." I dig my toes under the pillows at the head of

the bed and nod at my laptop. "Had to do some homework. I put all my clothes away, though." I don't mention that other than that and Buffy's food and water bowls, I haven't touched a thing.

Mom looks at the closet, her expression dubious. "What about your pictures and posters? Your books?"

I shrug. "I'm still trying to figure out where they should go."

Lie. I just don't see the point in unpacking when I'll be leaving for college in ten months. Ten months really isn't that long, and considering Mom's track record with guys, we'll probably be out of here before then anyway. The longest she's ever been with someone was five years, and she hasn't come close to that record in a while.

"Well," Mom says slowly. "Okay. You can get your stuff put away on your own time. I won't rush you." Then she smiles and looks around the room, like the beige walls and puke-green curtains are the greatest thing she's ever seen. "But isn't this room nice, Amber? A king-sized bed and your own bathroom. Pretty cool, huh?"

It is nice, if you like that hotel room vibe. Which I don't. "I still don't see why I couldn't keep my bed."

"Because this one's bigger," she says, like that explains everything.

"I guess." It may be bigger, but it isn't *mine*.

Mom sighs, clearly frustrated that I'm not willing to buy into her enthusiasm. "Are you hungry? Kevin and I thought we could go to New Market to try that new salad place."

Ugh. The last thing I want to do is go to dinner with Mom and Kevin. All they'll want to talk about is where to put Mom's furniture, and whether all her baking pans are going to fit in the kitchen cabinets, and how life is going to be snowflakes and rainbows from now on. I doubt I'd be able to keep a straight face. Or keep myself from asking Kevin if he's aware that he's the sixth guy my mother has called The One.

"No thanks," I say, pushing myself upright. "I'm gonna take Buffy for a walk."

Mom starts to protest, but I've said the magic word: *walk*. Buffy's tags jingle as she pads over to the door. She looks back at me over her shoulder and wuffs softly, and I get up to grab a sweatshirt and shoes.

"Okay," Mom says, her mouth a thin line again. "I'll go back down with you."

Downstairs, I hear Kevin in the kitchen. "Just have him put wax on the end to get him through the night," he's saying, "and then we'll get that wire snipped first thing in the morning. Yup, come on in at eight. Uh-huh. No, I don't think so . . ."

Kevin is an orthodontist—he and Mom met when she decided to get Invisalign after her last breakup—and it seems like there is always some kind of crisis happening with one of his patients. This morning he got a call from a middle school girl in hysterics because her rubber band colors didn't match the dress she bought for her school dance tonight. He spent twenty minutes on the phone consoling her, and then left me and my mom to finish loading the U-Haul so he could go help the kid. Luckily we only had smallish boxes left at that point, but it still sucked.

"Well is it really digging into his cheek?" Kevin says now, as I bypass the kitchen and head for the front door. "I think the wax will work, but if you want, I could—"

Bingo. Looks like I had the right idea about taking a walk

now instead of later. Something tells me Mom and Kevin's dinner is going to get pushed back awhile.

Buffy sits patiently while I clip on her leash. When that's done, I turn back to see Mom standing in the middle of the living room with her arms crossed tightly over her chest.

"I'll see you guys later, I guess," I say.

She nods. Opens her mouth like she wants to say something, then closes it. I wait a beat, to see if maybe she'll try again. But she doesn't. So I open the front door and go.

The air is crisp, cold for October, and the sky is already getting dark as Buffy and I set off down our new street. Buffy's ears are pricked forward and she's checking everything out, but I stop paying attention to where I'm going as soon as my feet hit the pavement. I know this neighborhood well, weirdly enough. My best friend, Hannah, and I drove through here all the time when we first got our licenses sophomore year. She had a huge crush on Will Hoefling, this senior who lived here, and seeing his car, in his driveway or elsewhere in the neighborhood, always gave her the ultimate thrill.

Those drives helped me learn pretty much all the twists and turns of this place, which I guess is a good thing since I live here now. Even after Hannah got over Will we still came through here every once in a while to check out our favorite houses, which were usually so big or so ridiculous that we couldn't imagine actual people living in them. Our absolute favorite, for both the bigness and the ridiculousness, was The Castle.

The Castle is just like how it sounds, complete with turrets and a tower and a porte-cochère over the driveway, with an iron gate that drops down to close it. It looks too big to be allowed. Like it was scooped up from some fairy-tale world and dumped here on a lot so tiny it doesn't even have a front yard. I didn't know this until a few weeks ago, when Mom was giving me the hard sell about us moving in with Kevin, but the other guy in Kevin's practice lives there. She said that they "do dinner" a lot and that we would probably be invited. The prospect is a little disturbing. I can't help wondering if I'll have to put on a big, poufy dress and a wig like old British royalty in order to be let inside.

I don't realize I'm heading toward The Castle until I'm turning onto the street. It's automatic, I guess, a route so worn into my brain that I don't even have to think about it. I stare at it as Buffy and I come around the bend and walk slowly around the cul-de-sac, wondering how much schmoozing I'm going to have to do in there before Kevin gets dumped.

Suddenly I notice a sound, different from the rest of the night sounds. Someone's dribbling a basketball. There's a pattern to it: three dribbles, then the swishing of the net. Like how my dad taught me to shoot free throws when I was little and he was still around. I look over my shoulder, trying to figure out where the dribbling is coming from, but before I can pinpoint it the pattern is interrupted. Instead of the swish I'm expecting there's a loud *bang*, and then a guy's voice is yelling, "Watch out!"

I duck on instinct and there's a whooshing sound as something large flies over the top of my head. A second later there's a rubbery *thwack* as that something—the basketball, I assume—lands somewhere very close behind me and rolls off down the street.

"You okay?" that same voice asks as I straighten back up. "That was a close one."

"I'm good," I say, but it comes out strangled because I can see him now, standing at the end of the driveway to the left of The Castle, lit up from behind by the motion light hanging over the garage. And I know who he is. Jordan Baugh. I can't believe I didn't notice him before.

"You sure?" Jordan says, taking a step closer.

"Yup," I say, nodding furiously and backing away. I jerk my thumb over my shoulder and say, "I'm just gonna go get your—ball."

Oh my God, I am an idiot.

"Oh, it's okay," he says, and to his credit he doesn't laugh at my weird stumbling over the word *ball*. "I can get it, just let me—"

But I don't let him finish. I drop Buffy's leash, say, "Chill," and turn and run off down the street.

It takes me a while to find the ball where it's gotten wedged under a neighbor's car, so when I finally make it back to the end of Jordan's driveway I'm half expecting him to have given up and gone back inside. He's still there, though, standing next to Buffy, who hasn't moved since I left except to lie down on top of her leash. She's staring up at him and he's looking back. As I watch he smiles down at her and says, "Aren't you a good dog?" and it's almost too adorable for me to handle.

God, forget that I can't believe I didn't notice him when I started down the street—I can't believe I didn't know he lives in this *neighborhood*. That seems like something I should have known, at least through Hannah, who views it as her life's mission to keep track of the permanent residences of the hot boys at our school.

And Jordan *is* hot. He's one of those guys I've always noticed. He's got this sort of effortlessly cool thing going on—blond hair that can't decide if it wants to fall over his forehead or stick up all over the place, these light icy-blue eyes, and a pretty amazing set of biceps thanks to his tenure as the star shooting guard on the basketball team. I haven't seen him shirtless since he volunteered for the dunk tank during Spirit Week freshman year, but if his arms are any indication of what he's got going on under there, I wouldn't mind getting a chance to look again.

But wow, that is not what I need to be thinking about right now. Not if I want to act semi-human when I'm face-to-face with him again. So I take a deep breath and steel myself as I walk back over to him, basketball held out in front of me. He takes it and tips his head to the side, watching me now instead of Buffy. "Thanks. Did you just tell your dog to chill?"

"Um, yeah," I manage.

"Nice." It comes out like *Nice*. Like he's actually impressed.

"Thanks."

"Sure." He smiles at me and it's all too much.

I give myself a shake and bend to pick up Buffy's leash. When I straighten up, I clear my throat. "I'd better go. Sorry for interrupting you."

He shakes his head. "You're fine. I missed the shot, remember?"

"Right," I say, taking a step back. "I'll let you get back to it."

"Sure," he says, his smile fading a little. In . . . disappointment? That can't be right. He doesn't even really know me. "See you around, Amber."

"See you," I say, turning to leave. Buffy hesitates for a second before falling into step beside me.

I can feel him watching me as I walk away, and when I glance back after a few houses, he gives me a little wave. Heat rushes to my face as I wave back, then give a gentle tug on Buffy's leash so we can pick up the pace. Still, I can't help smiling to myself as we reach the end of the street and turn back toward Kevin's house. This move may be a total disaster, but maybe, if I'm lucky, my new neighbor could be a silver lining.

two

The next morning I have to open at work, which for me is The Pet Shop in New Market. I've loved it since the day I found Buffy tied up to a tree outside, and I've been working there since I turned sixteen, so over two years now. I do a little bit of everything, but since my eighteenth birthday in September the biggest part of my shifts has been teaching dog obedience classes. Normally Sundays are pretty busy for me, but this is an off week, so this morning I just have a couple of private lessons. The first is an hour-long class with a college girl named Mia and her lab-mix puppy Ringo. Ringo is sweet, but he jumps like he's spring-loaded, and Mia is totally afraid to tell him no.

"Okay, Mia," I say, smiling at her as she comes into the glassed-off training area. "Ready to get some work done?"

She gives me a nervous smile, nods, and unclips Ringo's leash. He makes a beeline for me, his awkward baby legs moving at warp speed as he runs across the floor. He gets one half jump in before I say, "Ringo, *off*," turning my body to the side and stepping back so he can't make contact with my legs. And, miracle of miracles, he doesn't try jumping again. He just comes over to my feet and waits patiently until I give him a click and bend down to scratch his head.

"How do you get him to do that?" Mia wails.

"It's all about the body language and the tone," I tell her as I straighten up.

Ringo trots back over to her and starts jumping up on her legs. He gets high enough to lick her face. Mia shoves him away with a mumbled "No," and I shake my head. Blushing, she stops and takes a deep breath.

"Show me that sidestep thing again," she says, squaring her shoulders.

By the end of the session, we've made some good progress. Mia's "off" command is much more powerful, and she's getting better at using her clicker and bending down to pet Ringo so he won't want to jump up and lick her face. Since I have a break before my next lesson, I walk up front with them when we're done.

"You're doing great," I tell her, grinning, as we stop by the exit and I bend down to scratch Ringo's head one last time.

"You really think so?" she asks, her tone eager.

"Really. You guys make a great team."

She beams at me. "Thanks, Amber. Same time next week?"

I nod. "Yep. I betcha you'll be even better by then."

"We'll try," she says, and then she wraps Ringo's leash tightly around her wrist and goes. Ringo makes it about three steps before he starts pulling so hard he could probably move a dog sled all by himself. I bring a hand up to cover my smile. We'll definitely have to work on leash manners next.

On my way back to the lesson area, I pass by Stephanie, my boss, who's out training a new cashier on register one.

"Any word yet?" she asks.

She means about KU. Stephanie is the one who told me about the behavioral science program I want to do there. She's been asking me if I've heard back every shift for the past two weeks, which is how long it's been since I applied. I shake my head. "Not yet. Rolling admissions don't roll as fast as I want, I guess."

"They never do," she says, laughing. "You keep me posted. And bring that dog of yours in soon, okay?"

Stephanie has always had a soft spot for Buffy and spoils her rotten whenever I bring her in. "Okay."

My last lesson ends at one, and my stomach is grumbling by the time I clock out and hang up my vest in the back room. I consider going back to Kevin's for lunch, but quickly squash that idea. I'm pretty sure he mentioned something about tofurkey sandwiches when I left the house this morning, and I have zero desire to find out if that was just a conversation topic or if it's something I'd actually be expected to eat. So instead of heading back to the house and a questionable lunch option, I walk across the parking lot to the sandwich place where Hannah works. She's on the clock today, which means I can probably get a smoothie for free.

There's still a decent-sized line when I walk in, but I spot Hannah right away, working behind the register closest to the door. I give a little wave and she grins when she notices me.

"How were the puppies?" she asks when I come up to her register a few minutes later, already ringing up my regular order. "Any cute ones?"

"Ringo," I tell her, handing over my debit card. "And Kitty." These two are Hannah's most recent favorites.

"Kitty. I can't even," she says, shaking her head and handing me back my card. She thinks it's hilarious that I train a dog named Kitty, even though I keep telling her this one was named after the dog on the *Titanic*. "Get a booth if you can. I'm due for my break once this rush dies down."

"You got it." I grab a water cup off the counter and step aside so that she can wave the next customer forward.

A little while later Hannah comes out to join me, food and smoothies for both of us in hand. "Thanks," I say, taking mine from her and immediately digging in to my sandwich.

"Of course," she says, sliding in across from me. The restaurant is a lot quieter now, and the line that was snaking to the door when I got here is now completely gone. "Ugh, my feet are killing me."

"Busy morning?"

She nods, reaching for her spoon and taking a bite of soup. "Totally wild. The post-church crowd always is though."

"Amen," I say, and we both laugh.

Then Hannah's grin fades and she levels me with an expectant look. "So. How'd it go yesterday?"

And there it is. I'm surprised it took her this long to bring it up.

"Fine." I reach for my sandwich again. "My room's pretty big, and it's on the opposite side of the house from Cammie's, so that's a bonus."

"That's good," Hannah says, still watching me carefully. She knows how much I've been dreading this weekend, and even though we got into a fight over me not wanting her to help with the move, she still wants to make sure I'm okay about it. Hannah has a big heart. It's one of the many reasons I've kept her around so long. "Was she there at all? Cammie, I mean."

I shake my head. "It was supposed to be her weekend with Kevin too. At least that's what Mom said."

"Awkward," Hannah says.

"Tell me about it."

Honestly, Cammie is the part of this whole move that's been stressing me out the most. Kevin is the fifth guy since my dad that we've lived with, the third who has kids of his own. But he's the first person my mom has dated who has a kid that goes to my school, and when you add in the fact that Cammie and I are only a year apart and that her parents' divorce was Big News last year, awkward doesn't even begin to describe it.

"Well," Hannah says, because there's really nothing else to say about this whole situation that we haven't covered ad nauseam in the last few weeks. "Is the unpacking going okay at least?"

I think of the maze of boxes I had to navigate this morning when I was trying to find my work clothes, and of the judgmental look Buffy gave me when I tripped over a stack of books on my way to get her more water from the bathroom. No way am I telling Hannah this though. It'd make her worry more, and she already does enough of that where I'm concerned. "Yeah. I mean, it's slow. But it's coming along."

"Good," she says, smiling now. "You know I'm always game to help if you need it, right?"

This last part comes out a little uncertain, and I get this prickle of guilt that she's still so clearly worried about our fight.

"I know you are. It's just, you know the rules, Han, and you know why they matter more than ever now. I don't want to mess with the status quo this early in the game."

She nods, her smile fading a little even as a grim sort of understanding settles over her face. "Of course," she says quickly. "I get it."

Desperate for a change of subject, I reach for my smoothie, take a long drink, and then say the first thing that pops into my head. "Did you know Jordan Baugh lives in Harper Ridge?"

"What!" Hannah sits up straighter in her seat. "How did I not know this? How do *you* know this?"

"I saw him while I was walking Buffy last night," I admit. "His house is next door to The Castle."

"No shit?" she says, her expression gleeful. "Maybe he can be, like, your escape plan if things get too weird at home. You can walk Buffy over to his house all the time."

"I think you're getting a little ahead of yourself, Han. I don't even really know him."

"Yeah, but you've always wanted to *get* to know him." She waggles her eyebrows at me. "So this new proximity can be your in."

I shake my head at her, but I'm fighting a smile now. And I can't help picturing Jordan how I saw him last night, lit up from behind, his expression earnest as he watched me leave. "Maybe."

"You should invite him to my Halloween party," she says.

Every Halloween Hannah has a *Buffy* viewing party at her house, where we eat tons of junk food, watch all of the Halloween episodes of *Buffy*, and generally have a fabulous time. Usually it's only me, Hannah, and our friend Ryan and whatever girl he's dating, but this year Hannah invited Elliot, a guy from her physics class that she likes. I don't mind being the fifth wheel to the two of them plus Ryan and whoever he brings, but it could be nice to have someone there for me. "Hmm. I'll think about it."

"Deal," Hannah says, looking pleased with herself. "You know what else you need to think about? When we're going to Lawrence to visit my brother. He was texting me yesterday asking about it."

Just like that the warm, fizzy feeling I got from thinking about Jordan Baugh is gone. Hannah's brother Matt is a sophomore at KU, and he and his best friend from the dorms have an apartment off campus. Hannah made a few day trips to Lawrence last year with her parents, but now that Matt has his own place with a roommate their parents trust, the Spencers are cool with letting her make a trip by herself. She's been dying for me to come with, and I so wish I could make it happen. I'm not optimistic though. My mom is pretty anti-KU, especially since we filled out the FAFSA last week and found out I might not qualify for any Pell Grants. She wants me to stay in town for school and live at home so I can avoid taking out loans, but I want to go away and live on my own no matter how much debt it puts me in. Eyes on the horizon and all that.

"I haven't talked to my mom about it yet," I say, fiddling with the crouton on the table. "With the move and everything . . ."

"I get it," Hannah says quickly, but she can't totally mask the disappointment in her voice, and that disappointment makes me feel so guilty.

"I'll ask her soon. I promise."

"Okay," Hannah says, though I can tell by the look on her

face that she doesn't quite believe me. She looks like she wants to say something else, but then she glances over my shoulder and winces. "Shit. There's a line again and Vince is giving me the evil eye."

"But you haven't even finished your food," I say, looking down at her mostly untouched plate. We've been too busy talking to really eat much.

"I'll stick it in the fridge in the break room," she says, getting to her feet. "See you in the commons in the morning?"

"Yeah," I say, nodding.

"Cool," she says, grabbing her plate. "Tell your mom hi for me, okay? And seriously, Amber, ask her about our trip. She might surprise you."

"I will. Now go before you get in trouble." I shoo her away.

She grins and starts toward the kitchen, but before she disappears behind the counter she calls, "Be nice to Kevin!" over her shoulder at me.

I smile in spite of myself and shake my head at her retreating form. Typical Hannah. I thought we'd be able to get through a hangout without her reminding me to be a good person, but no. Of course we can't. Yet another reason why I've kept her around so long.

three

When I get back to the house, Mom and Kevin are in the process of organizing Mom's baking gear. She has so much that it won't all fit in the kitchen, so Kevin bought her some new shelves for the dining room to display all her nice pieces and fit all her extra gadgets. He's been in there trying to put them together since before I left for work, and judging by the muttered curse words I hear coming from there the second I walk in the door, I'd say it's safe to assume things are not going well. He might be skilled at aligning jaws and closing tooth gaps and all the other orthodontic things he does, but assembling furniture is clearly not Kevin's forte.

They're so distracted by the project that I manage to slip past them mostly unnoticed, with only vague hellos as I move to let Buffy out in the backyard. We stay outside for a few minutes and then I take her up to my room to finally start on the weekend reading for English class. We're in the middle of *Beowulf,* which I am so not enjoying, but it'll be a good distraction from the maze of boxes that is currently surrounding my bed.

I've been reading for maybe half an hour when I hear footsteps on the stairs. I close my copy of *Beowulf* around my finger to mark my place and sit up on the bed just in time for Mom to poke her head in the doorway. Buffy is stretched out in my closet today instead of on the bed next to me, and the second my mom appears her tail starts thumping on the carpet.

"What's up?" I ask, as a faint *Ouch!* echoes from downstairs.

"I, ah, couldn't stop laughing at the situation downstairs," Mom admits, which makes me snort in surprise, "so I decided it was time for me to take a break."

We grin at each other for a second, and I wonder if I should ask her about Lawrence now, while she's in a good mood. Maybe she'll be more likely to say yes. But she clears her throat and speaks up again before I can get the words out.

"I also wanted to make sure you'll be here for dinner tonight."

I go still. "I was planning on it," I say slowly. "Why?"

"That's good. Cammie's coming over," Mom says. "We'd like for you to be here too."

Of course they would. I wish I would've said I was going to Hannah's, but it's too late now. I can tell by Mom's tone that this is not something I can get out of. So I nod. "I'll be here." And then, because it can't hurt to ask for reinforcements, I say, "Can I invite Hannah?"

Mom shakes her head. "No. Tonight will be the four of us. Family."

She doesn't even stumble over that last word, though I can tell by the way she averts her eyes that she knew I wouldn't like it and decided to use it anyway. Mom always wants to pretend like her boyfriends and their kids are our family. She doesn't seem to get that family means permanence. That you can't just go out and get new members when you get tired of the ones you have.

"Family. Right," I say. She flinches, which is satisfying. I hold up my book. "I need to finish this. What time is dinner?"

"We'll plan on eating at six," she says, studying me.

"Okay. I'll be ready."

"Thank you," she says, taking a step back into the hall. "I love you."

I don't say anything back.

Once I hear Mom's footsteps on the stairs, I pat my hand on the bed and softly call, "Buffy." Buffy, never one to turn down an invitation to get on people beds, comes right up next to me and curls into my side. She gently rests her head on my ankles and lets out one of her deep sighs, and I'm more glad than ever that I have her. At least when this thing with Mom and Kevin is all over, she'll still be here. Just like she was last time.

"Oh my God," Cammie says as soon as the door closes behind her a few hours later. "What is *that*?" I'm in the still-cluttered dining room setting the table, so I can't see her face, but it doesn't matter. Her tone tells me pretty much everything I need to know. So that's why Kevin was so weird about having Buffy here.

"That's Buffy," Kevin says. His voice is very soothing, the way I imagine he talks to particularly freaked-out patients.

"Buffy?" Cammie echoes.

I bristle at the sarcasm in her voice. She either doesn't know where the name comes from or she has bad taste in TV shows. I can't decide which is worse.

"Buffy," Kevin repeats. "She's Amber's dog. Very well trained."

"Speaking of Amber," my mother says. "Amber, honey, can you come in here, please?"

I sigh and dump the last of the silverware on the table, then go into the kitchen. Mom's at the stove, stirring something that smells like onions in a skillet, and Kevin is hovering halfway between the island and the door to the garage, where Cammie is watching Buffy warily. Buffy's a polite three paces back from her in a very nice sit, and she looks at me as I come into the room. Cammie follows her gaze and narrows her eyes at me.

"Can you get it away?" she asks, with her hands down at her sides like she's two seconds away from making a shooing motion.

I think about saying no to spite her for calling Buffy an *it*, but I don't want to make Buffy seem mean or bad. Plus my mom and Kevin are looking at me expectantly, clearly waiting for me to take care of this. So I sigh again and pat my thighs. "Buffy, here." With one last glance at Cammie, Buffy gets up and trots over to my side.

Cammie doesn't even say thank you. She just stalks past me and into the dining room, where she sits down with her back to me. I frown and open my mouth to say something, but Mom clears her throat. I glance over at her and she shakes her head at me, eyes narrowed. So I snap my mouth closed again and say, "Buffy, come on. Let's go." After one last sniff in Cammie's direction, Buffy follows me out of the room.

I take Buffy up to my room and tell her to hang out there. She gives me a wounded look but stays when I leave, curling into a ball inside the doorway and watching as I head back toward the stairs. I wish I could stay up here with her, but I know that's not an option for me. Mom would be all over my shit if I did that, would accuse me of being antisocial and rude. Which would be true, but it would probably be better than me being rude in person downstairs.

The food's ready by the time I get back to the kitchen, and I help Mom and Kevin move the serving dishes over to the dining room table so we can eat. The shelves are assembled now but not all of Mom's stuff is put away, so things are cramped and awkward as we try to get everything ready. Cammie doesn't offer to help; she actually doesn't say anything at all. She stays in her chair, messing with her phone, until the three of us sit down with her.

"Cammie," Mom says, smiling at her and holding out the bowl of black beans, "would you like some beans?"

"No."

Mom's smile falters. "Oh, okay."

"I'll have some, Mom," I say, and she shoots me a grateful smile and passes me the bowl.

For the next few minutes, we don't say much. There's just the clinking of plates and cleared throats and quiet muttering to pass this or that. Mom looks like she wants to say something else but doesn't know what, so she's compensating by smiling so wide I can see all her teeth. Kevin's really focused on his plate, probably because Mom accidentally made his gluten free enchilada recipe with flour tortillas. I eat a lot of chips and guac, because the enchiladas are burned on the edges (a sure sign Mom is nervous, because she never burns things) and I don't like the sauce anyway. And Cammie watches my mother and me like we are aliens who have crash-landed in her life, which I guess in a way is true.

In the past, I've usually been the one eyeballing people like that at dinner, as Mom's boyfriends and their families sat at our kitchen table and fed us their own bad food. It's weird to be on the other side of things. I like it even less than I thought I would.

"So, Amber," Kevin says, shooting a hopeful smile across the table at me once the silence has stretched beyond awkward and into uncomfortable territory. "I noticed Buffy has a KU collar. Does that mean that's where you want to go to school next year?"

"Um . . . yeah." I glance at my mom in time to see the corners of her mouth tighten in disapproval. But Kevin starts talking again before she can change the subject.

"I'm a Jayhawk, did you know that?" he asks. I shake my head and he nods. "Undergrad. Class of '93."

"Oh. That's nice." I don't know what else to say except *I don't care.* Which of course I *can't* say, because that would go over about as well as the enchiladas.

"It is," he says, and he sounds like he really means it. Weird. "That's where Cam is planning to go for school too. Right, kiddo?"

Cammie gives him a dirty look across the table. "I guess." Then she turns to my mother. "Did you know these enchiladas are burned?"

We don't talk at all after that.

Finally, finally, we finish eating, and I start clearing plates off the table without any prompting from my mother, just to have something to do. I'm coming back to grab more when I hear Cammie say, "I'm gonna go."

Kevin's chair is facing me so I see his face as it falls. "But, sweetheart," he says, "we talked about this."

Cammie pushes her chair away from the table and gets up. Her added height is not very impressive since she's so tiny, but the way she's avoiding her dad's gaze is. "I changed my mind," she says. "I'm going back to Mom's."

She leaves without another word to any of us, slamming the door to the garage loudly as she goes.

I finish clearing off the table and start on the dishes, trying to ignore the tension in my mother's face and the hurt flashing across Kevin's. Rule number eight is to stay out of any drama with the boyfriend or his family, no matter how tempting it might be to get involved. So even though I wonder what Kevin and Cammie talked about, and why Cammie said she was going back to her mom's instead of saying she was going home, I don't let myself dwell on it.

When I'm done cleaning up I go up to my room and get Buffy. I tell Mom and Kevin that I'm going for a walk, but they're deep in conversation in the living room and I'm not sure they even hear me. So I scribble a note on the whiteboard Kevin keeps on the fridge and then head out into the night.

four

This time, I head toward The Castle on purpose. I haven't stopped thinking about what Hannah said earlier today about inviting Jordan to her Halloween party, and thinking about him is way more fun than replaying dinner on an excruciating loop in my head. So I lead Buffy in the direction of his house and tell myself that if he's outside, I'll at least talk to him again.

The walk goes by a lot faster tonight. It feels like one second I'm reaching the end of Kevin's cul-de-sac and the next I'm turning down Jordan's. This street is longer and curves around on itself, so Jordan's house and The Castle aren't visible from the main road. I don't hear any dribbling, but that doesn't totally kill the rush of anticipation I get as Buffy and I come around the bend. Anticipation turns to disappointment about a second later though, because his house is dark and quiet, and there's a little blue Honda parked right under the basketball hoop.

Well. At least walking here was a good distraction in and of itself. Hopefully Mom and Kevin will have gone to bed by the time Buffy and I get back.

I debate turning around and calling it a night, but Buffy gives me a look when I slow my pace. She will clearly be miffed if she doesn't get a chance to sniff every single house on this block again. So we keep moving, a little slower this time. And even though I tell myself not to, I sneak glances at Jordan's house as we go.

I check out the car, too. It's not Jordan's—his Jeep is parked on the curb next to the mailbox—but I'm pretty sure I've seen it at school before. There's a sticker in the corner of the back windshield that looks vaguely familiar, and I squint at it in the semi-darkness as Buffy and I go, trying to make out what it says.

It isn't until Buffy and I are level with Jordan's driveway on his side of the street that I can see the main part of the sticker—a falcon, our school's mascot. A lot of the student athletes have the same sticker on their cars, so I'd guess this belongs to one of Jordan's friends from basketball or the dance team. I can't read the name and sport on the sticker, though, and without really thinking about it I take a step closer to the car. The motion light over the garage clicks on when I do, and I snap my gaze to Jordan's front door, worried someone will come out and catch me here creeping.

But the night is still quiet, and after a beat I realize no one is coming. So I blow out a breath, reach down to scratch Buffy's head, and look at the car again. It's bright enough now that I can finally make out the full sticker, but it takes me a second to process what I'm seeing.

Harper High Falcons CHEER, it says, in an arc above the mascot. And below, one word that makes me go absolutely still.

Henning.

There's only one person at our school with the last name Henning, and I just saw her about twenty minutes ago. Cammie.

Apparently she didn't go straight back to her mom's place. She came here. Which makes no sense to me, because I had no idea she and Jordan were even friends. They don't hang out at school. I would have noticed if they did, because as soon as Mom told me she was dating Kevin Henning, I did some covert recon on his daughter to figure out who I needed to avoid at school to keep the awkwardness and life overlapping to a minimum. Jordan was definitely not on that list. He and his friends hang out with the senior dance team girls, not the junior cheerleaders. And when Cammie's not with her cheerleader friends, she hangs out with show choir people, not basketball players.

But this is her car. No question about it. And the fact that she's here after that disaster of a dinner means he's important to her in some way. Which means he is officially off-limits to me. Rule number seven for surviving my mother's love life? Don't get involved with guys who are connected to my mom's boyfriends or their families. Even if said guys are mega-hot, like Jordan Baugh. I learned that lesson the hard way my freshman year and I have zero plans to go through anything like that again. So I tear my gaze away from Cammie's car and walk away from Jordan's house without looking back.

The next morning I text Hannah from the parking lot asking her to meet me at my locker instead of the commons, where we usually get a table and hang out with Ryan before the first bell rings. She's already waiting for me by the time I get there, and makes herself comfortable leaning against the locker next to mine while I switch out my books and binders for first period.

"Hey," she says. "How'd dinner go yesterday?"

Dinner. Right. I forgot that I texted her about my impending "family" dinner yesterday after Mom dropped that bomb on me.

"It was okay." I slam my locker closed and start off down the hallway in the opposite direction of the commons. "I mean, super freaking awkward, but not, like, worse than I expected, so at least there's that."

"Hear, hear," Hannah says, taking a step after me. But then she frowns. "Wait, where are you going?"

Shit. I was hoping Hannah would go with it and follow me in the direction of my first period class, which just so happens to be in the opposite direction of the commons. The commons I'd like to avoid, since Jordan and Cammie and their respective friends usually hang out there before school too. I take a second to school my features into what I hope is an innocent expression before turning back to face her. "I, uh, figured since I'm running so behind I might as well go put my stuff down now."

Hannah frowns. "But I haven't gotten any caffeine yet. And also we still have fifteen minutes before the warning bell."

"Oh," I say, shifting from one foot to the other. "Right."

Hannah narrows her eyes at me in suspicion. "I know what you're doing."

"I'm not doing anything!" I blurt, so panicked-sounding that it is basically an admission of guilt.

"Yes you are," Hannah says, reaching forward and tugging me back in the direction of the commons. "You're totally trying to avoid seeing Cammie after all the weirdness at dinner last night."

"I mean, can you blame me?" I ask, wriggling out of her grip. "Besides, you know the rules."

"I do know them, but you can't let them keep you from living your life at school. We've talked about this."

"I haven't forgotten," I mutter, because she's right. We have talked about this, many times, mostly because Hannah thought my Cammie recon when Mom and Kevin first started dating was a little much. Apparently not, though. Because if I'd been thorough, I would've figured out Cammie's connection to Jordan and known not to talk to him when I saw him Saturday night.

"Great!" Hannah says, clearly choosing to ignore the snark in my tone. "Then let's go."

I do a quick scan of the commons when we finally get there, and breathe a sigh of relief when I don't see Jordan or Cammie anywhere. We find Ryan at a table near the edge of the room, reading a graphic novel and eating a giant bag of Peanut Butter M&M's. While Hannah fishes quarters out of her pocket and heads to get in line for the vending machines, I plunk myself into the chair opposite him and reach for the chocolate.

"That's my breakfast," he says, not bothering to look up from his book.

"There are like twenty servings in this bag," I say, grabbing a handful and sliding the goods back across the table to him. "I think you'll be okay without one or two of them."

He sighs, but I can tell by the smile tugging at the corners of his mouth that he's not really mad. That isn't surprising though, since Ryan is probably the most laid-back person I know.

"Rough weekend?" he asks, looking up from his book now. Ryan has a huge blended family and all the drama that comes along with one, so a lot of the time he gets how I feel about my home life even better than Hannah does. I haven't talked to him about it too much, but I know he knows I've been dreading the move this weekend.

I shrug. "About what I expected."

"Yeah," he says, studying me carefully. "Still sucks though."

"It does," I agree, and when he nudges the bag of candy closer to me, I gladly take another handful.

We're munching on M&M's and Ryan is telling me about his graphic novel when Hannah comes back from the vending machines.

"You guys," she says, slapping her granola bar onto the table and sliding into the chair next to me. "I saw Bailey Whittaker in line for my drink and I finally got her to switch with me so Elliot and I can be lab partners this quarter!"

"No shit?" Ryan says, widening his eyes as he looks at her. I'm just as surprised. Hannah's been trying to persuade Bailey to switch with her since the beginning of the year, when her monster crush on Elliot started.

"What'd you have to do?" I ask, because there's no way Bailey agreed to this without any incentive.

Hannah fidgets in her seat for a second, and then she sighs. "I had to pay her twenty bucks and take notes for her for the rest of the semester." Ryan and I both crack up laughing, and she quickly adds, "But it was worth it! He still barely speaks to me but we've been making progress. I mean, he does at least use full sentences every time we talk now. So I figure getting to work on lab stuff together will help with the conversation part, right?"

"Oh, definitely," Ryan says, coughing a little.

"It totally will. And he did agree to come to your house on Halloween," I add, taking a deep breath and holding it for a second to stop myself from laughing. Elliot is almost painfully shy and Hannah is most definitely not, so watching this whole thing between them unfold has been pretty entertaining. "That's still happening, right?"

"Duh," she says, sticking her tongue out at me. Her gaze catches on something over my shoulder, and her expression goes sly. "And *speaking* of my Halloween party, your hot new neighbor just got here. In case you were still thinking about inviting him."

I absolutely should not look, but I do it anyway. Sure enough, Jordan is now standing at a table of his friends in the center of the room, grinning at something one of them said. He's still grinning when he looks my way, and when he catches me watching him, his smile widens. Sucking in a breath, I whip back around in my seat, way too aware of the heat rushing to my face.

"What neighbor?" Ryan asks, looking between us.

"Jordan Baugh," Hannah says. "He lives in Harper Ridge, apparently. And he is totally checking you out right now, Amber. You should go talk to him."

I resist the urge to look back at Jordan and shake my head instead. "I'm good. And I'm not gonna invite him to your party, Han. The neighbor thing, it could get weird, you know? For the rules."

Hannah pulls her head back and furrows her brow in confusion. "I'm sorry, what happened between yesterday and today that made you change your mind?"

"I thought about it more," I say, gathering up my stuff and

stacking my books neatly in front of me. "And I decided this is for the best."

Hannah's mouth flattens into a line. "That is total bullshit and you know it."

I sigh, because I can tell she's not going to let this go. So I glance around to make sure no one else is paying attention to our table and say in a low voice, "Look, I found out he's friends with Cammie, okay? And you know what that means."

"What?" she asks, her eyes widening. "How do you know that?"

"Her car was at his house last night after dinner. I went over there to see if he was outside again to ask him about—" I cut myself off, take a deep breath, and start again. "Anyway, she was there. So please let this go, okay?"

"Shit," Hannah says. She chews on her bottom lip for a second and then adds, "What if—"

But Ryan cuts her off with a shake of his head. "You heard her. Let it go, Han."

I give him a grateful look. I haven't been friends with Ryan for as long as I've been friends with Hannah, but he knows about my rules as well as she does. Or as well as she should, anyway, since she was there the day I wrote them.

"All right," Hannah says, sighing. The warning bell rings a second later and she gets to her feet, offering me a hand as she does. "Come on. We'd better get to class."

five

The next week and a half passes by pretty quickly. The boxes in Kevin's house slowly disappear as Mom settles her stuff in downstairs, though my room stays basically the same way it looked on move-in day. We suffer through two more "family" dinners with Cammie, each more awkward than the last one. And I take Buffy on long walks through the neighborhood every night, just to get a little bit of space.

The only street I avoid is The Castle's.

On Halloween I have to stay after school to finish up a lab for my physics class. The halls are totally deserted by the time I'm done working, and my footsteps echo around me as I shoot a quick text to Hannah to tell her I'm on my way to her house. She's been stress cleaning all week since Elliot is coming over, and I promised her I'd get there early to help with the final touches.

I feel a little silly as I cross the nearly empty parking lot. Sort of like I'm on display. We were allowed to wear costumes today as long as they were appropriate, and to get in the spirit of things for Hannah's party later I dressed up like Buffy the Vampire Slayer circa season one, when she wears all those sixties-style short dresses and has big, swingy hair. I figured it was fitting because my hair, which is long and dark and wavy, is kind of big and swingy every day. I added leggings underneath my dress because it's cold and because Mom insisted, but it's still really short and my shoes are chunky and huge. It's fun, but not my usual T-shirt and jeans style, and it's a relief when I make it to my car.

My relief, however, is short-lived, because my car won't start. It's been acting finicky lately and will do this sometimes, but usually I can get it going after a few tries. But not today, apparently, because when I turn the key over it makes this awful churning noise like nails on a chalkboard. Then nothing. Great.

After a few tries—and after I hit the steering wheel a few times to vent my frustration—I pull out my phone and call my mom's cell. It goes straight to voice mail. Figures. I remember her telling me this morning that she had a late bridal cake tasting at the bakery today and would be crazy busy, which is fine. But would it kill her to leave her phone turned on?

I consider trying Ryan or Hannah, but decide against it. Ryan isn't good with cars, and Hannah's out since she's got party setup and Elliot-induced freaking out to do. Which leaves me one other option before I call my mother's work number: Kevin. I finally put his number in my phone the other day at Mom's insistence, but I never planned to actually *call* him. Rule number six for surviving my mother's love life? Never ask the boyfriend for help, unless it's a legitimate emergency. I follow that one to a tee, because when Mom was dating Leo in middle school, I used to ask him for help with all kinds of things. School projects, boy advice, rides to and from school and Hannah's house. He was always happy to do whatever I needed, and he acted like I wasn't any different from his own kids. Basically, he was nice, and dad-like. Which made it even harder after he was gone.

I stare at Kevin's number for a second, trying to decide. And then I pass it by, because while this situation sucks, it's not exactly worth breaking the rules over. Especially not this early in the game.

Right as I'm searching through my contacts to pull up Mom's work number there's a knock on my window.

I scream, loud and long and embarrassingly shrill, and fling my phone into the passenger seat. Someone laughs and I look up and there's Jordan Baugh, in full pirate attire, standing outside my door.

He stops laughing and presses his lips together. I use the crank to roll down the window—no automatic windows in this baby—and say, "Jordan. Hey."

"Hey," he says, his voice a little strangled still. "Do you need a ride?"

I sit up straight in an effort to regain my dignity. "Um, hopefully just a jump. My battery has been acting weird lately."

He nods and thumps the roof of my car. "I can do that. Let's take a look."

I pop the hood, then slowly get out of the car, wishing I was wearing my normal clothes instead of this costume. When I'm finally out and upright, Jordan's gaze follows my hands as I reach down and smooth my dress. Heat rushing to my face, I make myself think of rule number seven.

"Let me get my jumper cables," I say, taking a step back toward the trunk.

At my words Jordan starts and looks away. "Yeah, go ahead." He moves toward his Jeep and jerks a thumb over his shoulder. "Give me a sec to move this and then we'll get them hooked up."

Once Jordan's car is in the space right next to mine, we get everything connected and start his car. After a few minutes of awkwardness while his engine rumbles, I try to start mine. Nothing. Not even the churning noise.

"One more time?" Jordan asks, frowning. I nod, so we try again.

Twenty minutes and two more tries later, still nothing. I'm not surprised, since this car is basically junk on wheels, but I am a little disappointed. Jordan shuts his car off, unhooks the cables, and then shuts his hood and mine. "We could run to Walmart and get another battery."

I shake my head. "It's been acting weird for a few months now and the battery's only a year old, so I don't think it's that."

"Oh," Jordan says. "Okay. I could call Triple A or something, if you want."

"Don't worry about it. I'll have my mom help me figure it out tomorrow." I'm sure my car will be fine in the school parking lot overnight, and if it isn't, well, it isn't much of a loss.

Jordan nods. "Come on, then. I'll take you home."

I hesitate, wondering if I should figure out something else just to avoid being trapped in a car with him. But it's not like I have any other easy options right now, and I have somewhere I need to be. So I take a deep breath and say, "That would be great. Um, but actually, after we stop at the house, could you take me to Hannah Spencer's? That's where I'm supposed to be going. We have a thing tonight."

"Oh, yeah," he says, his eyebrows going up in surprise. "Sure."

"Thanks." I take my jumper cables back from him so that I

can toss them back in the trunk. "Let me lock up, and then we can . . . yeah."

He nods and fidgets with his keys. "All right."

❊

Jordan's Jeep is clean, but cluttered. Loose change rattles in the cup holders, school and library books are spread out over the backseat, and his backpack is unzipped and overstuffed with papers and notebooks.

"Sorry," he says, reaching over to scoop up a stack of CD cases in the passenger seat. As I climb in he puts them into the little compartment built into the driver's-side door.

"It's all right." I smooth my dress down again and tuck my bag between my feet. "You make mix CDs?"

"Yeah," he says, grinning a little sheepishly. "No aux hookup in here, so this is the closest I can get to playlists when I'm driving. Anything in particular you want to hear?"

I shake my head and reach for my seat belt.

"Okay." He turns the key in the ignition. "Let me know if you change your mind."

We stay quiet for the first few minutes, the only sounds in the car coming from the alt-rock mix Jordan has going in the CD player. At the first red light we hit, I look over at him and ask the question that's been lingering in the back of my head since he offered to drive me home.

"Do you need me to give you directions?"

He flicks his eyes over to me and then quickly focuses them back on the road. "Not to your house. I'll need them when I take you to Hannah's though."

50

Something tightens in my chest.

"Um, how did you . . ."

"Know where you live?" he asks, giving me another one of those brief glances as the light turns green and we pull forward again. I nod, and the corner of his mouth tugs up. "Cammie told me."

"I didn't think she was really telling anyone," I say. Cammie is popular enough that people would be gossiping about our new roommate situation if they knew about it. No one at school has said a word to me about it though, so Hannah and I assumed that Cammie wants to keep this quiet just as much as I do.

"She's not, really," Jordan confirms. "But we go way back, me and Cam. Our moms have been friends since we were in daycare together. So we don't really keep secrets."

"Oh." I want to ask him what *exactly* Cammie told him, and also why, if they're since-diapers-friends, they don't hang out at school, but I force myself to keep my mouth shut. Neither answer would change anything at this point.

He's friends with Cammie. *Close* friends. Which, according to the rules, means he's off-limits to me.

When we pull into Kevin's driveway a few minutes later, I scramble out of the car the second he puts it in park, and say, "I'll just be a sec," before I slam the door behind me and rush up the front walk.

I take a little longer than I probably need to let Buffy out and double-check her food and water bowls. Partly this is because she's so excited to see me and get some ear rubs that I don't want to make her feel rushed, but partly it's because I need the extra minutes to regroup before I have to go get back in Jordan Baugh's car. My phone buzzes with a text from Hannah right as I'm finishing up.

Where are you??? Elliot will be here soon and you were supposed to help me finish stress cleaning!

Sorry! I text back immediately. **On my way now. Had a car issue.**

"All good?" Jordan asks me a minute later, when I'm climbing into his car for the second time today.

"Yeah, sorry."

"It's no problem. I'm not in a hurry."

I don't really know what to say to that, so I give him directions to Hannah's house and start fiddling with my phone so that I have something to focus on besides him.

This part of the drive is as quiet as the last, but as we're waiting to turn into Hannah's neighborhood, Jordan surprises me by breaking the silence. "You have Ms. Ulbrich for English, right?"

I turn to look at him, thrown off by such a random question. "Yeah. How'd you know that?"

"I have her last hour. She used your paper on *Beowulf* as an 'example of excellence' for us."

I frown. "How do you know it was mine? When she reads stuff to us she never uses names."

The backs of his ears turn red again. "I had to stay after today to do some makeup stuff. It was on her desk."

"Oh."

There is a long pause. So long that there's been a break in traffic and we're moving forward again before he says, "I hated *Beowulf*."

"Oh my God, me too!" I can't help my enthusiasm, because Hannah loved *Beowulf* and totally did not understand why I bitched about it so much. "I don't think I'm cut out for epic poems. I like my stories regular, thanks."

Jordan laughs, and I get this fizzy feeling in my chest at the sound of it. Shit.

I think of rule number seven and force myself to look out the window, where I see that, thank God, we're turning onto Hannah's street. Jordan's still chuckling to himself a little when he pulls to a stop along the curb in front of her house, but his face is mostly serious when he turns to face me, drums his fingers on the steering wheel, and says, "Your stop, right?"

"Yeah." I glance up at Hannah's front door. "Thanks for the ride. Or rides, I guess."

Jordan smiles. "Anytime."

I gather up my stuff and reach for the door handle. I need to get out of this car, stat, and not just because I'm sure Hannah has already seen us and is planning to give me the third degree. "I'll see you around, I guess."

"For sure," Jordan says, and I don't think I'm imagining the warmth in his tone.

Which is why I'm out of the car and shutting the door before he can add anything else.

I'm halfway to Hannah's front door when Jordan calls my name. I turn around to see him leaning across the seat so he can see me out the passenger window. Did I forget something in his Jeep? I do a mental check: wallet, keys, backpack, phone. It's all here. "Yeah?"

"I like your costume."

Oh my God. Rule number seven. Rule number seven. "Uh, thanks."

"You're welcome," he says, grinning. "Happy Halloween."

six

Hannah's waiting by the door when I finally make my way inside, wearing an expression so similar to the one her cat gets when he's stalking his toys that it's kind of terrifying.

"Hi," I say warily, kicking off my shoes and dumping my backpack on the floor next to them.

"*Hi*," Hannah says. "So. Car trouble, huh?"

"Yeah. It was making that churning noise again only it wouldn't start at all this time, and when we tried to jump it nothing happened."

"*We?*" she asks, with that same weird emphasis.

I sigh. At least she's going straight for the kill instead of dragging it out indefinitely.

"Me and Jordan. Who I'm assuming you noticed dropping me off."

Hannah taps a finger to her chin and pretends to look confused as I push past her into the living room. "I mean, I *thought* it looked like him, but then I was like, that can't be right. Amber would never fraternize with the enemy."

"Are you done? I thought I was supposed to help you stress clean before everyone else shows up. When are Ryan and Megan and Elliot getting here, anyway?" I ask, plopping onto the couch and waving to her parents, who are out on the back deck grilling burgers for us to eat later. They both grin and wave back at me.

"They should be here any minute. You know for a fact that I already cleaned everything so I only needed you here for moral support. And I'm almost done," Hannah says. "I just have one more question."

I wave a hand at her and adopt the snooty, formal tone we use whenever we imagine what the people who live in The Castle sound like. "Proceed."

"I will, thank you," she says, going snooty right back. Then she gets this sly grin on her face. "What'd Jordan say to you before he drove away?"

I will myself not to react as I flash back to Jordan saying *I like your costume.* And to how his gaze traveled down my body when I first got out of my car at school. "Nothing really," I say, working hard to keep my tone even and disinterested. There are cans of soda set out on the coffee table, so I grab a Sprite and pop the top open just to have something to do with my hands. "He was asking about English class. We both have Ms. Ulbrich."

"Lame," Hannah says, right as I take a sip of my drink. "I was hoping for something about how hot you look in that dress."

I splutter a cough and almost choke.

"Whoa, you okay?" Hannah asks, leaning forward and reaching around to thump my back.

"Fine," I wheeze. "It went down the wrong pipe."

Her eyes narrow in suspicion. "Are you sure that's all?"

Thank God the doorbell rings before I have to respond.

Hannah's *Buffy* watch party is a ton of fun, as per usual. Elliot hardly talks for the first hour, but Ryan's new girlfriend, Megan, chatters more than enough to fill his silences. We all gorge ourselves on burgers and chips and puppy chow and then settle in front of the TV in the living room.

By unspoken agreement Ryan and I shuffle the seating arrangements around so that Hannah and Elliot have to share the oversized armchair that can almost but not quite pass for a love seat. She flashes a grateful smile in our direction once the first episode starts rolling, and I give her a thumbs-up back. By the second episode they're holding hands and Elliot is somewhat joining in on the debates about the best moments and characters on the show, so I'm calling that a win.

And what's even better? Hannah is so distracted by Elliot's presence that she doesn't ask me about Jordan Baugh again.

✳

The next morning when Buffy and I come downstairs, Kevin is sitting at the kitchen island eating a bowl of Kashi and scrolling through something on his iPad, two steaming hot mugs sitting in front of him. Mom is nowhere to be found.

"Morning, Amber," he says, glancing up from whatever he's reading as soon as I step into the room.

"Um, hi," I say, hesitating for a second before going over to the pantry and grabbing a scoop of food for Buffy. She digs right in, but unfortunately she's a slow eater. Which means I'm stuck here for at least a few minutes before I can use taking her outside as an excuse to leave the room.

"We'll probably want to get going soon," Kevin says. I look back up at him and frown, confused. "So we have time to look at your car before school," he adds.

"Oh," I say. "I, uh, figured I'd just have Mom give me a ride. Is she still getting ready?"

Kevin's smile is hesitant. "Actually, your mom had to open the bakery this morning. Apparently Stella called in sick, so I'll have to take you. She said she left you a note in your bathroom."

"Oh," I say again, because that seems more appropriate than *Jesus Christ, why couldn't she have texted me like a normal person?*

We stare at each other for a second, and then Kevin reaches out to nudge one of the mugs closer to me. "I made oatmeal for breakfast. You like it with two scoops of brown sugar, right?"

"Uh, right."

"Great!" he says, getting to his feet. "You can eat in the car. Do you need to do anything else before we go, or are you all set?"

"I just need to let Buffy out for a second."

He nods. "All right. I'll grab my briefcase. Meet you in the garage."

The whole time I'm outside with Buffy I debate ways to get out of this impending carpool without looking like a complete asshole, but I come up empty. It's seven and it takes at least fifteen minutes to get to the high school, so with the first bell at 7:25 we're already cutting things close. The bus would have come and gone like twenty minutes ago. Hannah would have to backtrack to come pick me up, meaning we'd most likely be late. Ryan's probably barely gotten out of bed since he has a first period teaching assistant class and doesn't live very far from the school. Plus telling Kevin I'll wait for either of them would go over like a lead balloon, and would most definitely earn me an earful from my mother later.

With that depressing thought in my head, I sigh and call Buffy over to come back inside. Chauffeur Kevin it is. So much for never asking him for help. Though I guess I didn't actually *ask* him to do this. So not a total rule break, technically speaking.

Kevin's car is some fancy Mercedes that looks like a box and is high enough off the ground that I have to use the little step thingy on the side to climb in. It still has that new-car smell from the dealership, even though I'm pretty sure he's had it for a few years. I can't help comparing the pristine interior of Kevin's car to the lived-in clutter of Jordan's Jeep yesterday, and I decide I like Jordan's better even though I really shouldn't like either of them.

I stay quiet as I shove my backpack down by my feet and buckle my seat belt. Once I'm all set, Kevin holds out the mug with my oatmeal and says, "I got you a glass of water too, in case you're thirsty."

"Thanks," I mumble, taking the mug from him.

I hurry to shove a bite in my mouth in the hopes that he won't talk to me while I'm eating, but the silence only lasts for about two minutes. As soon as we're out of the neighborhood he starts peppering me with questions, mostly about my car and what exactly happened yesterday. *Hmm, and has it made that noise before? Were you able to get the key to turn over at all? What did the dash lights look like? Has it done this before? When did you say you last replaced the battery? Was it acting funny when you drove to school yesterday morning, or did things seem normal?*

"Huh," he says finally, when we're sitting through our third red light at the last intersection before the high school. "It sounds like it might be your alternator, but I'm not sure. We'll have to have my buddy Pat look at it. He's got a great auto repair shop and—"

"That's okay," I say, cutting him off. No way am I having one of Kevin's *buddies* look at my car. Having to get a ride from him this morning is bad enough. "Mom and I have a place we use. We can take the car there."

There is a beat where the only sound in the car comes from NPR, which Kevin has had turned on low volume for the whole drive. Then Kevin says, "Of course. Whatever you guys want."

"Good." I shift to look out the window and we don't talk again until we finally make it to the school parking lot.

"What row?" Kevin asks, and I point him in the right direction. The lot is filling up quickly around us, echoing with the sound of slamming doors and laughter as all the upperclassmen park and head into the building, and I shrink lower into my seat, hoping no one who'd care will notice who my ride is.

My car, a beat-up old Buick I bought for five hundred dollars (the Kelley Blue Book value, which I think might actually have been exaggerated) from one of Eric's ancient female relatives before he and Mom broke up, is in one of the middle rows, about a third of the way up to the school. There's still a space left to the right side of it, though it isn't the roomiest, and for a second I wonder if I should tell Kevin to park somewhere else. But he whips the Mercedes box into it like it's no big deal, puts it into park, and glances over at me.

"This will probably be easier if you leave your keys with me. That way I can wait for the tow truck while you go inside."

"Are you sure that's okay? Really, I can just wait for my mom to help me after school—"

He holds out a hand to me, palm up. "Keys, Amber," he says, tone firm for the first time this morning. "Your mom wants me to look at the car before we have someone pick it up. I can get the info for whatever place you want to use from her, but I *will* be looking at it first."

Whoa. I didn't know perpetually cheerful Kevin had that kind of attitude in him. I get my keys out of my backpack, unclip the house key (which has a KU key cap on it to remind me that escape from this place isn't that far in the distance) from the carabiner I use to keep everything together, and hand the rest over to him.

"Thank you," he says, shutting off the Mercedes and reaching for the door handle. "I like the improvements you've made to your house key. Have you heard back from them yet?"

I blink at him, surprised both at the abrupt change in subject and the fact that he seems genuinely interested in my answer. "Not yet."

"I'm sure you will soon, and I'm sure it'll be good news. Keep me posted, okay?"

"Um, sure," I say, but I won't. I don't want to bond with Kevin over college. Not when odds are he won't still be with Mom by next fall.

"Great," he says, opening his door. "I'm gonna go ahead and take a look at your car now so I know for sure what to tell the mechanic when I call them. Do you need a ride home after school?"

I shake my head. Hannah can take me, and if she can't, I'll figure something else out.

"All right," Kevin says, getting out of the car. "Have a good day, then. See you at home tonight."

He closes the door without waiting for a response, and by the time I grab my bag and hop out of this giant box, he's already in my car and putting the key in the ignition. As I walk past the back bumper, he gives a cheerful wave over his shoulder that I can't bring myself to totally ignore. So I say a quick "Bye," and scurry away, beyond grateful this carpool is over.

seven

Kevin ends up being right—it *is* the alternator that needs to be replaced in my car. Mom calls me during the passing period before lunch to tell me the news, and to tell me that our usual mechanic won't be able to get it back to me until next Wednesday because they have to order the part.

"Wednesday?" I practically shout into the phone, which earns me several raised eyebrows from my classmates. I ignore them and duck into an empty chemistry room so I can finish this conversation without an audience.

"Yes," Mom says. "They're apparently swamped."

"Fantastic," I mutter, leaning against one of the lab tables.

"Easy on the sarcasm, sweetheart."

"Sorry," I say grudgingly, even as I roll my eyes and flip off the wall. "This just sucks."

"I know it's inconvenient for you," she allows. "Which is why I had Kevin check to see if there are any other options that would get it back to you sooner."

"And?" I ask, trying to keep my tone as neutral as possible even though internally I'm screaming *PLEEEEEEASE TELL ME HE FOUND SOMETHING.*

"And his friend Pat could get it back to you by Monday. For

the same price. But he wanted me to ask you about it first because he said you were pretty adamant about using Gage and Sons."

I tip my head back and reach up to pinch the bridge of my nose. Which do I want more? To avoid ever accepting help from Kevin again, or to reduce my time sans car by two whole days?

"Amber?" Mom prompts. She's using the overly patient tone she gets when she thinks I'm being ridiculous, which is so irritating. And which also seals the deal on my choice.

"Taking the car to Kevin's friend is fine." *Because the sooner I can drive myself around again, the better*, I think but don't add.

"Wonderful," Mom says, and I can actually hear her clap her hands in the background. "I'll let him know."

"You do that," I mutter.

"What was that?" Mom asks.

"I said tell him thank you for me."

"Hmm," Mom says, and I know she doesn't believe me. But she doesn't call me out.

❋

Between Hannah and Ryan I'm covered on rides to and from school for the rest of the week, and I take Buffy to Hannah's house for the weekend under the guise that it will be easier for us to carpool to work if we're coming from the same place. Really I don't want to be stuck at Kevin's house without a mode of transportation, but I don't explain that to my mom for obvious reasons.

Matt is home for the weekend to do his laundry—seriously, just to do his laundry—and I run into him in the hallway between loads on Saturday morning.

"Hey!" he says brightly, shifting the overflowing laundry basket he's carrying to one arm so that he can reach down to scratch Buffy, who is, as usual, close by my side. "I heard your car's in the shop. That's a bummer."

"Tell me about it. I get it back Monday though, so at least I don't have to wait too much longer."

"That's good," he says, nodding and grabbing the basket with both hands again. "Any updates on when you and Han are coming to visit? We're getting closer to finals so it might be better to wait until next semester, but if you've already gotten your mom to agree to a date, we can make it work."

I shake my head and force a smile. "No date yet, so waiting until next semester will be fine."

"Awesome," he says. "We'll make sure you guys have a good time, promise. Hey, have you thought much about where you want to live next year? Hannah's been talking about the dorms a lot, but I didn't know if you'd want to do that since you have the Buffster here."

A wave of panic washes through me. Hannah wants to live in the dorms? We've talked about being roommates at KU since before we really knew what it meant to go to college, and as far as I know that's still the plan. But there's no way I can do the dorms, because there's no way I'm leaving Buffy behind. And Hannah has to know that. Right?

"Not much, yet," I say, shaking my head and taking a step back so that Matt can move past me toward the laundry room.

"Well let me know if you need help researching any pet friendly places, all right?"

"Definitely."

On Monday I'm distracted, because all I can think about is how close I am to getting my car back. First period doesn't matter since it's Family and Consumer Sciences; we're baking pies today, something I could do in my sleep thanks to my mom, so I don't exactly need to pay close attention. But second period I have English with Ms. Ulbrich, who is a notorious hardass. So when she calls for me to come to her desk when the bell rings, I'm convinced I'm in deep shit.

Figuring it's better to head off her lecture with an apology, I blurt, "I'm so sorry for being sidetracked today."

Her fuzzy white eyebrows practically become one with her hair they go up so high. "I did notice you seemed a bit preoccupied," she says, cutting me off, "but that's not what I wanted to talk to you about. I've got an opportunity for you, if you're interested. Something to put on your scholarship applications."

"Oh," I say, totally thrown off by the fact that she's apparently not upset with me. "Um—"

"Come back at lunch, okay?" she says, already turning around and heading for her desk at the front of the room.

"Sure."

I text Hannah to fill her in on Ms. Ulbrich's strange request, and she promises to save me a seat and get me nachos from the à la carte line. So when the bell rings to signal the start of the lunch period, I head straight back to Ms. Ulbrich's classroom.

When I get there, I stop short in the doorway. Ms. Ulbrich is sitting in my usual seat and Jordan Baugh is at the seat next to her. They're both leaning into the center aisle to look at the paper in Ms. Ulbrich's hand. Jordan notices me first, and when he does his eyes crinkle at the corners like he's happy I'm here. Oh no.

"Hey," he says. "How's your car?"

"Hey. It's, uh, good. I get it back today." And since I agreed to take it to Kevin's friend to get fixed, Mom even said she'd pay for it, so. Bonus there.

"Oh, that's good."

"Yeah."

Ms. Ulbrich clears her throat, and I look over at her, startled. For a second I forgot she was in here.

"Miss Richter. Have a seat and we'll get started." She waves a hand in the air and motions me toward them, then points to the seat in front of Jordan.

I go over to them slowly and lower myself into the chair. Jordan's sitting sideways and leaning forward, with his forearm all the way at the front of his desk. I brush it with my butt as I sit down and almost die, especially when he quickly moves it away, the backs of his ears turning red. Jesus Christ. Ms. Ulbrich doesn't notice this, or else she doesn't care, because she just flaps the paper in her hands and peers over the top of her glasses at both of us.

"Mr. Baugh. Do you want to start?"

I look at Jordan, whose cheeks turn as red as his ears at being put on the spot. But he's a Mr. Congeniality if I've ever seen one, because the discomfort only lasts about a second before his face slips back into its normal easy expression and he turns to look at me. "I was wondering if you'd help me edit my papers."

Edit his papers? That is so not what I was expecting. "What, like tutor you?"

"No," he says quickly. "Not exactly. I—" And then it's like he's at a loss for words and he looks at Ms. Ulbrich for help.

She jumps right in, flapping the paper in her hands all over the place again. "Mr. Baugh is having difficulty with the writing assignments. His ideas are solid but some of the grammar and spelling isn't up to snuff. He asked if perhaps someone from my other class could help go over his paper drafts with him to make sure they're cleaned up before he turns them in. I thought you would be a good fit since your work has been solid all semester."

"Oh. Um, thanks."

She furrows her bushy eyebrows at me. "So you'll do it?"

"Well . . ." I say. I really shouldn't. Like, should not even. Because rule number seven exists for a reason, and I've already had to remind myself of it way too many times in Jordan's presence.

So that's it. It's settled. I'll tell them, no, sorry, I can't right now. I take a deep breath and open my mouth. And then I look at Jordan. He's staring at his hands, which are laced together in front of him, and his shoulders—which are broad and just as impressive as his biceps, not that I notice—are tense. Like getting help with this is really important to him.

"Okay," I say.

Jordan's head bobs up and he shoots me a smile that makes my stomach flip. Shit. Shit shit shit.

"Wonderful," Ms. Ulbrich says, smacking the paper she's holding onto the desk so hard that the sound makes me jump. "Let's go over the rules."

The rules are pretty self-explanatory, and no matter what she calls it this whole arrangement sounds a lot like tutoring. I can make suggestions but he has to make the changes himself. She'll be checking each assignment for plagiarism. I shouldn't mess with the ideas, because, as we've established, his are already good. I'm only supposed to help with the mechanics. And once we hit midterms we will reevaluate to see if Jordan still needs my help or if he can handle spring semester on his own.

I do a quick calculation in my head—not counting the week of Thanksgiving, there are only six weeks between now and Christmas break. Okay. I can handle that. That's plenty of time to whip him into shape so that when we come back in January, he won't need me anymore. I just have to keep things professional. No boundaries crossed, no rules broken. Easy.

Once she's done explaining everything, Ms. Ulbrich peers at us over the top of her glasses. "Sound good?"

"Sounds good," I echo. Jordan nods.

"All right," Ms. Ulbrich says, getting up and starting toward the door. "I'll leave you kids to it. I'll see you tomorrow morning, Miss Richter, and you later today, Mr. Baugh."

"Later, Ms. Ulbrich," Jordan says.

She waves and disappears out the door, leaving us alone.

"So," I say, turning to Jordan. "How do you want to do this?"

He shrugs and runs a hand through his hair, making it stick out all over the place like he's suffered an electric shock. "Whatever's easy. I can just email you stuff, if you want. That might be better since basketball practice starts next week. I'll be busy every day after school until late."

I shake my head, even though the idea of having a strictly email tutoring setup is tempting. "Email is okay for some things, but I think it would be helpful to meet in person at least once a week. It's easier to talk about the bigger issues that way."

Jordan nods. "All right. When and where?"

"Not my house," I say immediately. That would be too weird. Tutoring Cammie's friend in Cammie's house, under the watchful eyes of Mom and Kevin? No thank you.

He shakes his head and smiles a little. "My house, then? We could go somewhere else, but then we'd have to worry about when places close."

"Okay," I say. "Your house. That's fine."

"Cool," he says. "Is eight good?"

"That works. Thursday?"

He hesitates for a second, and then he nods.

"Okay then," I say, getting to my feet and ignoring the fact that my heart is racing. "I guess I'll see you Thursday at eight."

eight

By the time I get to the commons and spot Hannah at a table near the edge of the room, it still hasn't completely sunk in that I just agreed to spend one-on-one time with Jordan Baugh. I'm kind of shell-shocked from the whole thing, to be honest, and it must show because when I reach my friends' table Hannah frowns and says, "What's with the face? Did Ulbrich end up chewing you out after all?"

I shake my head and sink into the chair next to Ryan, who has his nose buried in one of the Song of Ice and Fire books today. His lunch is already gone, but he's got a bag of Reese's Pieces that he holds out to me wordlessly. I take a handful, because I need some sugar to deal with what just happened. "No, she didn't chew me out. She wanted me to tutor someone, actually."

"That's it?" Hannah asks, passing my nachos across the table. "Then why do you look like someone died?"

"Because." I pause to eat a chip loaded with cheese and taco meat to fortify myself.

"Because . . ." Ryan says, nudging me with his elbow when I take too long to continue.

I sigh. "Because the tutoring is for Jordan Baugh." And then, because it's better to get it all out there, I add, "And I said yes. Because I know you guys were gonna ask."

Ryan laughs and goes back to reading in response to this, but for a second, Hannah's expression doesn't change. Then a slow, gleeful smile spreads out over her face. It's like watching a light on a dimmer switch get turned all the way up, and the brighter her expression gets, the more wary I am of how much shit she's going to give me for agreeing to do this. Most likely an exponential amount.

"Well *that's*—" she starts, but I hold up a hand to stop her. Her tone is already too much, and I need to process everything before I let the ribbing start.

"Give me like five minutes, okay? It's been a weird day so far. I need to at least eat before you start giving me a hard time."

I expect some kind of pushback, but she nods, leans back in her seat, and says, "I'll make you a deal."

I raise an eyebrow at her in question and she grins.

"Ask your mom about the Lawrence trip by the end of the day today and I won't tease you about this at all."

Oh, she is *good*. And really, there's only one option. "Deal."

❋

Mom picks me up from school early so that we have enough time to pick up my car before my shift at work tonight. It's the first time I've been really alone with her in weeks, and even though I've been waiting for this exact scenario to ask her about Lawrence, I'm still way nervous about bringing it up.

"How was your day, honey?" Mom asks as we pull out of the parking lot. She's got the radio tuned to NPR like Kevin did last week, which is new for her. She used to only listen to audiobooks in the car.

"Fine," I say.

"Just fine?" Mom asks, glancing over at me. "Nothing exciting or unusual happened at all?"

Normally I would lie and say no, because Mom and I haven't exactly been at a sharing place lately. But telling her about my new tutoring gig is a decent way to circle around to the Lawrence trip, so I say, "Not crazy exciting, but Ms. Ulbrich asked me to tutor someone today. Well, help him edit, actually. She said it would look good on scholarship applications."

"Oh." Mom grips the steering wheel a little tighter at even this slight mention of college. "That's a good idea. I'm sure she's right."

"Yeah, she really knows her stuff. She looked over my application essays when I applied everywhere and she gave me really good notes."

"I would hope so, since she teaches senior English," Mom says lightly.

"Ha-ha," I say. My smile fades quickly though, because this is the best opening I'm going to get. So I take a deep breath and add, "You know, actually, I've been wanting to talk to you about some college stuff."

"What about?"

"You know how Matt Spencer got an apartment this year?" I ask. And then without waiting for her to respond, I blurt everything out. "He wants Hannah and me to come visit sometime next semester. He'd have his roommate go stay with his girlfriend so it's not like we'd be alone with strangers, and I think it'd be fun to go up there and explore a little, you know? Hannah loved going up last year with her parents."

I manage to stop the word vomit and sneak a glance in Mom's

direction. Her mouth is set in a thin line and her shoulders are tense. Fantastic.

Finally, after a long pause, she says, "Would Hannah's parents be with you this time?"

I'm so shocked that she didn't refuse outright that I tell her the truth. "No, it'd just be me and Hannah. But it'd be totally legit, Mom. Matt's a peer leader or something, I can't remember the official title. But he gives campus tours to potential students and incoming freshmen at orientation in the summer, so he'd be able to give us a real tour and everything. And maybe even show us pet friendly apartments."

We pull up to a red light and Mom looks over at me, brow furrowed. "Pet friendly apartments?"

"Yeah," I say slowly. "I can't live in the dorms with Buffy, Mom."

"Apartments are expensive, Amber," she says, turning her focus back to the road. "If you do go to KU next year—and you know that doesn't make the most financial sense for our family— an apartment that allows large dogs probably wouldn't be in the cards. And if that's the case, Buffy would have to stay behind."

She cannot be serious. Like I would *ever* leave Buffy. "*When* I go to KU next year," I say, voice shaking, "Buffy is coming with me. I'll work as many hours as I need to and take out whatever loans I have to to make that happen."

Mom is quiet for a long, long moment. And then she says, "Let's talk about this another day, Amber. After you've gotten your college acceptances and found out for sure about grants and scholarships, when we can look at real numbers."

"Numbers aren't going to change my—"

"Enough," Mom snaps, and I shut up. I wish I'd just let Hannah crow at me about Jordan so that I could've put off asking Mom about going to Lawrence longer. Or maybe forever.

"You know what, until we have concrete numbers to look at," Mom says as the light turns green and we start moving forward again, "I don't think a trip to Lawrence is the best idea."

Of course she doesn't. She never did. "Fine."

We don't speak to each other for the rest of the drive.

Thanks to that frosty exchange with Mom, I spend the next couple of days avoiding the house. I was already scheduled to work Wednesday, but I pick up a closing shift working the cash register on Tuesday too, so that I can skip "family" dinner. Mom is pissed, but I don't care because it's so nice to be away from that awkwardness. And Buffy comes with me to work both nights, which always helps lighten my mood.

On Thursday night I call Hannah in a panic as I'm getting ready to leave for Jordan's house.

"Dude," she says when she answers. No hello or anything. "You have got to stop freaking out about this."

I dig through one of my boxes in search of my favorite Harper High hoodie, which was conspicuously absent when I unpacked my clothes. I think I used it to wrap this little ceramic treasure box my grandma gave me, but I can't find it. "I should never have said yes. What was I thinking?"

"That he's hot?"

"Hannah," I say, even though she's not totally wrong. Still, we had a deal. "You promised."

"Sorry," she says. She's done pretty well at holding up her end of the bargain so far, though to be fair it's only been three days. I think it helps that she's spent most of them scheming about how to get Mom to change her mind about our road trip. That's definitely taken up a lot of her time. I haven't said much during those conversations though, because I'm still too freaked out about what Matt said and I don't know how to ask her about it. "It was too easy."

"Well, try harder to resist next time. You know the rules, Han."

"I do," she says. "But the rules aren't what matter now, Amb. It matters that you *did* say yes. Which means you have to go."

"Actually, no. I could still cancel," I say, abandoning the boxes by my bed to go search for my hoodie in the closet.

"No," Hannah says, with an air of patience that makes me feel like she is my parent and I am her two-year-old child who is scared of the monsters under the bed, "you can't. That would be rude. It's just tutoring."

"Not technically. More like editing."

"Even better. Editing is less personal. Strictly business." I give another frustrated sigh, and she sighs back. "Look, I have an idea that might make you feel better about the whole thing."

"Oh really?" I ask, as I finally find my hoodie wedged back behind one of the boxes in my closet and pull it out, victorious. Buffy's tail thumps on the carpet as I crouch down next to her, now in search of shoes. "What's that?"

nine

Fifteen minutes later I'm ringing the doorbell at Jordan's house. It takes him a while to come to the door, and when he does, he doesn't open the screen right away. He just looks at me and then down and to my left, where Buffy is sitting patiently. Then he smiles and shakes his head, not even seeming surprised to see her with me. I guess Hannah was right about bringing her.

He opens the door and sticks his head out to say, "I'll come out through the garage."

"Okay," I say, and he disappears back into the house. I go back to the driveway to wait, and a minute later the third garage door opens and Buffy and I slowly make our way inside.

The main part of the garage is empty, with only oil stains on the concrete to tell me that Jordan's parents normally park there. But the space where a third car could go has been transformed into a kind of workout room. Treadmill, weight bench, one of those arm machines with the pulleys that I have no idea what it's called. I guess that explains why Jordan's Jeep is parked out on the curb. Wow. I know Jordan's a good basketball player, but I've never thought about what it takes to stay that way. No wonder his arms are so impressive. Not that I'm noticing his arms anymore.

Jordan's over by the back wall, flipping on light switches and turning on a little space heater. He glances back over his shoulder at me.

"What do you think?"

In spite of myself, I can't stop looking around. I go over to the side wall, which is covered in pictures of Jordan and a blond girl I assume must be his older sister. Every single picture involves some kind of sport. Basketball, T-ball, football, cheerleading, tennis. The more recent pictures are mostly of Jordan playing for our middle school and high school basketball teams. There's one of him laughing with Ethan Hawkins in the middle of a game from last year that makes me feel like a whole swarm of butterflies has taken over my stomach.

"It's nice out here," I say, forcing my gaze away from that last picture and focusing on the one below it. "Very homey."

Jordan chuckles a little and I look back at him, confused. He gestures in front of him, and I notice for the first time that there's a card table in front of the weight bench. His laptop is out and waiting, and he's got a space heater set up under everything to fight the chill. "Thanks, but I meant this. Will it work?"

Heat rushes to my cheeks and I look at his chest as I say, "Yeah. This is good."

"Cool. I was planning on being inside, but I figured with the dog we'd probably better stay out here." My cheeks get even hotter at this, but Jordan grins. "What's its name?"

"*Her* name is Buffy," I say, looking him in the eye now. His grin widens.

"Nice. I love that show." I raise an eyebrow and he adds, "My sister made me watch it last year when she was home for Christmas break."

"Oh. Right." I want to ask about his sister, who clearly has good taste in TV, but I don't because that would be personal and I'm not here for personal reasons, I'm here for business. School. I look around the garage again, my gaze tripping over the empty spots where his parents' cars presumably go. "Are your parents not here?"

The easiness of Jordan's face flickers to uncertainty for a second, and he rocks back on his heels. "Um, no. They do this . . . thing on Thursday nights."

"Thing?"

"This . . . bowling thing."

I raise my eyebrows. He sighs and goes flat-footed again. "They're part of a cosmic bowling league and the games are on Thursday nights. They just started last week and I forgot about it when we made these plans. I hope that's okay. That they're, uh, not here." He reaches up like he's going to run a hand through his hair, but drops it before he makes contact. "They know you're here, and they said it's fine, so I hope it is. Fine, I mean. Um."

"Oh, it's fine," I say quickly, even though I really should not say that. But I need this conversation to be over, badly. "Totally fine." I clear my throat. "Cosmic bowling, huh? Cool."

"Something like that." He shakes his head, grinning a little, and then looks from me to Buffy expectantly. "So. What's Buffy gonna do while we work?"

In answer I bend down and unclip her leash. "She'll hang out with us. Buffy, hang."

Buffy looks at me and then goes over to sniff the weight bench. Then she turns in a circle three times and curls up on the floor, head resting on her paws. Her ears stay up and her eyes flick from Jordan to me and then back again. I look at him too.

"I thought 'chill' was your word for 'stay,'" he says.

I'm surprised he remembered. "They mean different things. 'Chill' is for when we're outside or in an open space and I need her to stay close. 'Hang' is for when we're in a room I need her to stay in."

He looks around, his gaze lingering on the open garage door. "This counts as a room?"

"Yup. Open doors don't matter." I go over to the weight bench, sit down, and pull Jordan's laptop toward me. He slides in next to me, then leans back and looks behind me, where Buffy's still happy on the floor.

"What about 'stay'? What does that mean?"

"That's for the basic tricks, when we want to impress people."

"Basic tricks," he repeats.

"Right."

He looks at Buffy, then at me. "You're kind of impressive all the time." Then he turns forward and pulls the laptop a little closer to him. "Now, give me a sec and I'll pull up the assignment I need you to look at."

"Okay," I say faintly. He was totally talking about Buffy and her tricks. Right?

Thankfully, things get back to business after that. We spend half an hour going over the outline for the next paper for English, this one on Toni Morrison's *Beloved*. Ms. Ulbrich was right, he does have really good ideas. But I can already tell why they asked me for help.

"Why is 'incident' capitalized?"

Jordan leans forward a little to peer at the screen. We're close enough when he does this that I can feel how warm he is. It's chilly out here, even with the space heater and my hoodie, and I want to lean closer. For survival reasons, definitely not anything else. Instead I lean back and take a deep breath. He finds the word I've pointed out and leans back so he's in his own space. Shrugs. "I don't know. I just get kind of excited when I type."

"What?"

"Sometimes it seems like the next word should be capitalized to add extra oomph."

I stare at him. I don't know what to say. Especially since I find this enthusiasm for capitalization kind of cute. Very cute, actually. I give myself a little shake to snap myself out of it. Make myself think of rule number seven.

"Well," I manage to get out, my voice only a little strangled. "I like that, but I don't think Ms. Ulbrich will."

He grins. "Noted."

We get through the whole outline and then go over some of his old stuff that Ms. Ulbrich asked him to clean up, but we still have a few things left to do when Jordan pushes the laptop away and looks at me. "You wanna take a break?"

"Okay," I say slowly. I guess a break can't hurt. We've been working for a while, and I learned in psychology last year that people do better when they take a fifteen-minute break after working for an hour. Or something like that. "Sure."

He gets up and goes over to one of the shelves on the other side of the garage, comes back with a basketball, and tosses it to me. "You ever play horse?"

The only person I ever really played horse with was my dad. He loved basketball. Taught me how to dribble and shoot when I was so little I can't remember learning. "Not lately."

"You want to?"

"Shooting around is your idea of a break?"

He shrugs. "It's kind of ingrained."

I hesitate, worried this is crossing the line from business into personal. But my butt is kinda sore from sitting on this weight bench for so long, and with my rusty shooting skills I doubt one game could last very long. "All right."

"Awesome," he says, flashing me a bright smile.

We go out to the driveway and the motion light clicks on. I didn't notice that first night, but his driveway is almost totally flat. I wonder if they built it like that on purpose so it'd be easier for Jordan to play. This is the kind of neighborhood where you can do things like that.

He passes me the ball and I catch it easily. I look at him, surprised. "You aren't going to start?"

"No." He looks kind of sheepish as he adds, "It's not usually fair if I go first."

I don't argue. Based on the rumors I've heard at school, Jordan has gotten interest from tons of Division II and a few Division I colleges to play next year. I have a feeling I'm about to get my ass kicked.

"All right." I'm standing about where the free-throw line would be. In fact, when I look down there's a faint line drawn on the concrete. I put my toes on the line, take a deep breath, and run through the motions my dad taught me for free throws, the one thing he taught me to do really well before he left. The same ones I saw Jordan do that first night. Three dribbles, pause to take a breath. Let it out. Shoot.

Swish.

"Nice," Jordan says. He was waiting by the basket and catches the ball easily as it falls to the ground. "You practice that?"

I flex my fingers, my wrists, and savor the loose feeling I have from going through those motions. Maybe this was a good idea after all. "Not in a long time."

"Well, you've got good form."

I feel myself blush and hope he can't see it. "Thanks."

We're somewhere in the middle of the game when I call Buffy to come chill in the yard. She's been good tonight and I'm sure she wants to sniff around. Jordan watches as she trots out of the garage and goes to sniff in the grass. He just made a shot from the very end of the driveway, so I go over to where he's standing to mark his place. But instead of moving away to give me plenty of space for my turn, he stays close behind me. His proximity is distracting and I miss, but he doesn't even notice. He's still watching Buffy, who's now settled at the top of the driveway and biting an itch on one of her paws.

"That's S for me," I say, running to catch the ball before it rolls into the street. Jordan's still there at the end of the driveway, so I go back over to him and hold out the ball. I get this sense of déjà vu as he takes it, especially when he looks back at me and tips his head ever so slightly to the side.

"How'd you teach her to do all those tricks?"

Usually when people ask me this I explain about all the *Dog Whisperer* marathons I did when I first got Buffy, and how I read all the books I could find on animal behavior and stuff like that. But again, I don't want to get into something so personal. So I say, "I don't know. She's smart. It was pretty easy."

Jordan palms the ball with one hand and shakes his head. "I can tell she's smart, but she learned the meaning of the word 'chill' from you."

"How'd you get so good at basketball?"

He pulls his head back and slaps his other hand to the ball so he's holding it with both hands in front of his chest, elbows out like chicken wings. "I practiced."

"Us too." I reach out and tap the ball. "It's your turn."

"Right." He goes to the top corner of the driveway now, the equivalent of a three, and makes it easily. I catch the ball and jog up to him, take my turn, and miss.

"E. You win."

"You did good, though," he says, turning to grin at me. "Better than most people. You got me up to HOR." He says it like *whore*, which startles a laugh out of me.

"A story to tell all my friends." One I'm sure Hannah in particular will love. If I tell her.

"Cammie would be jealous. She's only ever gotten me to HO."

I can tell he wants me to laugh again, but I can only manage a weak chuckle. The mention of Cammie is like a dousing of ice water that immediately snaps me back to reality. I clear my throat and head back into the garage. "We should probably get back to work. It's getting late."

"Oh. Right." He sounds disappointed, but he follows me in anyway. "What about Buffy?"

She's followed us in and I know she'll be fine, but I say, "You try telling her what to do."

"Really?" His eyes light up at the prospect. I nod, and he tells her to hang. She goes over to stand by Jordan, then lays down by his feet. He looks up at me, his expression full of wonder.

"That's more than practice. That's like magic." I try not to show how much that gets to me, but I don't think I do a very good job.

A little while later, when we're done and I'm clipping Buffy's leash back to her collar for the walk home, Jordan says, "Same time next week?"

I look up. He's still sitting at the weight bench, fiddling with this place on the seat where the fabric's ripped and part of it sticks up. He reaches out to scratch behind Buffy's ears while he waits for me to answer, not quite meeting my eyes, and I have the same thought I did in Ms. Ulbrich's classroom on Monday.

He really wants me to say yes.

"Yeah," I say.

Jordan smiles. "Good."

One week down, I tell myself as Buffy and I head back down his driveway. *And only five more to go.*

ten

S o," Hannah says to me the next morning, as we're walking laps around the hallways to kill time before the first bell. "How'd it go? Did the Buffy thing work?"

I shrug my purse higher on my shoulder and readjust my books in my arms. "Yeah, we stayed outside. Thanks for that, by the way. You're a genius. And it was fine. We got a lot of work done." Hannah hums in disappointment and I look over at her. "What?"

"Oh, nothing. Just, when you say work, I know you mean actual schoolwork. Not, you know, a more fun kind." She grins at me, eyes twinkling. "Tell me you don't want to do that kind of work with Jordan Baugh."

"Hannah!" I hiss, shooting her a look before I glance around to see if anyone near us is listening. No one is, but still. "God."

Her grin widens. "You didn't say no."

"That's because the no was implied," I tell her. "Rule number seven. Remember?"

I glare at her until she holds up her hands in surrender. "All right, fine, I'll quit."

We walk in silence for a few seconds and then she brightens and looks back at me. "Hey, so I was thinking. What if we do movie night at your house this weekend? I've missed your mom's baking, and I really wanna check out your new room."

I shake my head. I've been looking forward to having another escape from me and Mom's cold war this weekend, and anyway, inviting Hannah over would be breaking rule number nine. In the past when Mom's boyfriends were in our house, it didn't matter as much if Hannah came over because those spaces were ours first and Mom's boyfriends were just glorified guests. Now that we live with Kevin, though, it's the other way around, and I don't feel comfortable fudging the rule this way just because Hannah misses my mom's baked goods. "I already told Mom we'd do your house."

"So?" Hannah says, nodding her head to the left to tell me that we should turn down the next hallway so we can stop at her locker. "Tell her we changed our minds. I'm sure she won't care, and I really think—"

"I said *no*," I snap. My voice carries down the hall, loudly enough that quite a few people stop to stare at me.

"Okay," Hannah says after a beat, her voice quiet. "My house it is. You'll bring the popcorn?"

I clear my throat. "I'll bring some of Mom's cookies too. She found a new chocolate-chip recipe the other day and she needs taste testers, so. It should be good."

She found the new recipe when she was stress baking because of our fight on Monday, but I don't tell Hannah this.

"Happy to be a guinea pig," Hannah says, smiling at me over her shoulder as she spins the dial on her locker to put in the combination. But there is still an edge of hurt in her expression—a tightness in the corners of her mouth and a guarded look in her eyes—that makes me look away.

Once Hannah has her books, we head toward the commons to meet up with Ryan before first period, our conversation thankfully back to normal. As we round the corner back to the main hallway, Hannah stops.

"What?" I ask, wondering if she's changed her mind and is going to start bugging me about movie night again. But she doesn't do that. She just grins and looks pointedly in front of us. I follow her gaze and there's Jordan, walking this way with a whole group of his friends. He's holding up one hand in a sort of acknowledgment, a sheepish, shy smile on his face. I glance at Hannah and she gives me a look. So I wave back, because I know if I don't I'll never hear the end of it.

And then we're past him and as promised Hannah doesn't say a word about it. Like me waving to Jordan Baugh is a normal part of the day, even though it's not.

On Tuesday night I find myself at the table with Mom and Kevin and Cammie for yet another "family" dinner. Buffy has been banished to my room as usual.

Though the food has improved since our first attempt at this, the atmosphere still leaves a lot to be desired. Cammie is sullen and quiet and picks at her food. Mom chatters endlessly about her day at work and some confrontation she had with a crazy mother of the bride. And Kevin has to leave the table halfway through the meal to answer a call from his business partner about some sort of plumbing emergency at their office, which is so gross. Why would you call someone about that over dinner? Why not send a text so the rest of us didn't have to hear Kevin gasp, "The toilet overflowed into the *lobby*?" while we were halfway through eating our bowls of French onion soup?

I try to keep eating my soup after Kevin leaves to deal with the shit-cident, I really do. But when he calls out, "Claire! What's the name of that plumber you like?" I give up and shove my bowl into the center of the table. Mom closes her eyes for a brief second and then shoves her own bowl away too.

"It's Tom's Johns," she calls back, getting to her feet and hurrying out of the dining room. "I have the number in my phone, hang on."

Which leaves Cammie and me sitting in silence, eyeing each other across the table.

Finally, after a long moment, she says, "How mad do you think they'll be if we put it all down the garbage disposal?"

There's no need for her to specify what she means by "it."

"I'm willing to risk it," I say, grabbing Mom's soup bowl and mine and pushing my chair back.

With a nod, Cammie grabs her bowl and Kevin's abandoned one and follows me into the kitchen.

Ten minutes later we've dumped the soup, loaded the dishwasher, gotten the not-brown parts of dinner divided into Tupperware and put into the fridge, and wiped down the kitchen counters and the dining room table. All without speaking another word to each other. Now that we're done I'm expecting Cammie to bail any second. Mom and Kevin still haven't emerged from

Kevin's office yet, which can't be a good sign, so "family" night is clearly over. But she's lingering by the island and fiddling with her keys, like she's not sure whether she should stay or leave. Which makes me feel like I should be polite and stay down here too, at least for a little bit longer.

"Thanks for helping me clean up," I say, just to break the silence.

She shrugs and studies the sparkling countertop. "You're welcome."

Insert long, awkward pause.

"Well." I take a step back. "I need to go get Buffy and take her on a walk, so . . ."

Cammie straightens up. "I'd better go anyway. I told J I'd stop by before I go back to my mom's."

"Oh, right." I assume by J she means Jordan, and I get a pang of anxiety at this reminder of how many rules I've bent when it comes to him. And at picturing her car in his driveway, if I'm being honest. I want to ask her what their whole deal is, why they don't hang out at school, but that breaks like half of my rules. So I keep my mouth shut.

"Right?" Cammie asks, one eyebrow raised. "Did he tell you I was coming over or something?"

"What? No." I take another step back. "I haven't talked to him since—" I cut myself off, not sure how or if I should mention the fact that I was at his house last week. I can't decide if talking to Cammie about the fact that I'm helping her childhood friend makes it more or less weird. Probably because the weirdness is going to be the same regardless of whether we ignore it or not, which is why I should have said no in the first place. This is what I get for making exceptions to my rules. So much cringing.

Cammie watches me for a second after my strange pause and then goes, "Since your tutoring thing?"

"Editing," I correct automatically.

"Right," Cammie says, a hint of a smile on her face. "That."

"Whatever it is," I say, "I haven't talked to him since then. I don't even have his number, actually. Just Facebook."

"Got it," Cammie says. "Want me to tell him you say hey?"

"No!" I blurt, and her eyes widen.

"Girls, I am so sorry about that," Kevin calls, and I send a silent prayer of thanks up to God or whoever else might be listening for this perfect timing.

I scurry back into the dining room right as Mom and Kevin come in from the living room. They stop short at the sight of the cleared table and look over at me.

"You girls cleaned up?" Mom asks. "Thank you. You didn't have to do that."

"It's not a big deal," Cammie says from somewhere behind me.

"Did you save the soup?" Kevin asks.

Cammie snorts. "Dad. No. Come on."

Mom and Kevin both smile, but Kevin still looks a little anxious. "Are either of you still hungry?" he asks. "We could order pizza or something. Or I could make omelets."

I shake my head and start toward the living room. "I need to take Buffy for a walk, and I can scavenge later if I need to."

"And I need to go," Cammie says.

"So soon?" Kevin asks, disappointment clear in his voice.

Though Cammie comes for dinner when she's supposed to, she never stays long and has never spent the night, and I can tell Kevin is really anxious about it. I don't stay to hear the rest of the conversation though. Instead I take the stairs two at a time to go break Buffy out of bedroom jail. She's lying in the doorway with her nose barely out in the hallway, and she wuffs excitedly when she hears me coming.

It only takes me a couple of minutes to grab a sweatshirt and Buffy's leash, and then we're heading back down the stairs. I call out to Mom on our way out the door to let her know that I'm taking Buffy for a walk and won't be gone too long.

Cammie's little blue Honda, which is much newer than my car and doesn't look like it's ever needed any major parts replaced, is still in the driveway when we get outside. As soon as we hit the grass the driver's-side window rolls down and Cammie sticks her head out. "Hey, Amber?"

"Yeah?" I ask, giving Buffy some slack in her leash so that she can sniff around the front yard.

"Next time I'm here don't worry about putting Buffy in your room, okay?"

I blink at Cammie for a second, completely thrown by this. "Um, okay."

"Cool," she says. "See you."

eleven

On Thursday it's cold enough that I'm shivering in layered sweatshirts when I walk over to Jordan's. Buffy pants beside me, her toenails clicking on the hard ground, ears pricked forward like she's already focusing them on our destination. When we turn onto Jordan's street and she realizes for sure where we're going, she pulls at the leash to get me to move faster, something she hardly ever does.

"Don't get too excited. This isn't a regular thing," I tell her. She looks up at me and tips her head to the side, like she doesn't believe me. "I'm serious. Up to winter break and that's it."

All I get in response to that is a disdainful blink.

Jordan's already out in the garage and waiting for us when we get there. As I step inside, he makes a wide, sweeping gesture at the weight bench and card table. "Hey. What do you think?"

I look behind him and see an extra space heater under the card table, a bowl of water and a makeshift bed of towels for Buffy at our feet, and the basketball out and waiting behind his laptop.

"Looks great," I say, bending down to unclip Buffy's leash. She makes a beeline for the water bowl and laps half of it up in about three seconds. Then she goes over to Jordan and nudges his knee with her nose. When she backs away there's a giant wet spot that I know can't feel good in this chill. "Sorry about that. She's just excited to see you."

"It's okay," Jordan says, reaching his hand down for Buffy to sniff and then running it over the top of her head. "I'm excited to see her too."

But he's not looking at Buffy. He's looking at me.

Four more weeks. That's it.

After a second, Jordan clears his throat and adds, "I actually got Buffy something else, if it's okay for her to have it."

"What is it?" I ask, taking a deep breath to soothe my jittery stomach.

He heads to one of the shelves on the far wall of the garage and comes back with a knuckle bone. Buffy immediately plunks her butt on the ground and stares at him with sad puppy eyes, silently begging.

"Oh man. Is that the peanut butter–filled kind?"

"Yeah," Jordan says, glancing from Buffy to me. "Is that okay? I wasn't sure what to get but the lady at the store said that these are better for dogs than rawhide, so I went for it."

"It's perfect," I tell him. "Seriously. Give that to her and you've earned a lifelong friend."

"That's the idea," he says, holding the bone out to Buffy. She delicately takes it from him, tail wagging at warp speed, and immediately goes to her towel bed to start chomping on it. At the sight of this, Jordan grins at me so brightly that my breath catches and I have to look away.

"Right," I say, hugging my coat more tightly around myself. "Well, uh, good. Should we get started?"

"Oh yeah." He waits until I get settled on the weight bench to slide in beside me. "Let me know if you get cold, okay?"

"Okay," I say, even though between him and the space heaters, I doubt I'll be feeling cold for days.

We work for about an hour before he gets distracted and starts glancing over his shoulder out at the driveway, where the basketball hoop waits.

"Break time?" he asks as soon as I finish the paper I've been reading.

"Sure." I could use some movement after sitting still for so long. And, okay, I could also use some time not sitting next to him on this weight bench.

He grins and grabs the ball off the table, palming it in his hand.

We don't talk too much for the first few shots of the game, and Jordan gets me to HO in the first two rounds without even breaking a sweat. But when he misses a three-pointer from the very edge of the driveway and I get the ball back again, I decide to try something a little different.

"Backward?" Jordan asks, raising his eyebrows when I position myself about six feet in front of the basket and turn my back to it.

"Yeah. Got a problem with it?" His eyes dancing, he shakes his head. "Good. Now, *shhhh*. I need to concentrate."

He mimes zipping his lips and takes a step back, and I fight a laugh. Then I tip my head back to look at the basket, getting a feel for what kind of arc I'll need to make this happen. Jordan is watching me when I pull myself upright again, and I know I'll miss if I can see the look on his face when I do this. So I close my eyes, take a deep breath, and blow it out as I toss the ball up and over my head. A second later I'm rewarded by the *thwack* of the basketball on the backboard and a *swish* as it goes through the net.

"Ah, shit," Jordan says, and I open my eyes to find him grinning at me. "Do I have to keep my eyes closed, or is it just the spot and position I need to get?"

I think about that for a second. "If you make it with your eyes closed, we can play one more game before we go back inside."

He narrows his eyes and points at me. "You're on."

He misses, barely, but it's still a miss, and I try and fail to keep a smug grin off my face as I go get the ball for my next turn.

"I'll get you next time," he says, pointing a finger at me, his expression mock-serious.

"We'll see," I say, turning to face him. His hair is halfway stuck in the hood of his sweatshirt and the rest is a crazy mess, like it doesn't know which way to go now that it's free. I have this urge to run up to him and smooth it down, but I clutch the basketball to my chest and take a step back instead.

"Yeah we will," he says. "Next week I'll—" But then he stops himself and frowns. "Actually, I guess we won't be able to meet next week, since it's Thanksgiving."

"Yeah, probably not," I say, ignoring the stab of disappointment I feel at the thought.

Giving myself a shake, I line up my next shot at the free-throw line, needing the ritual dribbling to steady myself. I make the free throw easily and so does Jordan, but on my next turn, I miss. And instead of watching as he takes his next shot, I look over at The Castle. I've been trying to avoid it all night, which is difficult, let me tell you. Now that we've brought up Thanksgiving even vaguely, though, it's kind of hard to ignore it.

"You gonna be there for Thanksgiving?" Jordan asks. I jump and glance over my shoulder to find him looking at me, standing closer than usual.

I take a small step away so that he's out of my bubble, even though my insides are screaming at me to move closer. "Yeah. How'd you know?"

"It's what Kevin does every year. Cammie hates it because it's so over-the-top. She usually comes over here after the big dinner, to fill me in on all the shenanigans." He pauses and taps his foot on the concrete. "I don't know if she will this year though. Since it'll be the first big holiday there without . . . well, you know. I think she'll want to go hang out with her mom."

"That makes sense," I say, nodding. It's what she does after all our regular dinners, so I don't see why this one would be any different. I know this whole split-up-parents situation has to suck for Cammie, but I still get a little jealous sometimes, because she has both of her parents around. She has somewhere else to go when she doesn't want to be at her dad's, and that must be nice. I've never had that luxury.

After a beat of silence, I sneak a glance at Jordan and add, "Do you know them very well? The Kleins?"

I've been wondering about them more over the past couple of weeks, since I knew we'd be spending Thanksgiving there. Rule number four for surviving my mother's love life is to get used to spending holidays with strangers, but it's one of my hardest rules to follow. So many of my holiday memories are just blurs of faces and strange traditions that they don't even feel like mine. That's a weird feeling to get used to, no matter how hard I keep trying.

"Yeah, a little bit," Jordan says. "They're not too bad. Sometimes Oscar comes over to drink scotch and talk basketball with my dad."

I crinkle my nose up. "Fancy." Then for some reason I add, "Did you know he also calls in the middle of dinner to talk about plumbing problems?"

Out of the corner of my eye, I see Jordan grin. "Yeah, Cam mentioned something about that the other day. I didn't ask for details."

"Good call," I tell him.

We're quiet for a moment, just looking up at that big house. Then Jordan steps closer and taps my arm, holding out the basketball with his other hand. "It's your turn, remember?"

I jump a little and turn to look at him. "Right. Sorry."

After I lose the game and we're back in the garage, me reading Jordan's papers, Jordan crouched down on the floor trying to figure out all the tricks Buffy knows, I'm still thinking about next week and how much I am not looking forward to it. I've never had what I'd call a normal holiday, and suddenly I need to hear about what it's like to have one. About what normal holiday plans look like. Since Jordan's mention of Cammie earlier didn't totally freak me out, I decide to bend the rule a little more and ask him something personal. "What are you doing for Thanksgiving?"

"Usually we go to my grandparents' house in Kansas City, but this year they're coming here."

Perfectly normal, just like I thought. "Nice."

"Yeah, I guess."

I narrow my eyes at him. "You don't sound very excited."

He hesitates, watching me for a second. "I'm just worried. My sister is bi, and she hasn't come out to my grandparents yet. She's got this awesome girlfriend now though, and things are getting pretty serious between them. So she's planning to tell Grandma and Grandpa when they're here next week."

"You're worried about how they'll react?"

"Yeah," he says, blowing out a breath and looking at his feet. "Tasha and my parents are too. Grandma and Grandpa have made some really hurtful comments about LGBT rights in the last few years. My parents always shut them down, but they keep saying those kinds of things. So I'm not super optimistic."

"That sucks," I say.

"Tell me about it."

The slump of his shoulders and the way he won't meet my eyes both tug at my insides. Clearly I'm not the only person with family issues and holiday baggage, and I wish I could help him with his instead of dwelling on mine. Which is probably why I blurt, "Well, hey. Maybe we can meet on Thursday after all."

His head comes up. "Yeah?"

Oh no. What did I just do?

"Yeah. I can promise you I'll need an escape plan. Like, promise. And tutoring—I mean editing—is the perfect excuse. And you'll be right next door."

His face relaxes a little. "It'd be nice to have something planned after dinner since I doubt Cam will be around. Plus, we wouldn't want to miss out on our game. Maybe all the food I'm gonna eat will give you an advantage and you'll finally beat me."

I snort. "I highly doubt that."

"You never know." He sits up straighter. "All right then. Gimme your phone."

"What for?" I ask, but I hand it over anyway. He gives me a look.

"What do you think?" And then he puts his number in it and calls himself so he'll have mine.

I eye him when he hands my phone back, remembering how I word-vomited to Cammie on Tuesday night about how Jordan and I didn't have each other's numbers. "Did Cammie say something to you about this?"

A crinkle appears between his brows. "About Thanksgiving? I told you she did."

"No, never mind," I say, shaking my head.

"Ooo-kay," he says, smiling slightly now. "Send *SOS* if you need to get out next week, okay?"

"You too," I tell him. He nods in agreement and I go back to his papers and in a minute everything is back to business.

It's just one extra week, I tell myself. *One extra day.* But it feels like more than that.

twelve

I barely have time to look at the inside of The Castle before I'm swept into a bone-crushing hug by a giant man. My face fits into his armpit. Happy Thanksgiving to me.

"You must be Amber!" the guy booms over my head.

"Yup," I say to his pit. "That's me."

"So nice to meet you. We've heard all about you. All good, promise!" And then, thank God, he lets me go. I suck in air like it's going out of style and put a hand to my chest so I can feel it expanding. He squished it so hard I'm a little worried, but everything seems to be okay. The Giant doesn't notice my distress. He's already moved on to hugging Cammie.

"Cammie!" he yells. "So good to see you, kid!"

Mom's next to be hugged, and then Kevin and The Giant do a grown-up bro handshake, with lots of back slapping. I try not to laugh while it's happening but it's hard not to. They look so ridiculous. It's only after that's done that we're allowed to move further into the house and The Giant starts calling out to the other people that "Kevin and the girls are here!"

I hang back and let Mom and Kevin take the lead after The Giant, who I am assuming is Oscar Klein, and find myself alone in the huge foyer with Cammie. She's lingering by the long mirror that faces the doorway. From where I'm standing I have a pretty good view of myself and I can see that my hair is puffed out around my head from Oscar's hug. Cammie's blond hair is sleek and smooth as usual. So not fair.

"Well," I say, reaching up to run my fingers through my hair in an attempt to smooth it down. "That was something."

"That was Oscar," she says with a shrug.

I give up on taming my frizz and take advantage of our aloneness to check out the foyer. It's all high ceilings and magazine decorating. I check to make sure Cammie isn't looking and sneak a picture on my phone for Hannah. I promised to document the evening since we've spent so many years wondering what this place looks like on the inside.

Delicious smells are wafting in from the room to my right, which is promising. Less promising are the loud voices coming from the same room. It sounds like a pretty big crowd. New people are always my least favorite part of holidays with Mom's boyfriends, because you never know what you're going to get. For example, in middle school when my mom was dating Leo, he had an aunt who loved to talk to me at holidays and always tried to steal my food.

Aunt Marin is the inspiration for rule number five: Protect your plate at all large meal gatherings, holidays or otherwise. She'd start a conversation with me about random things and immediately reach out to grab a bite of my pie or my stuffing or whatever else looked good, always with used forks. She said it was okay for us to share because we were "family," and didn't ever seem to hear me when I told her that I don't even share forks with my mother, who is my actual blood relation. I never got to eat very much around her. I was always too grossed out.

Hopefully since no one here is related to Kevin and Cammie I won't get anyone like Aunt Marin, but you never know. Turkey and stuffing do weird things to people.

When Cammie and I finally come into the dining room—which is just as impressive as the foyer, but too crowded for me to sneak a picture of—my mother shoots me a look and holds out her hand, beckoning me over. She's smiling through her teeth, which tells me she can't remember the name of the person she's talking to. For as long as I can remember we've had a rule that if Mom doesn't introduce me to someone it's because she can't remember their name. It's my job to find it out. This means that I'm the one who ends up introducing myself to her current boyfriend's mother/sister/best friend/ex-wife, which is . . . awkward, most of the time. Which is why rule number three is: Get used to introducing yourself to strangers. It's going to happen a lot.

I fix on a smile of my own and walk over to my mother, hoping that this isn't another ex-wife situation. That happened with Howard at his first Christmas with Mom, and it did not end well.

"There you are," my mother says, grabbing hold of my arm and turning me so I'm facing the tiny lady in front of her.

"Here I am." I shake free of Mom's grip and hold out my hand to her new friend. "Hi, I'm Amber. What's your name?"

"Michelle," the lady says, shaking my hand. "I'm Oscar's wife."

"You have a beautiful house," I say, and Michelle beams.

"Thank you," she says. We make small talk for a few more

minutes and then Michelle starts talking to Mom about the rolls and pies we brought over. Under the safety of dessert talk, I slip away, sure Mom won't miss me. She can talk dessert for forever and a day.

I do a survey of the room. There are about fifteen other people here, all adults in fancy clothes holding champagne flutes. Kevin's talking to Oscar and a bunch of other guys who look like they're in their mid-forties and above, and Mom and Michelle have been joined by the rest of the ladies. There's an invisible line separating the men from the women. It's like we're at a middle school dance or something.

I spot Cammie in a chair by the fireplace and decide that since we are the only people here under thirty-five, she's my safest bet.

"Hey," I say when I reach her.

"Hey. You met Michelle?"

"Yeah. God, she's tiny."

"I know. Did she offer to give you the tour?"

"No."

Cammie gets up. "Come on. Knowing them, the food's ready but we won't eat for another half an hour."

I eye her for a second, trying to decide if this offer is genuine or not. Rule number two for survival is to remember that children of the boyfriend are roommates to be tolerated, not friends. But this doesn't seem like a friendly gesture; it just seems like a polite one. That plus the fact that she didn't say a word about Buffy being loose in the house when she came for dinner on Tuesday make me decide it's safe to say, "Okay."

The rest of the house is like the foyer and the living room.

Big. Impressive. Decorated down to the smallest details. And all the beds have at least twenty throw pillows, which is the most impractical thing I have ever seen. I don't even bother trying to hide that I'm taking pictures as we go along. As we come out of the master suite, which has a bathroom and walk-in closet combo the size of the den at Kevin's house, I turn to Cammie and say, "And to think I thought your house was big."

She gives me a funny look. "It's pretty small for this neighborhood, actually." She turns and gives one last look to the cavernous bedroom and adds, half under her breath, "I like ours better."

I'm so surprised to hear her refer to the house as ours that I say, "Me too," without a hint of sarcasm.

Cammie glances at me, then shuts the light off in the bedroom and starts back off down the hall. "We better get back."

"Right."

With rule number five in mind, I stick close to Mom once we rejoin the group. Somehow we manage to get the four of us in a row on one side of the table, with Cammie and me in between Mom and Kevin. It's perfect, especially since the table is huge and long and the centerpiece is the most elaborate thing I have ever seen. It runs the whole length of the table and has so many tall parts that you have to move your head to one side or the other to actually look at the people across from you. It makes having a conversation with anyone who isn't right beside you difficult, which is fine by me. And reaching over or across it is totally out of the question, which means I can enjoy my food without fear of anyone stealing a bite.

By four o'clock almost everyone is still talking across and around the centerpiece at each other. I'm on my second slice of pie. I'm still doing okay but then Mom gets up to go to the bathroom and the lady on the other side of her starts eyeing me like she wants to suck me into a conversation. Oh, shit. I've been debating about whether or not to actually use the lifeline Jordan gave me last week, but now I'm thinking maybe I should. Right on cue, my phone buzzes in my pocket. I pull it out to see a text from Jordan. **SOS**. Perfect.

I get up and am surprised when Cammie grabs for me, a panicked look on her face. I notice that Kevin's gotten up and followed Mom into the kitchen, and that the lady on *his* other side is leaning across the empty seat and opening her mouth like she's about to start talking at Cammie. Cammie and I may not be friends, but it's not like I can leave her to that kind of fate. I lean forward and put on my best polite smile.

"Hey, Cammie, can you show me where the bathroom is again?"

"Sure!" She scrambles out of her chair. The lady looks disappointed but snaps her mouth shut, and before anyone else notices, we're out in the now-empty living room.

"Thanks for that," Cammie says.

"No problem."

"Go ahead and go. I'll wait here. I need to text my mom to see when she'll be back at the apartment. You remember where the bathroom is, right?" She's already going toward the fire and the cushy armchairs there.

"Yeah," I say slowly. "I remember."

I could leave it at that. Make my escape on my own. Go hang out with Jordan alone, because he told me himself he wasn't banking on his usual holiday hang-out time with Cammie today. But that feels wrong, somehow. Like, if Cammie found out about me leaving her here to go hang out with her friend, I would feel like a huge bitch. And if Jordan found out—ugh, I don't want to think about why it would make me feel *so* guilty. But it would.

Plus, it's Thanksgiving. A holiday. Niceness is important on holidays. It's not getting involved, or caring, if I invite her along. It's just being nice.

Also, it might be good to bring her along. As a buffer. Since I don't have my usual canine one with me today.

"Actually," I say, "I wasn't going to the bathroom."

Cammie gives me a weird, narrow-eyed look, like I have confirmed all her worst fears about me. "Uh, okay. Were you going home?"

I shake my head. "I'm going next door."

She pulls her head back a little, a reflex, as if what I've said doesn't compute. Then she says, "Oh. Right."

"Do you want to come? Jordan said you guys usually hang out after your dinners here anyway. This would just be bailing a little early."

For another long moment she just studies me, her expression unreadable. Then she gets to her feet and tucks her phone back into her pocket. "Yeah. Okay."

thirteen

Jordan's garage is already open and he's digging something out of one of the buckets on the back wall when we walk in. At the sound of our footsteps he turns around and smiles, the kind that's slow and takes a while to spread out all over his face. The kind of smile that definitely does not make me feel like someone is slowly cranking up my heart rate right along with it.

"Hey," he says, nodding to me. "Took you long enough."

"Sorry."

"It's all right." He glances behind me and brightens even more when he notices Cammie. "Hey, Cam."

I want to ask him why he sent the SOS but Cammie says, "Hey, J." So I don't.

Jordan turns back to the bucket, rummages around for a few more seconds, and comes up with a basketball. Of course. He holds it out in my direction, a questioning look on his face.

I glance down at my outfit. Jordan's in track pants and a long-sleeved Nike T-shirt, so they must keep it casual at the Baugh house for Thanksgiving. Either that or they ate super early. I'm in a sweater dress, tights, and boots, my peacoat buttoned up halfway. Not exactly the right clothes for shooting around, but I shrug, pull off my coat, and toss it on the weight bench. Just like it didn't feel right to leave Cammie alone next door, today it doesn't feel right to remind him that we're supposed to work first, play second. Stupid holiday niceness.

"You going first today?" I ask.

"Nope. Cam, you wanna play?"

"Play what?"

"Horse."

Cammie wrinkles her nose. "No thanks." She gestures down to her feet, at the nice heels she's wearing. "I can't play in these, and I don't want to shred my tights."

Jordan grins. "Fair enough." He bounce-passes me the ball and we go back out to the driveway. Cammie drags a chair to the edge of the garage and sits down to watch. Jordan hangs back near her but turns to me. "All right, Amber. Let's see what you got."

I'm wired and jittery. It must be all the pie. I put the ball down between my feet and do helicopters with my arms for a second, first forward, then back. I size up the basket, trying to decide my best move. Do I start off easy, or go for the kill right away?

"Come on," Jordan says in a teasing voice. "We don't have all day."

I scowl at him, grab the ball, and position myself in front of the basket. Turn around. Don't look when I toss the ball over my head. Smile like a maniac when I hear the ball swish through the net.

"Damn," Jordan says. I turn around and smirk at him before I go running after the ball.

"How many times has she made that shot?" Cammie asks. It's

clear from her tone that she knows this is a thing we do. I'm not sure if that's good or not. That she knows. Or that Jordan and I have a thing.

"Twice," Jordan says.

"And how many times have *you* made it?"

I'm back over to them now. I hand Jordan the ball and say, "None yet. You need me to show you the spot?"

He slumps his shoulders, an exaggerated frown on his face. "No. I remember." He gets the spot right, but misses.

"H," I say.

"Yeah, yeah. Go on, superstar. It's your turn."

"I'm not a superstar," I tell him, but I go pick my next shot anyway.

We go back and forth for a while. I manage to get him to HOR, tying my personal best, but I'm a letter ahead and earn my E before I can make him plural. I'm a little out of breath when we finish, and a lot sweaty. It's cold out but we've been moving around enough that I wish I could strip down to something cooler. I settle for pushing my sleeves up as far as they can go and pulling my hair back into a sloppy ponytail.

Cammie's quiet through most of the game, and when Jordan goes to get us all drinks from the fridge in the garage I realize she's watching me, eyes narrowed.

"What?" I ask.

She presses her lips together and shakes her head. "Nothing."

Jordan comes back out then. I reach for the water bottle he's holding out, but instead of handing it over he comes around behind me and says, "Hold up your hair."

"What?" I ask again, but for some insane reason I do what he says. The next thing I know the bottle is pressed against my neck. It's cold and it feels good and for one second that's all I think. Then my brain catches up with what's happening and I'm hotter all over than I was a minute ago. Rule number seven. *Rule number seven.* I step away and turn around to face him, snatching the bottle from his hand.

"Thanks," I say, working to keep my tone even. Short.

He grins. "Sure thing."

Cammie does this cough that sounds like she's trying to cover up a laugh. My face burns with embarrassment. I need to sit down, so I go into the garage and over to the weight bench, my usual spot. This is good until Jordan comes over and slides in next to me. Not touching, but close. All relaxed and comfortable and easy. I am none of those things. I am the opposite of those things. And I need to get away from him but I can't get up because I just sat down and getting up again would be weird.

I look over at Cammie. She looks like she needs to cough again. Jesus Christ.

"So," Jordan says, making me jump. "Thanksgiving dinner. You tell me yours, I'll tell you mine."

"Ugh," Cammie says, rolling her eyes. "Oscar practically suffocated Amber. She's not small enough to escape the pits."

Jordan winces. "Ouch."

"Yup."

They're both looking at me. I should probably say something. What comes out is, "At least he wears deodorant."

For about ten seconds there is total silence. Then it's like someone snaps their fingers and we all laugh and laugh like I am the funniest person in the world, even though I'm definitely not.

The laughter is a good icebreaker, and Cammie and Jordan start trading stories. They ask each other questions like they already know the answers, and I'm sure they do, since Jordan said they do this little tradition every year. Jordan asks how long it took Oscar to tell his African safari story and Cammie asks whether Jordan's grandparents have said anything nasty yet (twenty minutes, and yes, after Tasha came out to them, which resulted in Jordan's dad kicking them out). I don't have much to add to the conversation, but it's nice. Too nice, actually, though it's better than if I'd stayed next door.

Eventually Cammie's phone rings. "It's Dad," she tells us, glancing at the screen. She answers in a very upbeat tone that I'm betting Kevin will find suspicious since she's still been less than enthusiastic about spending time at his house. "Hey, Dad. What's up? No, sorry, we went next door. You know I always hang with J after turkey, and Amber had to help him with their editing thing." Jordan and I exchange a glance. Editing. Right. We were supposed to be doing that. "Well, I'm sorry. You guys were busy." Cammie sighs. "Yes, fine. Yeah, I'll ask him. *Yes*, God. See you in a sec. Okay, yeah. Bye."

She gets up, shoves her phone in her coat pocket, and looks over at us. "Dad wants me to head back. I guess we're going home soon, and then I need to go back to my mom's. He said to tell you he's very impressed that you're so studious on a holiday and to ask you, J, if you'll give Amber a ride home when you guys are done."

All of this comes out very fast, too fast for my brain to keep up. When it finally does, Cammie's still standing there, now with her arms crossed over her chest and her eyebrows raised as she waits for one of us to answer.

"Uh, well—" I should go with her since we aren't actually studying and I've bailed on a holiday and this whole situation is bending rule number seven so far I can feel it cracking. But Jordan interrupts me.

"I can do that no problem." His gaze flicks to my face, and then quickly away. "I mean, if you're cool with it."

I swallow; my throat is suddenly very dry, in spite of all the water I just drank. I should say no. But what comes out is, "Yeah. I'm cool."

"Cool," he says.

"*Cool*," Cammie says, and not in a mean way.

The door to the house opens up and a man who must be Jordan's dad sticks his head out and says, "Jordan, what are you— oh. I didn't realize you had company." He smiles warmly at Cammie. "It's good to see you, kiddo."

"Good to see you too, Tom," she says, smiling back at him. "Happy Thanksgiving."

"Same to you," Jordan's dad says. Then he looks over at me and his smile turns knowing and Jordan, who has this easy way of sitting most of the time, shifts and straightens up next to me on the weight bench. His dad's gaze flicks between us briefly. "And you must be Amber."

"Yeah, hi." I raise my hand in a weird attempt at a wave.

"It's nice to finally meet you," Jordan's dad says, his tone warm. To Jordan, he adds, "Are you going to invite the girls inside, or were you planning to hang out in the cold all night?"

"Actually, we were just kind of talking about that," Cammie says. "I have to get back to my mom's, but Amber and Jordan had some stuff to look over for their English class. Right, guys?"

"Um, right," I say, sneaking a glance at Jordan. His head is ducked a little, and there's a smile tugging at the corners of his mouth, and he looks so happy I'm staying that my breath catches and I have to look away.

"All right," Tom says. "Cam, tell your mom we say hello and Happy Thanksgiving, okay? Julie says they keep missing each other on the phone."

"I'll tell her," Cammie says, taking a step backward. I can't help noticing that her expression is guarded now, and that she won't meet anyone's eyes. "And I really do need to get going. I'll make sure your mom lets the dog out, Amber," she adds, and then she turns and starts walking away.

I stare after her, surprised and a little touched that she thought of Buffy at all. "Thanks."

She waves vaguely in our direction as she crosses into The Castle's tiny front yard. "Yeah. You kids have fun."

"Well," Jordan's dad says when Cammie disappears inside The Castle. "Come on, you two. We've got leftovers if you're hungry, Amber, but otherwise we'll let you get to work."

Jordan gets to his feet and offers his hand to help me up. Against my better judgment, I let him pull me to my feet, and I follow him inside. We step into a big, open kitchen that looks a lot like the one at Kevin's house except everything is white instead of brown. Two pretty blond women are standing at the island, and their heads whip in my direction when they realize Jordan didn't come back inside alone.

"This is Amber," Jordan says, gesturing to me. "Amber, this is my mom, Julie, and my sister, Tasha."

Jordan's mom smiles and echoes Jordan's dad, "It's so nice to finally meet you, sweetheart."

Tasha's eyes are a little red, but as she looks between Jordan and me a slow smile spreads across her face. "You're the one with the vampire slayer dog."

"Um, yeah," I say, shooting a look Jordan's way. But he's blushing and won't look at me.

"You guys—" Jordan starts.

"Sorry, honey," his mom says. But she doesn't sound sorry, and she winks at me when Jordan isn't looking. I decide I like her, even though I shouldn't be deciding things like that.

Jordan's dad, who's been watching this whole exchange with that same knowing grin on his face, says, "We got to meet your mom the other day. She's dating Kevin Henning, right?"

"Um, yeah," I say again. Apparently that's my entire vocabulary now.

"We liked her a lot," Julie says, surprising me a little since I know she's friends with Cammie's mom. I may not know a ton of details about Kevin's divorce, but it's pretty obvious that it was not exactly an amicable one. I figured their friends must have split down party lines or something, but I guess not. "She and Kevin seem so happy," Julie adds, yanking me out of my thoughts. "And I can definitely see the resemblance between the two of you."

"Oh, thanks," I say, surprised all over again. People don't tell me I look like my mom very often, so I'm never sure how to take it. We have the same eyes, but that's about it. Everything else is my dad's.

"We have that paper to work on," Jordan says, nudging me with his elbow.

I shoot him a grateful look. "Right. It was so nice to meet you guys."

"You too, Amber," Tasha says, and his parents echo her as Jordan leads me out of the room.

fourteen

I follow Jordan through the living room and down the stairs, where they have a family room setup similar to Kevin's. Big sectional, huge entertainment center, cushy recliner. I expect us to stop here, but we don't. We go through a door at the far end of the room, into what turns out to be Jordan's bedroom.

"Wow," I say, stepping inside and looking around at his walls, which are covered in newspaper articles about March Madness games from the last decade or so. "You have a great room."

"Thanks," he says, grinning. He hesitates for a second and then adds, "Sorry to bombard you with my family like that. They can be . . . well, you saw."

"I like them," I admit. "They seem really nice."

"Yeah?"

"Yeah."

"Good," he says, letting out a long breath. Like he's relieved I think his family is nice. I don't let myself dwell on this.

"Homework time?" I ask, trying to get things back on track.

Suddenly he looks uncertain. "We can, if you want. But, uh, I actually thought we could watch some *Buffy*. We don't have to," he rushes to add, as I bite my lip. "It just seems . . . sacrilegious to do homework on a holiday. Don't you think?"

I chew on my lip and stare at him, trying to decide. This would definitely be going against the rules. But *Buffy* is like my kryptonite. Maybe since we only have three more weeks of tutoring before all of this is over it'll be okay. I mean, it can't hurt to be friendly until then, can it? Not friends. Just friendly.

"All right," I say, sitting down on the bed too. But not next to him. Far enough away from him for at least two people to fit between us. Maybe even three. "One episode. And then we get to work."

"One episode," he says, grinning now. "And since you're the expert, you get to pick."

❋

The next day Hannah calls me at seven in the morning and tries to get me to go Black Friday shopping.

"Mom tried this two hours ago," I tell her. "Guess what? The answer is still no."

"But, Amber," she whines, "if we go now we can still catch some of the good sales!"

"The good sales are gonna last all weekend. We can go tomorrow. I've got more important things to do today."

"Like what?" she asks, not trying to hide the snippiness in her tone. Hannah is never happy when I turn down shopping.

"Like unpacking my room." When I got home from Jordan's yesterday, it was like I couldn't ignore the boxes anymore, and I figured maybe waiting until college to unpack them is a little excessive. Plus, I couldn't find my heavy winter coat, and it's getting cold.

For a long moment, there's silence on the other end of the phone. I can't even hear Hannah breathing. "Are you still there?"

"Yeah," she says quickly. "Do you want help with that? The . . . unpacking?"

"That'd be nice," I say, before I can change my mind.

Hannah squeals into the phone, making me regret my weakness and wish I'd just agreed to go to the stupid mall with her. I'm about to tell her I was April Foolsing her in November when she shouts, "I'll be there in fifteen minutes! Make sure there's food!" and hangs up.

She gets here in ten, and I manage to resist the urge to ask her how fast she sped on the way over. I bring Buffy out to the driveway with me to greet her and hopefully head off any more squealing.

"You want food first, or a tour first?" I ask, as she bounces out of her car and over to me and Buffy. Buffy picks up on her excitement and hops a little in place, stretching her head forward so she can lick Hannah's face when she bends down to pet her.

"Chill out, Buffster," Hannah says, laughing and gently pushing Buffy away. "Tour. As long as we make the kitchen the first stop."

"Got it," I say, shaking my head and leading her inside. "This is the living room, by the way," I add, as we pass through it.

"I figured. I love that wall. Is it stone?" The far wall of Kevin's living room looks like the side of an adobe building, which my mother loves because it fits in with her Southwest decorating scheme. This is one of the many reasons she's convinced Kevin is

The One, I'm sure. Like having the same taste in home decor is the most important thing when you're with someone.

"Fake stone. Apparently there was an incident with the fireplace a few years ago. They had to do that to cover it up."

"Well," Hannah says. "The end result is awesome, so I say worth it."

"I guess," I say, though secretly I agree with her.

Kevin's in the kitchen when we walk in, sitting at the island with his standard mug of coffee and newspaper in hand. He looks up at the sound of our footsteps and raises his eyebrows a little when he sees it's me.

"Morning, Amber. You're up early."

I jerk my thumb over my shoulder. "Hannah's got the Black Friday bug too."

"Ah," he says, nodding. Then he gets up and holds out a hand to Hannah, who takes it and shakes it, looking bemused. "Nice to meet you," he adds. "I've heard a lot about you."

Hannah shoots me a glance. "You too."

I sense that I need to get Hannah out of here before she starts asking probing questions, so I say, "I was giving Hannah the tour."

She frowns. "I thought we were stopping for food."

"Tell you what," Kevin says, before I can answer her. "You girls go check out the basement and the rest of the downstairs and then come back here. I'll put some plates together for you."

Hannah beams at him. "Thanks, Kevin!"

She takes my hand and drags me out of the kitchen before I can protest, or warn her that Kevin's idea of seven-thirty-in-the-morning food is probably a lot different than hers.

"I like Kevin," she says, as I lead her back through the living room and down to the basement.

I stop at the foot of the stairs and reach down to scratch Buffy, who's led us down the stairs like she's the one giving the tour. "Reserve your judgment until you see what he gives us to eat."

"Why?"

"He's one of those health food people. We had tofu for dinner three times last week." But even as I say this I can't help thinking about that mug of oatmeal he gave me in his car that day, exactly the way I like it.

"Ugh." Hannah makes a face. Then she sighs. "How do people do that? I could never make it as a vegetarian. I like meat too much."

"Ooh," I say. "Dirty."

"Oh, stop." But she's laughing and so am I, and for the first time in weeks things feel back to normal between us.

"Okay," I say, once we've calmed down. "This is the family room."

I watch as she takes in the big sectional, two huge, cushy recliners, and giant entertainment center, complete with a flat-screen TV that's at least twice the size of the one at her house. She stares at it for a second and then turns to me, one eyebrow raised.

"What?" I ask.

"We are *so* doing movie nights over here from now on. Don't even try to argue."

I hold up my hands in surrender and start for the guest room against the far wall, which is now overflow storage for Mom's kitchen gadgets and cookbooks.

"God," Hannah says, staring at the shelves along the far wall, which are crammed full to the brim and look like they might tip over from all the weight they're holding. "I forgot how big your mom's collection is."

"I know, right? And it's gotten worse since we've been here, now that she's got all of Kevin's stuff too. He has like fifteen cookbooks with the word healthy in the title."

Hannah groans. "Ugh. Do you think that's the kind of food he's getting for us? Healthy?"

"Probably." I back out of the room and flip off the light. "Come on. We'll do the rest of the main floor and then make a pit stop in the kitchen before we go upstairs."

Five minutes later we're back in the kitchen. As promised, Kevin has two heaping plates and two cans of Coke waiting on the counter for us. He gives them a wave as we walk in. "I tried to get all the most important food groups."

I stare at the plates. They're covered in leftover French silk pie, sweet potatoes with marshmallows, and rolls from yesterday's dinner at The Castle. Hannah brushes past me to scoop them up, grinning. "Dessert and carbs," she says. "That pretty much covers it."

Kevin laughs. "That's what I figured. When your sugar coma hits, there's turkey in the fridge. Please eat some."

Hannah nods and heads for the door to the living room. "Will do. Amber, you coming?"

"I—yeah." I grab the drinks and follow her, but at the last second stop and look back at Kevin. He's back to his coffee and newspaper, but he looks up when I clear my throat.

"Did I forget something?" he asks.

"No. Just . . . thank you."

"Sure thing, kid," he says, smiling at me. "Anytime."

✳

When we get upstairs, Buffy goes straight to her favorite spot in my closet. Hannah and I lay out the food on my bed and then turn to survey the disaster zone that my room has become in the last two months.

"Wow," Hannah says finally. "You could be on one of those hoarding TV shows."

"I could not!" I whack her on the arm and try not to look at the closest stack of boxes, which kind of looks like the Leaning Tower of Pisa.

"That was rude. And you need to get your eyes checked, because this is ridiculous. How do you *find* anything?"

"I don't," I admit, sighing and reaching for a slice of pie.

Hannah grabs for some pie too. "All right. Pie first, then sort. Deal?"

"Deal."

We start with my boxes of books, and we've only been working again for a few minutes when she gasps. "Holy shit, you still have this?"

I turn to see what she's holding. In one hand she has a battered Stephen King paperback, and in the other a familiar folded-up piece of paper. I know she's not talking about the book.

"Of course I still have it," I say, taking the paper from her and carefully unfolding it. My rules are written out on the page, one through nine in my hurried scrawl, and number ten added at the bottom in Hannah's neat block lettering.

I read the list over quickly, but instead of the usual wash of reassurance I feel when I look at it, my chest tightens with unease.

"I remember the day we wrote those down," Hannah says quietly.

"It'd be a hard one to forget," I say, getting to my feet and going over to my desk. I carefully tuck the rules into the smallest drawer, then close it firmly and come back over to help Hannah alphabetize my romance novels.

We're quiet for a few minutes, but then Hannah says suddenly, "You know, this bookshelf would be really perfect for when we're in Lawrence next year, don't you think?"

"I mean, I guess it would. But that shelf is Kevin's, so I'm not planning to take it with me."

"You could ask, though. Because seriously, I think this would be the perfect size to fit under a lofted bed. It's narrow enough that a desk could fit next to it."

The mention of a lofted bed makes me go still. Matt must have been right. Hannah really has been thinking about living in the dorms next year. I thought if I ignored that comment he made it would go away, but that was clearly wishful thinking.

"Why would I need a lofted bed in an apartment?" I ask slowly. "Buffy wouldn't be able to get her snugs in if I did that."

"Oh, duh," Hannah says. "I was just looking at decorating ideas on Pinterest the other day and saw one that looked really cute, so it was kind of fresh in my brain."

"Oh." I clear my throat. "Maybe for your room, then?"

"Yeah, maybe," she says, turning back to my books and shoving them onto the shelf a little more aggressively than before.

There's a weird tension hanging in the air now, and even though I think we should probably talk about it, all I want to do is make things go back to normal. So instead of asking Hannah to tell me more about her Pinterest binge or why a loft bed sounds so appealing, I blurt the first thing I can think of to change the subject.

"I can't believe you haven't asked me whether or not Jordan used his SOS."

She whips her head around to look at me. "Did he?"

"Yeah. Cammie came too. We did homework."

Hannah glances over at my desk before snapping her gaze back to me. "Cammie came with you? What about rule number two?"

"What about it? We're not friends. I was being nice. Niceness is allowed, especially on holidays."

Hannah smirks at me. "I know for a fact that's not on the list."

I can tell by her tone and expression that she's going to give me shit about this for at least the rest of the day, but I don't mind. Because the weirdness of a few minutes ago is gone now. Hopefully it'll stay away for a while.

fifteen

On Monday I come home to a letter from Wichita State, the only college in town I applied to. Mom's home early, and she sits at the counter and watches as I open it.

"What does it say?" she asks, as I stare at the letter in my hand.

"I got in." But that isn't all it says. It says I got a scholarship that covers all of my tuition for all four years.

"Let me see." Mom reaches for the letter and grabs it out of my hands. She reads it and then looks up at me, her face lit up like a ten-thousand-watt bulb. "Oh, Amber, this is wonderful!"

"Wichita State doesn't have the major I want, Mom," I say, trying to keep my tone neutral and hold off the panic that's creeping up at the idea of staying here next year.

"I know, honey," Mom says, "but try to be practical here, okay? If you stay here and accept this scholarship you would save *so* much money."

Practical? Right. This coming from the woman who dumped her last boyfriend because he didn't like kids, meaning he didn't like me. It sounds like a good reason for her to dump someone until you realize that Eric didn't like kids when my mother met him and that this didn't stop her from dating him for two years in the first place. How very practical of her.

"I can be practical and have goals, Mom. I haven't even heard from KU yet, so I don't know about scholarships from them." Another wave of anxiety rises in my chest at this thought, because what if KU doesn't give me a comparable scholarship? How will I ever talk Mom into letting me go then?

Mom must be having a similar thought, because she smiles at me sweetly. "We'll deal with that when you hear back from them. But in the meantime, I'm proud of you, sweetheart. So proud."

Then she comes around the island and hugs me tight, which almost makes me feel bad for wanting to get out of this place so badly.

Almost, but not quite.

✳

Hannah has a doctor's appointment the next morning, so it's just me and Ryan at our table in the commons. He shares his chocolate-frosted donuts with me and listens while I word-vomit about Hannah and Wichita State and dorms and KU's admission status page. It takes me like ten minutes of rambling to get everything out, and when I'm done I flop forward to rest my head on the edge of the table so that I don't have to see his reaction to everything.

There's a rustling sound, and then a little donut appears in front of my face. When I take it, Ryan pats the back of my head. "Well, first of all, the money thing is a problem, but you can do your best to fix it," he says. "Just apply for more outside scholarships. Try to line up a job in Lawrence. Start looking at apartments and comparing rent and stuff, you know?"

"I know," I mumble around a bite of donut. "I applied for

three more scholarships last night. But the apartment stuff is so overwhelming. And I don't know if most places even hire people this far in advance."

"It doesn't hurt to ask, though," he says. Another donut appears in front of my face. "And it wouldn't hurt to ask Hannah what's going on with her, either."

"Ugh, I know," I say, pushing myself upright. "I know you're right. I just . . ."

"You're afraid of what she'll say," he finishes, zero judgment in his expression.

I nod miserably.

Ryan sighs and glances around at the commons, which is loud and full of our chattering classmates. Cammie and her friends are at a table only a few away from ours, but Jordan and his friends aren't here. Not that I've been looking for him or anything.

"Look," Ryan says, and I glance at him, wondering if he's somehow read my thoughts. "I can't lie to you. Hannah has made some comments about next year that make me wonder if she isn't as excited about the apartment thing anymore."

"Shit. Like what?"

He shrugs. "Little things. Stuff kind of like what you mentioned. The other day she was asking me how Bri likes the dorms at K-State, and if Parker regrets living off campus his freshman year."

I wince. Bri and Parker are Ryan's twin siblings who graduated last year, and Hannah *has* been asking Ryan a lot of questions about their living situations ever since they moved to Manhattan at the beginning of the school year.

"For the record, I told her the truth—that Bri hates the dorms and that Parker loves living off campus. But I don't think the answer was as important as the fact that Hannah was asking the question in the first place, you know?"

"Yeah," I agree.

"So talk to her, okay?" Ryan says, watching me carefully.

"I will," I promise.

Eventually.

✳

On Thursday at Jordan's, I have a hard time staying focused on this week's paper. I think I'm doing an okay job of hiding my distraction, but after about twenty minutes he reaches over and pulls the laptop away from me.

"What are you doing?" I ask.

He snaps it closed. "It's break time."

"But we haven't even been working for half an hour."

"I know," he says, getting up to go grab the basketball. Buffy follows closely at his heels. "But if I have to sit through another thirty minutes of you sighing every five seconds just because the rule is we work for an hour before we take a break, I'm gonna go nuts."

I have to process that for a second. "Was I really sighing every five seconds?"

He smiles at me crookedly, head tipped to the side. "Yeah. It might have been more."

"Shit. Sorry."

"Don't worry about it. Just come on." He points to Buffy and adds, "You hang."

I laugh and follow him out of the garage, checking over my

shoulder to make sure Buffy stays in the doorway. She does, and Jordan bounce-passes me the ball so I can take the first shot. We play, and it isn't long before I feel myself relax. And when we finish the game—I lose, of course—I don't move back toward the garage.

His eyebrows go up in surprise. "Another game?"

I flex my fingers and shove them in the pockets of my hoodie. We shouldn't—we should go back inside, actually get some work done. But I need to be moving right now. "Yeah. You first this time."

For once he doesn't argue.

"So," he says as he watches his first shot swish through the net, "what's on your mind?"

"Right now? That maybe I should've stayed with the usual game plan and gone first." He jogs after the ball and then comes over to where I'm standing.

"Actually it's here." He taps his foot on the ground. I move to where he says and reach for the ball. But he doesn't let it go. He waits and looks me straight in the eye until I realize that I have to answer for real or we'll be standing here all night.

"It's nothing. Just college stuff. No big deal."

He lets go of the ball but doesn't back away. "College is a big deal. At least for you. I can tell."

"Oh yeah?" He nods. I sigh. "Okay, yeah. You're right."

"I know." He gives me this shit-eating grin. I thrust my arms out and hit him in the chest with the basketball. Not hard, but enough to push him a little off-balance.

"Shit, Amber," he says, and I worry that he's mad. But then he laughs and I know it's okay.

"Sorry. But it's my turn." He nods his head in acknowledgment and backs further away. I shoot and the ball goes in.

"Nice one."

He goes to shoot again and I think he's going to let me off the hook with the college thing, which would really be for the best. But then he says, "All right, so college. What's the deal?"

I hesitate. This feels too personal somehow. But then, maybe college talk is relevant. I am here to help him with school, after all. Or at least I'm supposed to be. "I got my acceptance letter from WSU earlier this week. They offered me a full ride."

"That's awesome! Why are you saying that like it's a bad thing?"

"I want to go to KU," I say slowly, "but I haven't heard back from them yet. And now, with this offer, my mom is pushing me to stay here even though I don't want to."

He's already got his arms in the air to shoot, but slowly he lowers them. Tucks the ball under one arm and looks at me. "Why not?"

This answer comes more easily, if only because I don't have to tell him the whole truth. "KU has this behavioral science major that I really want to do."

Jordan grins. "You want to be the next dog whisperer, don't you?"

"Maybe," I say, grinning back in spite of myself. I finally caved last week during our impromptu *Buffy* marathon and told him about my job and some of the books I read when I was training my Buffy. He didn't laugh at all. He told me he thought it was cool. "Or maybe work with people, I don't know."

"You'd be good at either one," he says, his voice quiet.

"Thanks." I clear my throat and look away. "Anyway, until I hear back from KU, I'm kind of stuck in limbo. And it sucks. Especially since I'm worried that even if I do get in, I won't get enough financial aid to convince my mom to let me go." I hesitate for a second, then add, "And also there's the fact that I'm pretty sure my best friend wants to live in the dorms instead of getting an apartment together like we've been talking about since we were freshmen. So my college situation kind of sucks right now."

"That does suck," Jordan agrees, and I nod. "Have you talked to Hannah about it? I'm, uh, assuming she's the roommate and not Ryan McKinney."

"She's the roommate," I say, fighting a grin for a reason I won't let myself name. But my grin fades as I shake my head. "I haven't talked to her about it yet though. I've been avoiding it since I'm in limbo with KU, until I find out whether I'm admitted or not anyway. Maybe it sounds dumb, but I don't want to have a fight with her about it if I can't even go there in the first place."

Jordan shakes his head. "It's not dumb. I hope you do have that fight with her eventually though. Because then that means you'll be admitted to KU and have enough aid money to go, right?"

"Right," I say, my face warming as he studies me.

We're quiet for a long moment, standing here watching each other, and then Jordan says, "I want to play Division-One ball in college, but it's not looking like that's gonna happen. That's why I asked for help with my papers. I've got an offer to play for a D-Two school but my grades aren't quite good enough to get the scholarship unless I bring them up this year. And we'd need that scholarship for me to go since it's a private school."

His tone is even as he says this, but I can tell by the tension in his shoulders and the set of his jaw that this matters to him a lot. There's no denying that Jordan is good at basketball. Like, really good. It would be a shame if he didn't get to play next year. Without thinking, I hold out my hands. He hesitates a moment and then bounce-passes me the ball. I look at it, feel the grit of it under my fingertips. Then I pass it back and say, "Okay. So we'll make sure your grades are where they need to be. Or your English ones, at least."

"Yeah?"

"Yeah."

His shoulders relax. "Thanks." Then he turns away from me, facing the basket to take his shot. It goes in easy and I run after the ball as it starts to roll down the driveway.

"Here," he says, tapping his foot in the right spot when I get back to him.

I don't shoot yet. Instead I look over my shoulder at Jordan and do something I shouldn't. "The D-Two school. Where is it?" I ask.

"Rockhurst. In Kansas City."

Only an hour from Lawrence, where I want to be. That's hardly anything, really.

Rule number seven, Amber. Remember the rule. I shake myself out of these thoughts, clear my throat, turn to face the basket, shoot, and . . . miss. "Damn."

"That's H," he tells me, and then he runs after the ball.

"I am aware, thank you," I call. All he does is laugh in response.

Later, when I've lost and we've gone back into the garage to get some work done, he says, "Are you coming to the game tomorrow?"

Tomorrow night is the first varsity game of the season. I've been planning on going for a while, because Hannah and Elliot are going together and she needs a wingwoman. But I shrug like it's no big deal. "Yeah. I might even cheer for you."

Jordan pulls the laptop toward himself and smiles. "I'd like that."

sixteen

Hannah and I carpool to the game with Elliot and Ryan—Megan has to work tonight, apparently—and the teams are already out on the court warming up when we get there. I spot Jordan right away—he's running for a layup right as we go in—and I watch as he runs back to the end of the line and laughs at something one of the forwards says to him.

"Amber." Hannah tugs my arm. Mentally scolding myself, I jerk my gaze away from Jordan and follow her up into the bleachers with the boys.

"So, what do you think?" Hannah asks once we're settled into our seats. "We gonna win?"

"Um—" I say.

"Hell yeah we are," Ryan says, leaning around me to look at Hannah. "Have you been paying attention to Baugh the last three years? He's gonna kill it out there."

Hannah raises an eyebrow and smiles slyly at me. "Not as much as some people."

I choke on my own spit and have a spectacular coughing fit, so bad that Ryan has to pound on my back to calm me down. "Whoa," he says, peering at me when I finally sit up, eyes watering. "You okay?"

"Yeah," I say hoarsely. I get up and motion toward the doors out of the gym. "I'm gonna go get a water. You guys want anything?"

Hannah glances at Elliot, who shakes his head, his face slightly flushed as usual. Then she turns back to me, eyes sparkling. "We're good."

Ryan comes with me so that Hannah and Elliot can get some alone time, and by the time we make it through the concession line and back into the gym, it's tip-off time. The centers are already facing off at half-court, with the rest of the players circled around them. Jordan is standing with his back to me, arms loose at his sides, shoulders hunched forward a little like he's ready to spring into action. "Shit." I trip a little as I take a too-quick step forward. "We're gonna miss it."

"Chill." Ryan grabs my shoulder to steady me. "We're good. Let's watch right here. Okay?"

I nod vaguely, eyes still on Jordan as the ref blows his whistle and comes out onto the court with the ball in hand. The ref says something to the players, and I see Cory Mitchell, our center, give a sharp nod and glance over his shoulder to where Jordan waits. Then the ball is up in the air and Cory swipes it away from the other team's center and back over his head. Jordan grabs it and races down the court toward the basket, the other players falling back with him.

Jordan passes to one of the forwards at the top of the key, ducks around a player for the other team, and ends up right on the outside edge of the three-point line. I hold my breath as someone passes back to Jordan and he shoots; it comes out in a cheer that blends in with the rest of the crowd as the ball goes in.

Someone taps my shoulder and I jump, surprised to find Ryan still behind me. I look back and find him grinning. He tips his head toward the bleachers, where Hannah and Elliot are waiting. "Come on," he says, prodding me forward. "A three-pointer already. Looks like it's gonna be a good game."

The rest of the first half goes a lot like those first few seconds, with our team scoring like crazy and Jordan making amazing shot after amazing shot. Every time he does it's like my heart races faster, and it doesn't help that Hannah and Ryan both keep elbowing me. I'm gonna have bruises by the end of this thing. With a minute left in the second quarter we're up by twelve points, mostly scored by Jordan, which has not escaped the other team's notice. They keep fouling him in the hopes that he'll miss his free throws, but he never does. He sinks them all.

With thirty seconds left until halftime, Jordan gets fouled again. Only this time he wasn't taking a shot, so he steps over the line to inbound the ball. He's under the basket, and right as he's holding up a hand to signal the play to his team, he looks up in this direction. He searches the crowd for a second before his gaze locks on me, and a wide grin spreads out over his face. My breath catches as we stare at each other for a second, and then, breathing hard, Jordan turns back to the game.

"Uh," Hannah says as Jordan lobs an overhead pass to Ethan Hawkins. "Did I imagine that, or did Jordan just look up here at you?"

"I don't know," I say, shrugging, trying to sound nonchalant and keep my breathing under control. But I know he did. Shit.

"Right." Hannah smirks at me and then turns back to Elliot and links her arm through his.

We win the game by fifteen points and I'm hoarse from cheering as we follow the flood of spectators down onto the court and then back out of the gym. People are already going out to their cars, which means traffic is going to be a bitch, so Hannah votes that we hang around for a bit and the rest of us agree. We're supposed to go to Hannah's house after this, so Ryan calls Megan to let her know that we're leaving a little later than we planned and get her vote on what movie we should watch. I'm arguing in favor of either the newest Star Wars movie or *Black Panther* when a familiar voice calls my name.

"Well, well, well," Hannah says in a low voice, stepping closer to me so only I can hear her. "Look who it is."

"Shut it," I tell her, fighting off a rush of excitement as I turn to see Jordan picking his way through the crowd and coming our way. He's smiling and sweaty and still in his uniform, and he looks amazing. He's also not alone, and at the sight of a few of his teammates trailing him, my excitement turns to anxiety. Hanging out with Jordan by myself is one thing, but all of our friends in one place like this is another thing entirely. One I don't know if I'll ever be ready for.

"Hey," Jordan says when he reaches me, tugging at a spot where his shirt is sticking to his chest. "You came."

"I did," I tell him, all too aware of my friends and his closely watching this exchange. I can feel the rules bending as we stand here, and I'm worried that one wrong move is all it will take for them to break. "Great game. Seeing you play like that makes me think you've been going easy on me."

His smile turns shy as he shakes his head. "I really haven't been."

"He's not kidding," Cory Mitchell says, grinning and stepping forward a little bit. "He won't stop bitching about that backward shot you keep using on him."

"Oh really?" I ask, swallowing hard. Jordan's talked about me to his friends. I guess I shouldn't be surprised, since he'd talked to his family about me. This explains why Cory has been smiling at me in the hallways lately.

"Really." Cory nods. "Did you know you're the only one to get him to HOR status? That's serious business, Richter. You should be proud of yourself."

My face flushes red, but Ryan saves me. "Whore status?" he asks. "Whoa, Amber. Is there something you need to tell us?"

Everyone cracks up but Jordan, who looks at me steadily, the corners of his mouth tugging up in a smile. My stomach swoops, and I look away. I need to get out of here.

"Hey, listen," Jordan says once everyone's calmed down. "You guys doing anything after this? Cory's having people over. You should come hang out for a bit."

"Um." I glance at Cory to see if this is true, even though I'm not planning to say yes. He nods. So weird. "Sorry, but we already have plans."

"Oh," Jordan says, the smile slipping off his face. "All right." Behind him, his friends exchange confused glances.

"Flexible plans," Hannah says, and I shoot her a look over my shoulder to tell her to shut up. Going to this party would break more than one rule, so movie night it is.

"Not really," I hiss, and Hannah frowns.

"Bummer," Cory says, looking between me and Hannah and Jordan like he's not sure what's going on. "Maybe next time?"

"Maybe," I agree, grabbing for Hannah. "See you guys later, okay?"

"Yeah," Cory says, his brow furrowing a little. Behind him, the corners of Jordan's mouth are turned down and he's looking at his feet. "See you."

"Bye," I say, tugging Hannah's arm to get her moving. I need to get out of here ASAP, because if we stay much longer I won't be able to handle it. She's narrowing her eyes at me now, so not the glowing version of herself she was earlier tonight when Elliot was holding her hand. But she lets me pull her away.

I'm anxious and jittery all weekend, and though I try to tell myself it has nothing to do with what happened after the game on Friday and everything to do with my worry about KU, I know that's total bullshit. I can't stop thinking about Jordan's expression when I told him we had other plans. How disappointment was written all over his face. The knowledge that I hurt his feelings makes me sick to my stomach, though I refuse to examine the reasons why too closely.

I feel guilty enough about how I handled everything that on Sunday night I do something I've never done before: text Jordan about something unrelated to studying.

Hey, sorry again that we couldn't come to that party. Hope you got some good celebrating in.

I regret it as soon as I hit send, because what kind of idiot texts an apology about a party two days later? But before I have a chance to get too worked up about it he texts me back and I'm scrambling to unlock my phone so I can read it.

No big deal. It was a last-minute thing.

It sure seemed like a big deal from his reaction, but maybe I was imagining things.

I still feel bad, I tell him, because it's true and because for some reason I really need him to know this.

This time it takes him a long time to answer, and when he does, it's only one word: **Don't.**

Somehow, that makes me feel even worse.

seventeen

Tuesday night before dinner I'm in my room browsing pet friendly apartment complexes in Lawrence when my phone dings with an email notification. I glance over at the screen, expecting it to be junk, and freeze when I see that it's from KU's Office of Admissions. It takes about ten seconds for this to sink in, and then I unlock my phone at warp speed and pull up my email app, holding my breath while I wait for it to load.

Dear Amber, the message starts. *We are pleased to inform you that—*

I stop reading and sit bolt upright on my bed, letting out a shriek of delight. From her spot in the closet Buffy startles at the noise and barks at me like, *Mom, what are you doing???* Which only makes me laugh.

"We got in, Buffster! It's all happening!"

She starts barking at me again, this time happy and joyful because of my tone, and jumps up on the bed so that she can get her face as close to mine as possible. I jump with her, which she totally digs, and for a minute it's just jumping and barking and laughing and joy.

But then the sound of footsteps interrupts my celebration, and I flop into a sitting position as Mom and Kevin come rushing into my room.

"Amber?" Mom says, casting a frantic look around. "Is everything okay?"

"We heard yelling," Kevin adds.

Buffy lets out a loud *wuff* that makes both of them start, and I laugh.

"I'm fine. Everything's great, actually!" I scramble off my bed and clutch my phone to my chest, hesitating for only a second before handing it over to my mom. "See for yourself."

She takes it from me and starts to read, her eyes scanning the screen. But Kevin, who is leaning in beside her, figures it out faster, because after about two seconds he looks back at me. "You got in to KU? That's amazing!"

"It is, isn't it?" I say, and it hits me that I'm glad he's here for this moment, because he is genuinely excited for me.

"Yes," he says, beaming at me. Then he turns to my mom. "Claire, this calls for a celebration, don't you think? I was going to make tofu stir-fry tonight but maybe we can order takeout instead? Amber, what do you want? Pizza? Chinese?"

"Um, I don't know," I say, a little overwhelmed by his enthusiasm, and by the fact that he's willing to ditch a tofu dinner for me. "Maybe we could do Emperor's?" Emperor's is like a faster version of hibachi, and their fried rice is amazing. Mom and I used to get it pretty often, but we haven't since we moved in here. It's way too much grease for Kevin's usual diet.

"Done," Kevin says without hesitation. "What do you want? I'll go pick it up."

I rattle off my usual order and watch as he carefully makes a note of it in his phone.

"Got it. Claire, anything in particular you want?"

Mom shakes her head. "Surprise me."

"Okay. Be back in a little while." Then he turns and leaves, tapping out something else on his phone as he goes. As he starts down the stairs I hear him say, "Cam, you like the steak and shrimp from Emperor's, right?"

"Amber, honey," Mom says, drawing my attention back to her. She's smiling at me, but I can't help noticing that her smile is nowhere near as joyful as Kevin's was. "This is wonderful. I'm so proud of you."

"Thanks, Mom."

She holds out my phone and I take it back, watching her warily and waiting for the other shoe to drop. And I'm not disappointed, because after a second she clears her throat and says, "Did you check your financial aid package yet? The email mentions logging into the portal to see what aid you were awarded."

There it is. I shake my head. "Not yet. You guys came in right after I opened the email."

"Ah. Well, let's check then, okay? I promised we could talk about Lawrence when we had numbers to look at, so let's see if we do."

"Sure," I say, even though I don't want to. I'm worried that no matter what I find in the portal it won't be enough, and I'd like to hold on to this happiness for a little bit longer.

But it's rare that Mom actually wants to talk about college stuff, so I guess I should take advantage of this moment while I have it. I grab my laptop off my desk and settle back on my bed, where Buffy is calm and curled up now after all the excitement.

It only takes me a minute to navigate to the right page and log in to my account. It takes about thirty seconds after that for me to realize I was right: what I got in grants and scholarships isn't going to be enough to convince her. It will barely cover tuition and books. I'd have to take out loans to cover room and board. Not to mention food and vet bills and incidentals.

"Can I see?" Mom asks when the pause has stretched out for too long.

I hand the laptop back to her without a word and then reach for Buffy, needing the comfort of her presence right now.

"Is this per semester or per year?" Mom asks, taking a seat in my desk chair and leaning closer to the laptop screen.

"Per year." I don't manage to look away in time to miss her frown.

"Amber," she starts, and that one word is enough for me to know what she's going to say. *It doesn't make sense for you to go. We can't afford it. What would you do with Buffy? Wichita State offered you almost twice as much, which would really even out to more if you live at home.*

But I don't want to hear any of that right now. I don't want to talk to her at all. So I get up, reach around her, and snap my laptop shut.

"I changed my mind," I say, not meeting Mom's eyes. "I don't want to talk about this right now. I need to take Buffy for a walk before dinner anyway."

"Amber," she says again, and this time her tone is sharp. But I'm already stuffing my feet into shoes and motioning for Buffy to follow me.

"Don't worry. I'll be back in time to eat. I promise not to mess up *family* dinner."

Then I rush out of the room, Buffy hot on my heels.

✳

Kevin and Cammie are at the kitchen island pulling takeout boxes out of plastic bags when Buffy and I get back from our walk. Kevin looks up and smiles as I close the door behind me.

"There she is!" he says. "KU's newest incoming freshman. I might have gone a bit overboard with the food, so grab a plate and take a little of everything, okay?"

I nod in response to this and bend down to unclip Buffy's leash, because I can't trust myself to speak right now.

To buy myself some more time to calm down, I feed Buffy and refill her water bowl before going over to get my own dinner. Cammie is lingering near the crab rangoons, and she gives me a cold look when I reach over to grab one.

"What?" I ask, pulling my hand back.

She shakes her head and snatches her plate off the counter.

"There's a KU game on tonight," Kevin says, "so I thought we could eat in the living room. What do you think, Claire?" he adds as Mom comes into the room.

"That's fine with me," she says, avoiding my gaze.

Glad for a reason to escape the kitchen, I load a few scoops of chicken fried rice onto my plate and then head into the living room, settling on the floor at the far end of the coffee table so I don't have to worry about balancing my plate on my knees while I eat. Buffy, who has already scarfed her food down, settles in beside me, resting her head on my leg.

Mom and Kevin and Cammie join me after a few minutes, and Kevin hurries to get the game pulled up so we don't miss anything. We're playing Florida, and Kevin gets super into it, yelling and cheering when we make a good play and cussing when we don't. The first time he drops the f-bomb I have to do a double take because I've never heard Kevin say that before. Even when he was putting those shelves together for Mom. He doesn't notice my glance, but Mom does; she's got a hand over her mouth to keep from laughing, and she flashes a hopeful smile in my direction that I ignore. Cammie is rolling her eyes from her spot on the love seat, but she's smiling too; she looks happier than I've seen her in a long time. Until she notices me looking. Then it's back to the ice-bitch expression from the kitchen earlier.

Whatever.

We're up by eleven at halftime, and Kevin is so pumped that he waves off my attempts to help him take our plates into the kitchen.

"We're celebrating you tonight, remember? That means no dishes."

And with that he sweeps off into the kitchen with the stack of dirty plates, reappearing a few minutes later with clean forks, a stack of small plates, and napkins piled on top of a box from the bakery.

"A celebration wouldn't be complete without dessert," he says, grinning when he sees my expression. He passes out the plates and forks to all of us, opens up the box to reveal my favorite of Mom's sheet cakes. "Dig in."

I glance at my mom, surprised, because there's no way Kevin would have known to get this cake if she hadn't told him. But she's busy cutting slices for all of us and arranging them just so on the little plates and doesn't notice me looking.

"I think we're gonna win it," Kevin says fifteen minutes later, after we've all eaten two slices of cake and the game has come back on again.

"Yeah?" I ask, scratching a spot on Buffy's shoulder that makes her lean into my hand.

He nods. "I've got a good feeling. Man, I wish I could be there right now. You ever been to a game in Allen Fieldhouse?" I shake my head. "Oh, that's a crime. It's the best place in the world to watch basketball. I can't even describe it."

"When's the last time you were there? College?"

"Oh, no. Ellen and I used to split season tickets with the Kleins. We'd go to three or four games a year. Wouldn't we, Cam?" Slowly, Cammie nods. Kevin grins at me, not seeming to notice the stricken look on his daughter's face.

"Oh," I say.

"You know," Kevin says, turning to my mother now. "I might need to talk to Oscar about splitting the tickets again next year. We used to go in on them together with a friend of ours from college who still lives up there. What would you think about that, Claire? We could go visit Amber. See a game."

Mom shoots him a tight smile. "That could be nice. If that's where she goes."

"Cam," Kevin says, twisting around so he can look at her, apparently unaffected by Mom's strained tone. Or by her implication that I won't be in Lawrence next year at all. "What do you think? Would you want to go see some games next year?"

148

"It could be fun," she says, her voice hesitant and unsure. She looks like she wants to agree but doesn't know if she should.

"It's just an idea," Kevin says, his voice slipping into soothing territory. "Something to think about. Okay?"

"Okay," Cammie says.

Mom doesn't say anything and neither do I. But while she probably stays quiet because she doesn't want me to go to Lawrence next year, I stay quiet because I'm too busy thinking about how to make sure that's where I end up. I'm not naive enough to wish for the whole family trip to a basketball game, because I know better than to think Mom and Kevin will for sure still be together a year from now. But me living in Lawrence, going to school where I want and doing the major I want, and watching a basketball game at Allen Fieldhouse? That's a reality I can picture. I'll do whatever it takes to make sure it happens.

eighteen

At lunch on Thursday I get a voice mail from Stephanie asking if I can come into work after school.

"Sean called in sick so I need another body on the floor until seven thirty or so. Also Mia called in a panic earlier today asking about scheduling an emergency session with her pup. Something about family coming into town this weekend? Anyway, she asked for you specifically, so I thought I'd check. I know you have something else on Thursday nights though, so I understand if you can't do it."

I chew on my lip as I listen to Stephanie's message a second time. When I agreed to tutor Jordan on Thursdays I made sure I'd always have those nights off, but technically I have enough time to fit in a shift before I go to his house. Tonight will be the first time I've really seen him since the game and our awkward text exchange on Sunday, so it might not be a bad idea to have a distraction before we're face-to-face again. The money wouldn't hurt either. I'll need every penny I can get for next year.

Got your message. I can do it, I text her.

Thanks, kid. See you then.

❋

"Okay," I say, glancing up at Mia, who is struggling to restrain a very excited Ringo. We've managed to curb his jumping habit, but he still has endless amounts of energy and erratic leash manners. Right now he's doing little hops in place and keeps straining toward the end of his leash to get to me and Buffy, who I ran home to grab after school today since I don't want to go to Jordan's without her. "The first thing we need to do is get him to sit. Ideally his right shoulder should be touching your left leg, so that when we're ready to start walking he'll step out when you do."

Mia nods, gathers the leash into her hands more firmly, and says, "Ringo, *sit*."

Ringo sits, but he doesn't stop moving. His whole body wriggles and his front paws *tap tap* on the ground, like he's a little engine that's idling, waiting for driver Mia to step on the gas. He's so cute I want to laugh, but I don't let myself. "That's great! Now, remember when we start, to step with your left foot first. That way he'll take it as his cue to go and you'll be a step ahead."

"Got it," Mia says. She looks down at Ringo, who looks back up with a doggy version of a smile. Then she looks over at Buffy and me. "How'd you get her to be so good again?"

"Practice." I smile as I think of the last time someone asked me something like that. "And we started with things like this, just like you. You ready to go?" Mia nods, so I take a step forward and say, "Buffy, heel." She does easily, falling into step beside me, and behind us I hear Mia give Ringo the same command.

We get about halfway around the little training space before I hear Mia say, "Ringo, *sit*." I turn just in time to see Ringo plop his butt down on the floor, back to his idling engine pose, and

Mia gives him a click. She notices me looking and shrugs a little, blushing. "He started to pull forward again."

"You did exactly right. We'll let him calm down, and then start up again. You first this time."

"Really?"

"Really." I reach down to scratch Buffy behind the ears. She is, of course, already sitting at my side, shoulder brushing my leg. What an angel dog. "You're doing great, especially with a munchkin who has so much energy."

"Thanks." Mia beams at me. Then she takes a deep breath, squares her shoulders, and says, "Ringo, *heel*." I tell Buffy to do the same, and we start the process all over again.

By the end of the hour, we can make it two laps around the room before Mia has to stop and make Ringo sit. This is a huge improvement, and I tell Mia so as the four of us walk up to the front doors. "You've got a good one on your hands. Just keep practicing, and before you know it you'll be able to teach him how to chill."

"I don't know." Mia shakes her head and smiles as she looks at Buffy, who is unleashed and sitting patiently by my side. "We'll see. Anyway, thanks for squeezing me in today. I feel a lot better about having him around my mom this weekend. She's not a dog person, so I don't want her to hate him on principle just because he's jumpy, you know?"

"I definitely do," I say. "And it was no problem. I'll see you Monday, okay?"

"See you, Amber!" she says. "C'mon, Ringo." And she tugs Ringo toward the doors. He walks by her side in an almost perfect heel all the way to them, only stopping to lunge once as they pass a woman with a chihuahua coming inside.

When they're gone, I go in search of Stephanie. I find her at her desk, poring over a thick stack of paper. She looks up when I knock on the door and smiles, waving me in and then holding out a hand to Buffy to beckon her over.

"Hey, kid," Stephanie says, as Buffy sniffs her hand and then rests her head in her lap so that it's easy for Steph to rub her ears. "I was wondering when you were going to bring this cutie in to see me."

"She comes with me to my Thursday night thing, so I figured I'd pick her up before we came in."

"I'm glad you did. Gotta get all my Buffy time in this year, before you guys go off to college and leave me to find some new trainers."

"Yeah," I say, trying to laugh and not doing a very good job. "Totally."

Steph looks up at me. "Everything okay in college land? You know I would love nothing more than to keep you two here forever so we can train all the puppies in Wichita to be as good as the Buffster. But not if I have to listen to you fake-laugh like that."

I laugh for real this time. Ever since Steph told me about the behavioral science program at KU, she's been joking about somehow getting me to stick around in town for school. But I know she doesn't mean it. She knows how much I want to go, even if she doesn't know all the reasons why.

"It's okay," I say. "I found out I got into KU this week, actually."

"That's great!"

"Yeah. The financial aid package wasn't as good as I was hoping, but I'll figure out how to make it work. I've been applying for more scholarships, and I started researching apartments and jobs up there. I wanted to ask you about a pet store I read about, actually."

Stephanie smiles at me. "Pet Universe?"

"Yeah." I scoot aside a pile of papers so I can sit down on her desk. "You've heard of it?"

She nods. "Of course. They've been around since the eighties, I think. I worked for them my junior year when I was in undergrad. It's what made me sure I wanted to open my own store someday. I've been meaning to tell you to check it out, actually, but you've been so busy during your shifts that I haven't gotten a chance."

"Everything I've read about them sounds amazing," I confess. "Would you mind being a reference for me if I apply? They already have applications up for next fall, I guess since they get a lot of students who work just for the school year."

Stephanie narrows her eyes at me. "I hope you mean *when* you apply, not if. And of course I'll be your reference. You didn't even need to ask, kiddo. That's a given."

"Thanks, Steph," I say, a little overwhelmed by the matter-of-fact kindness in her tone.

"You're welcome." She grins at me and tosses Buffy a treat. "Now get back out on the floor for a little bit before you go, okay?"

"Okay," I say, smiling as I push myself off the desk.

As I head back out to the front of the store with Buffy at my side, I can't help thinking of rule number one. I don't want to jinx it, but I think my horizon just got a little brighter.

✳

I get caught up helping a customer toward the end of my shift, so I don't actually end up leaving work until 7:55. When I realize the time I shoot off a quick text to Jordan to let him know Buffy and I will be a few minutes late.

No worries, he says, but I feel guilty anyway and drive ten over the speed limit to minimize how long I leave him hanging.

The garage door is open when I pull up to the curb in front of Jordan's house, and light is spilling out onto the driveway. I cut the engine and sit for a second, fighting off a rush of nervousness as I try to psych myself up to go in.

"This is no big deal," I say to Buffy, who is sitting primly in the backseat. "It's just Jordan. And he told me not to feel bad about Friday, so I totally shouldn't. Right?"

Buffy tips her head to the side and blinks at me in the rear-view mirror, clearly skeptical. I sigh. Maybe it's not too late to bail?

But then she looks up at the house and barks, and I see that Jordan is standing at the top of the driveway, watching us. A second later my phone vibrates in the cup holder, and I pick it up to find a text from him.

Hey, creeper.

I grin in spite of myself. Okay, so it's too late to bail. And maybe I've been making a bigger deal out of this than I should be.

"I'm not a creeper," I call as I get out of the car and open the back door to let Buffy out.

"Just giving you a hard time," Jordan says, watching as we come up to meet him. "Looked like the two of you were having a pretty serious conversation in there. Everything okay?"

"Fine." I follow him into the garage. "It's just been a long week."

He eyes me for a second. "All right. We should try to make this quick, then."

"Oh no, we don't have to," I blurt, and then I realize how desperate that sounds and heat rushes to my face. "I mean, it's fine. I'm not in a hurry or anything."

There's a beat of silence, and then he says, "Okay."

I feel strange and off-balance as I settle into my usual spot on the work bench, and judging by the stiff way Jordan holds himself as he slides in next to me I'm not the only one feeling awkward. I'm even more aware of him than usual, which is saying something, but I force myself to focus on the assignment he needs me to read. It takes a while, but I do finally start to relax. And as I start to get more comfortable, so does he, until it almost feels like we've traveled back in time to last week, when we were talking about our dreams.

That feeling makes me brave, so when we get to a stopping point between assignments I say, "So. You want to take a break and shoot around for a bit?"

It's the first time I've ever been the one to suggest this, and I don't let myself think too hard about why. I just know that I could go for a game of horse right now and the inevitable conversation that would come along with it. I find myself holding my breath, hoping he says yes.

It takes a long time for him to answer, and when he does he won't meet my gaze. "No, that's okay. We've only got one more paper to read through, and it's been a long day. Better to just finish up, don't you think?"

"Oh," I say, letting my breath out in a *whoosh*, my heart sinking. "Right, yeah. That makes sense."

"Right," he says, fiddling with that tear on the seat. "Great."

He doesn't sound like he means it, but I don't push. I just settle back into work and tell myself it's better this way. This thing we're doing, it was starting to push against the rules too much. Better to curb that impulse now than to keep going. Because this rejection? It hurts. But it would hurt more if I had really let him be an exception.

nineteen

The next night Hannah comes over for our traditional pre-Christmas sleepover, which we've done every year since second grade. We watch Disney movies and exchange presents and are generally obnoxious and loud and revert back to our eight-year-old selves. It's my favorite part of the holidays because it's the one thing that's been the same since I was a little kid.

We've barely gotten the snacks laid out and the first movie going when Mom yells down the stairs that Cammie is here to spend the night. Hannah and I exchange confused glances. While Cammie has come over for dinner every night she's supposed to be here since that first time, she has yet to stay over. I don't remember her saying anything about spending the night when she was here on Tuesday, but I was so distracted by the whole KU thing that I could have easily missed something.

"We should invite her to hang out with us," Hannah says.

"Are you serious?" I ask, looking at her. "No." I don't bother to add that tonight is me and Hannah's time. That I look forward to this sleepover every year, with no intrusions by Mom or her boyfriend or his kids. I don't add this because I shouldn't have to. Hannah should already know.

"Why not?" Hannah asks. "You hung out with her at Jordan's

on Thanksgiving." There is a challenge in her tone that I don't like, a reminder that she's still mad about me turning down Jordan's invite after the game last weekend. We still haven't talked about that, even though I can tell she wants to. I'm worried that if we talk about Jordan, we'll have to talk about everything we've been avoiding, including the fact that I'm pretty sure she doesn't want to be my roomie next year anymore. So I've been changing the subject every time she brings it up.

I know it's stupid, but I just want things to stay normal for a little while longer, even though with all this awkwardness lingering between us they really aren't.

"That was different. They've been friends since they were in diapers. It would have been weird not to invite her. I was being nice."

Hannah narrows her eyes at me. "Okay, well, this is her house. And I think we should let her know that, if she's interested, we will be screening Disney movies and romantic comedies in her basement all night. It's the nice thing to do. Don't you think?"

I open my mouth and snap it closed again. I can't believe she's throwing my words back at me. "Fine," I say through gritted teeth. "But you can tell her that. Not me."

"Great!" Hannah says, and before I can stop her she's out of the recliner and up the stairs. She goes so fast that Buffy doesn't even move from her spot on the floor to follow her. She just looks at me, her brown eyes confused, like she doesn't get what all the fuss is about.

"I don't either," I tell her, and she tips her head to the side so her tags jingle, like she's telling me she understands.

Five minutes later Hannah's back downstairs with Cammie in tow. She shoots me a challenging smile, then turns to Cammie and says, "Welcome to girls' night. I hope you like *Mulan*, because that's what we're watching first. Amber's pick."

Cammie eyes me for a second, and I bristle at the cool expression on her face. "That's one of my favorites, actually," she says.

Hannah grins. I look away, back at the TV. It's going to be a long night.

We make it through *Mulan* fine, and when it's over Hannah insists we rewatch the "I'll Make a Man Out of You" part three times. Normally I love this part—actually normally *I'm* the one who insists we watch that clip over and over again—but tonight it grates on my nerves. I want this movie to be over so Cammie will go upstairs and leave us alone.

But that doesn't happen, because when Hannah finally gets tired of swooning over Shang, she says, "I think Cammie should pick the next movie. Amber, you good with that?"

And I say yes, because saying anything else would be rude, and for the next few minutes, while Cammie debates what to pick, I sit and seethe in silence, wondering how this night went so wrong.

She picks *Tangled*, which gets me a raised eyebrow from Hannah because *Tangled* is another one of my favorites and I'm sure she thinks this is a sign that Cammie and I are destined to be friends. *But it isn't*, I want to shout. *Because that's against the rules. The RULES, Hannah! Don't you remember them?*

I don't though, because if I did Hannah would point out that *I've* been having trouble with the rules where a certain someone is concerned this year. So it's better to keep my mouth shut.

When the movie ends, Hannah flips on the lamp on the end table by her and reaches down for her overnight bag. She starts digging in it and finally comes up with a small package in hand. "Ha!" she says, and tosses it at me. "Here."

I hesitate for a second, not wanting to do this little ritual in front of Cammie. But Hannah raises her eyebrows at me so I grab my own little package from the back of the couch and toss it at her, a little harder than I should. "Here's yours."

"Is it someone's birthday?" Cammie asks, looking very confused.

"Nope," Hannah says.

"So what are the presents for?"

"Christmas." I open mine and laugh. I can't help it. "Darth Vader? Nice."

Hannah holds up hers. "Bugs Bunny! I've missed this guy."

"Wait," Cammie says, and I look over at her. She's looking from Hannah to me and back again. "You guys give each other bobbleheads?"

"Yup," Hannah says, grinning. "See, my dad has this bobblehead problem. Like, he's gotten me bobbleheads for Christmas every year since I was five."

"And," I jump in, because I love this story, "the year we turned eight, he started getting them for me too. And not just one."

"Oh no," Hannah says. "Like a ton of them. 'They're collector's items, Hannah,'" she adds in a perfect imitation of her dad. It's so good I lose it all over again and a little bit of my irritation with her goes away.

"And he still gets these for you?"

"No, he stopped last year. But we have so many and we never

161

got the same thing, so we started trading. How old were we? Thirteen?"

"Twelve," I say. "The Star Wars ones are our favorites."

Cammie takes a second to process this. Then she goes, "Huh." Which sets Hannah and I off again.

After that, Hannah decides we should put in another movie. "My pick this time," she says, getting up and going over to the rows of movies. She's quiet for a few moments and then she says, "Ha!" and puts one in. I know what it is as soon as I hear Al Green over the opening credits. *Love & Basketball.*

"That's an interesting choice," Cammie says, raising an eyebrow, and my whole face burns.

I keep quiet, staring at the TV until my vision starts to blur. I miss the first ten minutes or so of the movie because I'm not paying attention to anything except keeping my face blank. By the time I tune back in, it's almost to the high school years, and Hannah and Cammie are having an intense conversation about Omar Epps and his hotness.

"He's definitely on my boyfriend list," Hannah's saying.

"Boyfriend list?"

"Yeah. Don't you have one?" Out of the corner of my eye I see her nod toward me. "Amber does, but hers are all fictional. Like Barry Allen and Harry Potter."

"Oh," Cammie says. "I've never made an official one, but I see what you mean. My number one would probably be Paul Walker, may he rest in peace." I raise my eyes at her in surprise and she says, "What? I like The Fast and the Furious movies, okay?"

Hannah nods, holds her hand over her heart for a brief second, and then grins approvingly. "Noah Centineo for me. That boy is *so* good-looking."

We make it through almost all of the rest of the movie in silence, with only the occasional comment about something funny or hot on the screen. It gets so close to the end that I think maybe it really was a coincidence that Hannah picked this movie and I'm being paranoid for no reason. But then we hit the part where Monica challenges Quincy to a game of one-on-one for his heart.

"So, Amber," Hannah says. "Is this how your games with Jordan go?"

Startled, I blink at her for a few seconds while emotional music comes out of the speakers. "What?"

"Your one-on-one games. Are they this intense?"

"No," I snap, glaring at her.

"No," Cammie agrees, and I shoot her a grateful look, surprised she's backing me up on this. But then she adds, "I'd say it's more like that earlier scene, where they strip while they play." And I remember why rule number two exists in the first place.

"Yeah, well," I say, "in case you weren't paying attention, nobody asked you."

She jerks back like I've slapped her, and I catch Hannah's expression out of the corner of my eye. Like she doesn't even know who I am anymore. Pretty ridiculous, since this whole situation is her fault.

What feels like an eternity but is really only about five minutes later, the movie ends and I hurry to get up and take it out of the Blu-ray player. Hannah gets up too and flips on the lights.

The sudden brightness makes me squint. I stay on the floor in front of the TV instead of going back to my seat, hoping my outburst means this charade is finally over.

"Well," Hannah says, clearing her throat. "Thanks for hanging out with us." She says it nicely, but it's clearly a dismissal, and Cammie thankfully gets the hint.

"Yeah," she says. "Thanks for letting me. It was—fun." She yawns big and long. "I'm gonna go up to bed. Night."

Hannah waits until we can't hear Cammie's footsteps anymore before she rounds on me. "What is your *problem*?"

"*My* problem?" I ask, whipping my head around to look at her. "Are you kidding me?"

Hannah stares at me. "Uh, no, I'm not."

"My *problem*," I say, mimicking her tone, "is that you invited her down here when you knew I didn't want you to."

"You said it was okay!"

"Only after you backed me into a corner!"

Hannah looks at me for a second, blinking rapidly like maybe that will make my angry mood go away. "God, Amber, you know what? You really need to get over this."

"This?" I say, using air quotes. "What is 'this,' Hannah?"

"*This* is the way you explode at *everyone* anytime you have one second of connection with whoever your mom is dating, or his family, or, God, his neighbor or something. And you know what? I am tired of it, Amber. I get that it sucks for you to have all these people come and go, but you make it so much harder than it needs to be!" She takes a step toward me. "That girl is nice. Tonight was fun. Sue me for trying to be nice to someone you have to live with.

164

And Jesus, Amber, what if things really do work out with your mom and Kevin and you have to deal with Cammie long-term? What are you going to do then?"

I scramble to my feet, my hands shaking, and back away from her. Buffy gets up too and puts herself between Hannah and me. "Don't. Just stop. You know it doesn't work like that. You know the rules."

I've been letting them slide too much lately, but I have to stop. Because every time I do, it's like Mom knows and decides that's the best time to end things and move on to the next guy. I don't ever get a choice. I just get hurt. So the rules, following them, that's my choice. It's the only one I get. How can I break them, knowing that?

Hannah's face softens, and she gets this look of understanding that I hate. Like she can see some part of me that even I can't. "Amber," she says, taking a tentative step forward, reaching out one hand to Buffy, who sniffs it delicately, and the other to me. "Maybe this time will be different. Your mom really seems to like Kevin, and he—"

I'm already heading for the stairs, shaking my head and fighting back sudden tears. I don't want to talk about this anymore. Or ever. "Just drop it. I'll see you upstairs."

twenty

Hannah leaves early the next morning, when it becomes clear to her that I am going to fake-sleep until she goes away. I hear her stop in my doorway, and then she says, "You can keep this up for as long as you want, but I'm the one who taught you how to fake-snore in the first place. Don't even pretend like I don't know what you're doing. When you want to talk about this—about everything—I'll be here. Until then, snore away." Then she goes, and I feel like something heavy is sitting on my chest.

At school on Monday, Hannah and I pretend like nothing happened, though I can tell by the way she watches me that she's still mad-at-slash-worried-about me. Luckily she has Elliot as a distraction and I have Ryan to pass me bites of cinnamon crunch bagels under the table. Without them there'd be frigid silence at our lunch table, though things are pretty quiet even with the boys as buffers.

I avoid Cammie. Partly because the last week was a wake-up call that I need to be stricter about the rules, about remembering she and I aren't friends and never will be. But I also avoid her because I'm embarrassed about how I treated her. It's been a long time since I lost control like that in front of one of my mom's boyfriends or their families. Even longer since I took my anger out on them. It makes me feel small.

Jordan I do not avoid, but it's not like I see him much, anyway.

We are strictly back to business. I go over to his house on Thursday night for not-tutoring session number six, and we keep things totally professional. We get through his fifteen-page midterm paper in record time and then I leave, because after last week horse is apparently off the table. I try not to think about how much this bothers me, but that night when I get home it takes me a long, long time to fall asleep.

Friday morning Ms. Ulbrich pulls me aside after English class again. "Can you come by during lunch?" she says. "I thought today would be a good time to check in with you and Mr. Baugh. See how your meetings are going."

Oh. Right. "Definitely. I'll see you then."

She nods and I leave to spend the rest of the morning with my stomach in knots, which is stupid. I knew this was coming. Six weeks was always the time limit. I'm only upset because I promised Jordan I'd make sure he kept his grades up and I can't do that if we don't meet anymore. That's all.

Jordan beats me to Ms. Ulbrich's room again. He gives a hesitant smile when he sees me.

Ms. Ulbrich comes over and plonks herself down in the seat across from us and says, "Let's begin."

Jordan and I both look at her. She's got Jordan's midterm paper in her hands, and I brace myself for her to go into some long, detailed conversation about it. But she doesn't. She just says, "Well, Mr. Baugh, this is certainly an improvement. Your argument is much more coherent, and the random capitalizations are gone. I think you're doing very well. This is a solid B paper, and the rest of the work you've turned in since you started working with Ms. Richter is as well."

"Oh." Jordan glances at me and then quickly away. "Thanks. Amber's been really . . . She's really helped me."

I can feel myself blushing, but luckily neither of them seem to notice.

"I'm happy to hear that," Ms. Ulbrich says. "However, since we only have next week left before the holiday break, I'd like to see how you do on your own for those assignments before we decide if this arrangement should continue next semester. Does that work for both of you?"

She says that last part like a question, but I can tell it's really not. So I ignore the sinking feeling in my gut and say, "That's fine with me."

"Yeah, no problem," Jordan agrees, staring at his feet.

"Wonderful," Ms. Ulbrich says. "We'll check back in after the new year, then." And with that, she gets up and leaves the room.

"Well," Jordan says. "I guess that's it."

There's a note of disappointment in his voice that makes my heart thump hard in my chest, but I force myself to keep my tone neutral as I say, "For now at least."

"Right." He gets to his feet and looks over at me. "I guess we should go get some food, then." As if on cue, my stomach rumbles, and he grins. "Hungry?"

"Starving," I admit.

"Then let's go."

We head out of the classroom and toward the commons. We're silent for a minute and then Jordan clears his throat. "So. You coming to the game tonight?"

"Yeah," I say. "And the dance tomorrow." This weekend is basketball Homecoming. Why the school administration decided to put it on the last weekend of school before winter break is beyond me, but there you go.

"Nice. You going with anybody?"

"Hannah," I say, resisting the urge to ask him why he wants to know. "I'm her second date." I still have this title, in spite of our fight. One of the perks of being best friends.

That surprises a laugh out of him. "Second date?"

I grin and feel myself relax a little. "Yeah. Elliot's her first, but she and I have a long-standing tradition. And besides, I'm a better dancer than Elliot anyway."

He shoots me a sideways glance, the corners of his mouth tugging up in a smile. "That I can definitely believe."

We're at the commons now. Ryan spots me and waves, motioning to show me that they've saved me a seat. "I'd better go," I say, nodding toward them.

"Right, yeah," Jordan says, looking over at my friends and then back at me. I start toward the table but I don't get very far before he says, "I'll be there tomorrow. At the dance."

He looks so serious. My heart starts pounding hard in my chest. I open my mouth to say something like, "Then I'll see you there," or "Awesome, it's gonna be so much fun!"

What comes out instead is, "If you win tonight, I'll save a dance for you."

His mouth opens in surprise. We stare at each other for a long moment.

"Amber!" Hannah calls.

I jump like I've been shocked and squeak, "Gottago-seeyoulaterbye!"

169

And then I turn and practically sprint toward my friends' table, trying to ignore the fizzing feeling that's happening in my veins. Jesus Christ. Why did I *say* that?

"What was that about?" Hannah asks as soon as I reach them. Ryan raises an eyebrow at me, clearly interested by the suspicion in her tone.

"Nothing." I flop into the seat across from Ryan and reach for his chips. "Just talking about the game."

Hannah looks at me with a knowing expression. "That didn't look like nothing."

"Hey, I wasn't done with those," Ryan says.

"Sorry." I hand the bag back to him and reach for the apple on his tray instead; he rolls his eyes, laughs, and hands the chip bag back to me. To Hannah, I add, "Well, what did it look like?"

"Something."

"Right. Well it wasn't, so don't worry about it."

She eyes me carefully for a second, clearly trying to decide whether she should push me on this or not. And I guess she decides not to, because she nods and says, "Okay. We're still carpooling to the game tonight, right?"

"Right."

I hope we lose.

❋

We win. By twenty points. And when that final buzzer sounds, my promise echoes in my head. *If you win tonight, I'll save a dance for you.*

Shit.

*

Hannah insists that we go out to get dessert after the game, so it's late when I finally get home, pushing close to my curfew. I'm careful to be quiet as I slip through the kitchen and head toward the stairs. Buffy greets me in the living room, her paws padding softly on the carpet as she comes over to stick her nose in my hand. I'm bending down to rub her neck under her collar when I hear angry voices coming from Mom and Kevin's room.

I freeze, hold my breath, and try to make out what they're saying. But I can't from here, can barely even tell it's my mother talking and not Kevin; I only know it's her because I have years of experience listening to her hiss at people behind closed doors. Slowly I let my breath out and take a step closer, and then another, until I'm across the living room and at the start of the hallway that leads to their bedroom.

". . . without asking me," I hear my mother say, her voice low and sharp.

"Claire," Kevin says, "I really think you're blowing this out of proportion."

"I'm not," she snaps. The words are cutting even to me, so I can imagine what they must feel like to Kevin. I hear her saying something else, but I don't catch the first part of it. I just get ". . . don't appreciate it."

Kevin says something back, his voice muffled now too. They must be walking toward the bathroom, or their closet or something. "Shouldn't you let . . . say . . . ? You don't know . . . might . . . future."

"I do know," my mother says, her voice clear again. "And I'm done talking about this. I'm going to bed."

With that, the strip of light under their door goes dark, and I hear the sound of rustling covers. I stay where I am for a second, waiting to see if Kevin will push back or if the conversation really is over. But he stays quiet and the light stays off, so I back away from the hallway and hurry toward the stairs.

This is how it always starts. Angry voices behind closed doors lead to tense silences at dinner, which turn into clipped words and sighs of irritation, and then full-on fights with actual yelling that my mother couldn't hide even if she wanted to. And then it's over and she finds someone new and convinces herself that this guy will be The One. That this will be the last time we have to rearrange our whole lives again.

I never believe it. I just wait for the signs that show me the end is coming, so that I'll be ready when it does. Usually it's a relief when I spot the first one, because waiting takes a lot of energy and it's hard to always be on edge. But this time I don't feel relieved.

I feel like crying.

I wake up early the next morning to let Buffy out and feed her, then go back to bed and sleep until it's almost time for lunch. When I come downstairs again, Mom is at the kitchen island, nursing a cup of coffee and aggressively flipping through one of her favorite recipe books. Kevin is nowhere to be seen.

"Um, morning," I say, hesitating in the doorway, and she jumps at the sound of my voice.

"Oh, Amber, you scared me," she says, setting her coffee cup down and putting a hand over her heart.

"Sorry." I come further into the room and head for the fridge in search of food.

"That's all right, sweetheart. Are you and Hannah still planning to come back here after your dance tonight?"

I hesitate. Part of me wants to say no, that Hannah and I are staying at her house now, but if I do that Mom will ask why we changed our minds. I don't want her to know that I overheard her fight with Kevin last night, and maybe knowing Hannah and I are coming back here will make them less likely to give a repeat performance.

"That's the plan," I say, emerging from behind the refrigerator door with an apple and some Babybel cheese. At the sight of the cheese Buffy gives me sad eyes, so I take pity on her and start unwrapping one for us to share.

"Good," Mom says, smiling now. "Any snack requests? Stella has the bakery covered today, so I figured I'd play around with some new recipes."

"Hannah liked those s'mores cookies you did over the summer. Otherwise just surprise me."

"Deal," Mom says. Then she glances at something behind me and stiffens in her seat.

I turn to find Kevin coming into the kitchen, his coat halfway on and his keys and a pair of sparkly high heels in hand.

He smiles warmly at me. "Morning, Amber." Then he turns to Mom and adds, "I've got to run Cam's shoes over to Ellen's," in a tone that for normal humans would be considered friendly but for him is downright frosty.

"All right," Mom says, not meeting his gaze.

Aaaand that's my cue to leave.

"I've got to head to Hannah's to get ready," I say, loudly enough that both of them start and look at me. "Mom, you guys can still take care of Buffy tonight, right?"

"Yes." She nods and gets to her feet. "We've got her covered."

"Thanks," I say, turning to go.

"Have fun," she and Kevin say together, and I look back in time to find them watching each other warily. I don't wait to see how the standoff turns out. Instead I hurry out of the room and back upstairs to grab my stuff, glad that for today at least, I have a place to make my escape.

twenty-one

Hannah and I spend the whole afternoon getting ready for the dance. She keeps changing her mind about her lipstick color and yelling at Matt, who is already home from KU for winter break, to turn down his music. After what I heard last night and witnessed this morning I'm having a hard time caring about the dance, but I know there's no way I can get out of it. So I do my best to act like I'm having a good time and to keep myself from thinking about the drama that's waiting for me back at Kevin's. I do a pretty good job at faking enthusiasm. Not so good at keeping my thoughts in check.

Hannah and I do each other's hair—I put hers up with a bunch of loose braids and she curls mine so the waves are bigger than usual—and she lets me borrow her favorite pair of blue heels to go with my dress. This is her version of a peace offering. Some people say they're sorry or try to talk things out with you after a fight, but not Hannah. She lets you wear her shoes.

We meet up with Elliot and Ryan at Megan's house, and Megan's mom has us line up to take a million pictures in front of her fireplace. I'm exhausted by the end of it and feeling very much like a fifth wheel, but I don't say anything because I don't want to ruin the night for anyone else.

The music's already blaring when we get to the dance. Hannah and Megan have to go to the coat check, but I skip it because I left my coat in the car and everything else I need fits in my bra. Instead I take a bathroom break to double-check my hair and makeup. I have to skirt around the dance floor—which is really the floor of the commons decorated with snowflakes and flooded with strobe lights—to get there. It's still early, so not many people are dancing yet. Just a few awkward baby freshmen and some of the die-hard girls who never miss a song.

I walk into the bathroom and stop short at the sight of Cammie in a poufy pink dress, leaning close to the mirror to touch up her lip gloss.

She catches sight of me in the mirror, and smiles warily. "Amber. Hi."

"Hey." I hesitate for a second and then go over to stand next to her so I can check my makeup too.

She studies me carefully in the mirror. "I stopped by the house on the way here. Your mom said to tell you to make sure Megan's mom gives her pictures."

I roll my eyes. Mom has already texted me this like ten times. "Will do."

"Okay," Cammie says. She's quiet for a beat. Then: "So. Where's your date?" I must look confused because she adds, "Hannah."

"Oh, right." I laugh uneasily. Jordan must've told her about me and Hannah's arrangement. How else would she know? "She's in line for the coat check with Megan and the guys."

"Ah." Some other girls come in and Cammie backs away from

the mirror. I think she's going to leave but then she turns to me and says, "Well. Jordan and some of the other guys from the team got here a little bit ago."

My stomach flips. "Uh, okay."

"Just so you know," Cammie says.

"Right."

She peers at me for a second, frowning a little. Then she shakes her head and says, "I'll see you out there, Amber."

I have butterflies when I leave the bathroom, the big, swooping, scary kind. I tell myself to go find Jordan and end this whole stupid thing now, but Hannah and Megan and the boys find me before I can and start pulling me toward the dance floor. It's kind of a relief, to be honest. I'll deal with Jordan later. Or maybe he'll forget about what I said to him and won't come find me at all.

We push our way through the growing crowd until we're right next to the DJ booth, where the music is so loud it's like I can feel it in my bloodstream. The first song melts into the second and then the third and then the fourth, and somehow I manage to lose myself in the music.

It's hot and it doesn't take long for me to feel sweat trickling down my back. My hair feels heavy so I gather it up in one hand and pull it over my shoulder, not ready to give up and pull it back yet. Hannah's dancing with Elliot—his arms are around her waist and he keeps leaning down so his mouth is near her ear. They look happy.

She smiles a huge smile at me and holds out her wrist, the one with the ponytail holder. I shake my head no. Then her smile gets even bigger and she waves at someone behind me, and I turn around and there's Cammie. And I wonder why Hannah's smiling like that, because I know she likes Cammie but that's the smile she saves for whenever important boy things are about to happen.

And then I see Jordan following right behind Cammie and I get it now, and my heart starts beating so hard that I can feel it in my fingertips.

"Hey," Cammie shouts at me. She shoves Jordan in my direction and then melts back into the crowd. After a moment of hesitation, he comes close and leans down until his mouth is right next to my ear.

"I think you said something about saving me a dance." I feel his breath on the side of my neck as he speaks to me, and it sends a shiver skittering down my spine.

I did, I think, pulling back and staring up at him. *But I shouldn't have.*

"Amber?" he asks, after a moment. I took too long to answer. He's smiling but he looks unsure now, like he thinks my silence means no, that I don't remember my promise or don't want to keep it anymore. Why don't I want to say no to him? When did that get so hard?

"Yes," I tell him. One dance. That's all I promised. What can that hurt?

"What?"

I go up on my toes a little so that now I'm talking into his ear. He smells like . . . something I haven't quite figured out yet. Something sporty, either his deodorant or his cologne. It's how he smells after we've been shooting around for a while. Right now it's doing crazy things to my head. "Yes. I owe you a dance. You cashing in?"

He swallows and nods.

"Okay," I say.

He reaches out to me, but before his skin makes contact with mine the song changes to something slow. I freeze and he falters and we stare at each other for a long moment. Then, slowly, cautiously, he steps closer and loops his arms around my waist, settles his hands on the small of my back. The heat from his palms seeps through my dress and it's almost like he's touching my skin. I take a deep, shuddering breath and hook my arms around his neck, and then we're dancing and I think, *Okay. This is going to be okay.*

Then he whispers, so low I can't believe I hear him over the music, "I like your dress. It's pretty." And then he adds in a quieter tone, "You look beautiful."

My breath catches. It's not going to be okay. Because I did something really, really stupid. I broke the rules. I got involved. No, worse.

I got attached.

By the time the song ends, I'm shaking so bad I know he has to notice. So I make myself take a step away from him, a big enough one that he's forced to let me go, and put on the best smile I can do right now. "Promise paid," I say in that quiet moment before the next song comes on. "Thanks for the dance."

A flicker of confusion passes over his face, like he's not sure he heard me right. He studies me for a second, and then, as a rap song starts blaring out of the speakers, reaches out to catch my arm. Sparks race up from his fingers as he gently tugs me closer and leans in again. "Are you okay?"

"Fine," I breathe, nodding. And then I make another mistake. I look up at him.

His face is so close to mine, and I feel fluttery all over, and maybe he can tell because something in his expression changes. He starts to lean down. I close my eyes. I can feel his breath on my lips.

For one second, I think I'm going to let him kiss me. But then I hear Cammie's laughter nearby and everything from the past twenty-four hours comes rushing back and my eyes fly open and I stumble away from him. He loses his hold on me and my skin is cold where his hand used to be.

"I'm fine," I repeat, louder this time, and now he looks hurt and the hurt doesn't go away. Like it's too big for him to hide it.

"Are you sure?" he asks.

"Yeah," I say, my voice high and strange. "I'm just hot. I need a drink. I'll see you later, okay?"

I don't wait to hear if he says anything back. I'm already moving, shoving through people until I'm out of the crowd, and I don't stop until I'm in the deserted bathroom, locked in the accessible stall. I press my back against the door and try to slow my breathing, but I'm having a hard time.

After a few minutes, someone says, "Amber?"

I take a deep breath and then turn around and open the stall door. Hannah's there in front of the first sink. "Here."

She gives me a look that's half exasperation, half worry. Worry wins, and she comes to join me. "What happened?"

I shake my head. I can't talk about it. If I do, I'll start crying.

"Amber. Come on."

I shake my head again and press my lips together. But staying quiet isn't working either, because my eyes fill with tears that spill over and rush down my face. Furiously I reach up to swipe them away.

"Hey, whoa," Hannah says, reaching out to grab my arm, peering at me. "I didn't mean to make you cry. I'm sorry."

"It's fine," I choke. "It's not you."

"Do you want to go?"

I nod.

"All right, let's go." She unlocks the stall door and starts marching me toward the exit.

"What about everyone else? What about Elliot?"

But Hannah's already pulling out her phone. "I'll text him. He can ride home with Ryan and Megan. He'll understand."

"Thanks," I whisper, and I let her pull me out of the stall.

We get Hannah's stuff from the coat check. Her phone buzzes as we're walking out the door and she checks it, then smiles reassuringly at me. "We're all good."

"Good," I say, relieved. I can't believe I'm ruining her night with Elliot. I'll have to make it up to her.

We walk to the car in silence and I'm reaching for the door handle automatically before I realize that Hannah hasn't unlocked it yet. I look over the top of the car to find her watching me.

"What?" I ask.

She studies me for a second longer. "You like him."

I don't answer. I don't need to.

"I thought so," she says, and then the horn beeps as she finally unlocks the doors.

twenty-two

Hannah and I go back to Kevin's house and set up camp in the basement. We put on Star Wars, our go-to comfort movie series, and she doesn't even get mad when I pick the prequel trilogy instead of the original or sequel ones. Halfway through *Attack of the Clones* I get a text from Jordan.

I'm sorry if I freaked you out tonight.

I stare at it for a long time. Long enough that Hannah notices.

"Who's that from?" she asks, scooting closer to me. We're both on the couch tonight, Buffy on the floor between our feet.

I show her and she looks at me, her expression unreadable. "What?" I ask, flipping my phone over so she can't see Jordan's text anymore.

"Can I say something without you getting mad at me?"

I flinch and look away. I hate that she feels like she has to ask that. "Yeah."

"Okay." There's a pause and I hear her fishing in the bag of chocolate-covered pretzels we brought down here with us. Mom's s'mores cookies are long gone. "Screw the rules."

I snap my gaze over to her.

She bites into the pretzel, crunching loudly. "You said you wouldn't get mad."

I take a deep breath in through my nose to keep myself in check, then let it out slow. "I'm not mad. Just . . . you helped me write the rules." I swallow hard, thinking of Mom and Kevin's fight, of Jordan's face when I ran away tonight, of how much it hurts me whenever Mom dumps someone even though I tell myself it doesn't. "You know why they exist."

"I do," Hannah says, nodding. "We made them because you felt safer having them, and that was good for a while. But, Amber . . . are they making you feel safe right now, or are they making you unhappy?"

I open my mouth to answer her, then snap it closed again.

"Think about it." She holds out the bag of pretzels to me and turns back to face the TV.

"Okay," I say in a small voice, settling deeper into the cushions.

We're quiet for a few minutes, back to watching the movie. But then Hannah pauses the movie and says, in a voice even smaller than mine, "Can I say something *else* without you getting mad?"

"Is it about you wanting to live on campus next year?" I ask, looking over at her.

"Not for sure," she says in a rush. "But yeah. I've kind of been thinking about it. How'd you figure it out?"

"Matt said something to me a while ago, on one of his laundry trips. Ryan said you'd been asking about Bri and Parker. And that loft bed comment you made the day we unpacked my room wasn't exactly subtle."

Hannah winces and lets out a little laugh. "Yeah, that was pretty bad. I just . . . didn't know how to talk to you about it."

"It's okay," I tell her. "I didn't know how to ask you about it either."

"Part of me loves the idea of an apartment," Hannah says, "but part of me really wants to live in the dorms freshman year. Matt loved it so much, you know? I think I'd love it too."

"I'm sure you would," I say. "Which means we should add a dorm tour to our plans when we finally go up to visit your brother. I'll talk to my mom about it tomorrow, okay?"

"Really?" Hannah asks, her voice a mixture of hopefulness and disbelief.

"Really," I promise. "I've been doing my research on jobs and apartments for next year, and I made a budget and everything. I'll have to tweak some of the numbers so that I have a plan for if Buffy and I need to live alone, but—"

"I'll help you," Hannah says with a firm nod. "We can look at it in the morning, okay? But I don't want you to think you living alone is a done deal, Amber. I just want to see what my options are, you know?"

"Of course." But I have a feeling I know how this is going to go. Hannah is so much more social than I am. She'll love the community aspect of the dorms.

"Okay." She lets out a huge sigh. "God, I feel so much better now. You have no idea how much that's been weighing on me."

"Mm, I think I have a little bit of an idea."

She throws a pretzel at me and hits play on the movie.

"You know," she says, "on top of thinking about the rules, you should really think about at least talking to Jordan. Speaking from experience—"

I snort. "Experience of like five seconds ago?"

This time she throws a pillow. I catch it easily and toss it to the side. "Speaking from experience," she starts again, giving me a look, "worrying about the conversation you're afraid of is a lot worse than actually having it."

"Thanks, Yoda."

"I'm just saying." She holds up her hands in surrender. "It's something else to think about."

A little after one in the morning, somewhere in the middle of *Revenge of the Sith*, I look over and see that Hannah is passed out next to me. I'm tired too, but I can't sleep. I've got too much on my mind—I'm still *thinking* about everything we talked about earlier. The dorms and the rules and me having a real conversation with Jordan instead of running away all the time like I've been doing. That last one in particular is terrifying, but I can't get the thought out of my head.

Buffy has picked up on my nervous energy. She keeps lifting her head to sniff me, tags jingling every time. Finally, after about five rounds of this, I get up, slip carefully past Hannah, and head up the stairs. Buffy follows, quiet except for her tags, and the two of us go quickly through the living room and into the kitchen, where her leash is hanging on the hook by the garage door.

Two minutes later we're out in the neighborhood and I'm trying to tell myself that I'm not going where I'm actually going.

But I know exactly what I'm doing. I can't stop picturing Jordan's face when I pulled away, and I can't leave it like that. I have to explain why I can't be like that with him. Why that part of me is broken and I don't want to fix it, at least for now. He probably won't even be outside, but I have to try. I have to see.

It's snowing and I'm shivering in my coat, so I stuff my hands in my pockets and let Buffy lead, because she knows the way. We loop around the golf course, where the grass is brown and crunchy-looking, and go on past the clubhouse and the empty pool. Then Will Hoefling's street. Then another, and then another, and then Buffy bumps into my legs because she's trying to turn right. I take a deep breath, holding it until it hurts.

Then we go right. Down Jordan's street.

I hear it as we come around the curve in the road that hides the end of the cul-de-sac from the main street. Someone dribbling a basketball. At first I think *No way*, because really, what are the odds? But then I hear it again, three in a row this time, and I get this rush that starts in my heart and spreads out to my fingers and toes. I'm here to apologize. To explain. That's it and that's all.

But it doesn't feel like that anymore.

We make it past the bend and there's Jordan, shooting free throws in his driveway, lit up only by the motion light above the garage door. Buffy pulls at the leash when she sees him. I drop it and let her go.

She runs right up to him and he drops the ball in surprise. I watch as he crouches down to grab at her collar. I think he's saying something but I'm still too far away to hear. He scratches her behind the ears and then looks up and around, but it's inky dark tonight and I'm sure he can't see me yet. I keep walking, breathing in through my nose and out through my mouth to keep myself from freaking out. Which works fine until I almost trip over something in the gutter at my feet and realize it's the basketball. At that, my heart kicks into overdrive and I have to shake myself a little. I pick up the ball and tuck it under my arm and then I jog the rest of the way to Jordan's house.

I stop at the end of the driveway, and there's this moment where we just stare at each other. I wonder if he's thinking about that first night I walked by his house; I know I am.

Finally the silence is too much and I have to do something. Talking would probably be good, but I can't seem to make words. So I toss him the ball. He catches it easily, and I think maybe he'll shoot it or go put it away or challenge me to a game of horse or something. He throws it into the yard. I pull my head back and give it a little shake, like, *what are you doing*? But he doesn't answer me.

Instead he looks down at my dog, who's been standing next to him this whole time. He holds a hand out to her and says, "Chill." And then he starts walking over to me.

He stops about a foot away from me and then he waits. The proverbial ball is in my court. I close my eyes to steady myself. Then I open them and say, "Did you . . . did you just tell my dog to chill?"

He takes a step closer. "Uh, yeah."

"Nice," I whisper.

"Thanks." He studies my face and I study his, and then he sighs. "What are you doing here, Amber?"

I'm so caught up in looking at him that it takes me a second to remember. "I wanted to say sorry. About earlier."

"It's fine." He looks away. "No big deal."

"It is, though."

"It's really not," he says, shaking his head. "Look, *I'm* sorry, okay? For a while I thought that maybe . . . but then after that first game you didn't seem . . . but then yesterday you said—" He cuts himself off and blows out a frustrated breath, reaching up to run a hand through his hair. The motion sends snow fluttering to the ground, and I realize we've been standing here staring at each other for longer than I thought.

When he starts again, his voice is low and quiet, and he can't quite meet my gaze. "I'm sorry if I made you uncomfortable or pushed for anything you didn't want. I promise it won't happen again."

I take a step forward, and it's like something snaps into place and I get what Hannah meant about the rules making me unhappy. At least in this case. I've spent all this time moving myself away from Jordan when what I really wanted to do is move closer. All staying away from him does is hurt.

Slowly, I shake my head. "You didn't."

Jordan swallows, hard. "Didn't what?"

"Didn't push for anything I didn't want. Anything I *don't* want." I take another step closer. We're almost touching.

His head comes up and his eyes search my face. "There were a lot of negatives in that sentence, so I'm gonna need you to clarify what you mean."

"I mean I like you," I blurt.

Oh my God. I can't believe I just said that.

He goes very still and gets this look on his face like he wants to believe me but doesn't quite dare. "You do?"

"Yeah."

"Why'd you run away from me, then?"

Here's my chance to get back on track. To tell him all the reasons that we can't, we shouldn't, I won't. But I can't make myself say it, because that's not what I want. So I tell him the truth, or at least the part of it that I can share. "I got scared."

He nods like this makes sense. "Are you going to run away now?"

Somehow I manage to shake my head.

"Okay." He moves so there's no more space between us and brushes the snow off my shoulders before gently cupping my face in his hands. "For the record," he says, his voice shaky, "I like you too."

"Yeah?"

"Yeah," he says, and then he kisses me. And I kiss him back.

God, I kiss him back.

twenty-three

The next morning I wake up to the sound of the shower running in my bathroom and light pouring in through my open bedroom curtains. This is confusing because when I went to sleep last night—actually really early this morning—I was alone in here. Hannah was still downstairs on the couch. I sit up slowly and discover Buffy lying in the doorway with her butt out in the hall. She lifts her head and stares at me, and oh my God, I blush. Because she's looking at me like *I know what you did last night*. And she does, too.

"Shut it," I tell her, but I'm smiling.

I kissed Jordan Baugh. A lot.

"Oh, good," a voice says from the hallway, and all of a sudden Cammie's standing next to Buffy in the doorway. What is she doing here? She steps carefully around Buffy and comes into the room, going over to the desk and leaning against it. "You're up."

"Um, yeah," I say. "What time is it?" I look over at my nightstand but I don't have a clock and my phone is nowhere to be found.

"Noon."

Only noon? I'm surprised it's not later than that. Jordan didn't drive me home until after three.

"Listen, I won't keep you very long because I'm sure you and Hannah have plans," Cammie says. She's got her arms crossed over her chest and is glaring at me so hard that a large part of me wants to dive under my covers and never come out again. Jesus, this girl has the whole murderous-expression thing down to a science. "I just came in here to tell you to knock off this bullshit back-and-forth thing you have going on with J."

For a second, all I can do is blink at her. "What?"

"You know exactly what," she snaps. "One minute you're making googly eyes at him in his driveway and the next you're blowing him off in front of his best friends. It's rude and it hurts him and it's pretty freaking stupid because any idiot could tell that you're actually into him."

I'm not sure how to respond to this, because she's not wrong. Up until about ten and a half hours ago, the hot-and-cold thing is exactly what I was doing when it came to Jordan. And I am definitely, definitely into him. Jordan's face pops into my head, all messy hair and flushed cheeks after he kissed me goodbye this morning. And earlier than that, how he looked when we went inside because I was shivering in the snow. How I told him I wanted to take things slow and he kissed me and said, "Slow is good. I like slow."

And just like that, I blush again. Full-on hot face, neck, ears. It all burns.

When I don't say anything, Cammie rolls her eyes and mutters, "At least you're not trying to deny it."

Even though she's right, I bristle at her tone. "Look," I say, pushing back the covers and swinging my legs over the edge of the bed. "I get where you're coming from, but I don't think—"

"Um, guys?" Hannah's voice says from the bathroom doorway, and I jump, startled. I was so focused on Cammie's anger that I didn't even hear the shower cut off. "Everything okay in here?"

"It's fine," I say.

"No it's not." Cammie glares at me again. "I don't know what your hang-up is when it comes to Jordan, Amber, but you need to figure it out ASAP or leave him alone. If you don't, I will totally lose my shit."

Hannah blinks at us for a second, then does a weird cough thing that is definitely actually a laugh.

I sigh right as Cammie says, "What's so funny?"

"Nothing really," Hannah says, coming over to sit on the end of my bed and unwinding the towel she's got wrapped around her hair. "It's just, I told her pretty much the same thing last night when we got back here. In a little nicer words, maybe. But the point was the same."

"Oh." Cammie glances from Hannah to me and back again. "Well, good. Someone needed to, because this whole thing is starting to get ridiculous."

"Okay," I say, getting to my feet. "I'm gonna take a shower now."

"Wait," Cammie says, and something in her tone makes me stop.

"What?"

She studies me carefully for a second, like she's trying to decide something. Then she sighs. "Look, J would kill me if he knew I was here right now, but he really likes you, okay? He was so upset when you guys left last night."

"I know," I say without thinking.

Cammie narrows her eyes at me. "How do you know?"

My phone rings before I have a chance to answer. It's muffled, coming from under my pillow, and I lunge for it, sure that if I don't, Hannah or Cammie will either grab for it first or tell me to ignore the call and focus on the conversation. More heat rushes to my face when I see Jordan's name flashing across the screen. I answer and press the phone tight to my ear, trying to ignore Hannah and Cammie's stares.

"Hi," I say.

"Hey," Jordan says. He sounds nervous, which is good because I am too. It feels a little silly to be nervous after how much my tongue was in his mouth last night, but there you go. At least I'm not the only one. "I didn't wake you up, did I?"

"No, no."

"Oh, good." He clears his throat. "So, uh, I have a question. Which is why I called."

"Okay," I say, laughing. "Hit me."

"What are you doing tonight?"

"Um, nothing really," I say. Out of the corner of my eye, I see Hannah lean forward slightly, like a hunting dog on point. I look away from her and focus on twisting the corner of my sheets around my fingers. "Why?"

"Tasha and her girlfriend will be home for winter break tonight. My mom's making a big dinner. Do you want to come? It won't be fancy or anything, but the food will be good."

I want to ask him if this means what I think it means, but I am way too aware of Hannah and Cammie watching me. So I take a deep breath to help settle the butterflies in my stomach and say, "Yeah, I'll come. That sounds fun."

"Yeah?" The happiness in his voice makes me grin.

"Yeah. What time?"

"Six thirty? I'll pick you up a little before."

I hesitate for a second, thinking of the awkwardness that's lingering between Mom and Kevin. But I want to go to Jordan's tonight more than I want to avoid any weird run-ins. "Okay. I'll have to double-check with my mom first, but it shouldn't be a problem."

"Great," he says. "I guess I'll see you tonight."

"See you then," I say.

"Bye," he says. I get the feeling he's having a hard time hanging up. Which is good, since I am too.

"Bye," I say, and force myself to hang up.

A throat clears and I look at the foot of my bed, where Cammie has come to sit next to Hannah. Both of them are gaping at me.

"Who was that?" Hannah asks.

"Um . . . Jordan."

"And," Cammie says, her expression wary, "you're hanging out with him tonight?"

I look at her. "Yeah."

"And," Hannah says, giving a little bounce, her voice full of barely suppressed glee, "how, exactly, did this happen?"

"Um." I hesitate for a second before I decide, to paraphrase Hannah, to screw it and tell them the truth. "I took Buffy on a walk last night after you fell asleep. By his house."

"You *did*?" Hannah says, her smile at full wattage.

"Yeah. He was outside. We're, uh, we're good now."

She tackle-hugs me, squealing, and I laugh and squeal with her. "Tell us everything!" she demands when she finally lets me go. "Every detail." And even though Cammie's here and I'm still not sure about breaking rule number two, I do.

Once I'm done with my story—during which Hannah interrupts me about a million times and Cammie's expression morphs from suspicious to happy as I go on—we head downstairs in search of food. Cammie makes a vague comment about how she should probably go back to her mom's place since Mom and Kevin apparently aren't even here, but Hannah waves her off and insists that she stay and eat with us. So she does. And even though she basically came over here to yell at me before she realized I'd already fixed things with Jordan, it's surprisingly not weird.

Later, after we've eaten and Cammie has left, Hannah and I go back up to my room to look at all the apartments I've been researching and make a game plan for when I talk to my mom later today. I'm in the middle of taking screenshots of all the most promising apartments I've found when Hannah says, "You didn't mind that I asked Cammie to stay earlier, did you?"

"No," I say. "It was kind of nice."

Hannah grins. "I thought so too."

❋

It's after six by the time Mom gets home, and I'm so antsy about my talk with her and my impending dinner with Jordan's family that I corner her in the kitchen while she's hanging up her keys and coat.

"Hey," I say, skidding to a stop near the island. "Can you come look at something with me before I go to my dinner thing? It's really important."

"Oh hi, honey," Mom says, turning at the sound of my voice. She looks tired and half her hair is lighter than the other, probably from sugar or something from the bakery. But she still smiles gamely at me. "Of course. Give me a second to change out of these clothes, okay? I feel like I'm covered in flour."

"Okay." I take a step back out of the kitchen and turn toward the stairs. "I'll be up in my room."

I should probably change too, because there is no way I'm wearing yoga pants and a sweatshirt over to Jordan's house for dinner with his whole family.

A few minutes later I'm standing at the foot of my bed in jeans and a bra, staring at the ten different shirts I've got spread out over my bed. Buffy is lying at my feet, watching me with her ears pricked and her head resting on her paws. She lifts her head up, tags jingling, at the same time Mom says from the doorway, "Is this what you needed help with?"

"Oh, no," I say, jumping a little. "I mean, I only have like twenty more minutes to figure out what to wear, but no, I wanted to ask you something else."

"Okay," Mom says slowly, looking a little bemused as she comes further into the room.

I go over to my desk and open the top drawer enough to pull out the folder Hannah and I stashed there earlier this afternoon. Steeling myself, I turn back to face my mom and hold the folder out to her.

"What's this?" she asks, taking it from me and carefully flipping it open.

"I've been doing some research," I say. "On what it will cost me to live in Lawrence with Buffy next year. I hit a little snag because I don't think Hannah really wants to live off campus anymore, but I made a plan B just in case, and I think I've got everything covered with the aid package I got. It'll be tight and I'll probably still have to take out loans, but I did the calculations on exactly how much I'd need to make my budget work, and—"

"Amber," Mom says, cutting me off. "Stop. Breathe. Okay?"

I nod and suck in a huge breath, then let it out slow.

She holds up the folder, which I realize she flipped all the way through while I was rambling. "This is wonderful. It's very detailed. Can I take some time to look it over before we talk about it? I know you have dinner with your friend tonight." She tips her head to the side a little and smiles at me. "And I'd rather you go fully dressed."

"Oh, right." I look down at myself. "Um, okay." I grab a shirt at random off the bed, take one look at it, and throw it back down again. "Does this mean you'll let me at least do a campus visit with Hannah though? Because that's what I was leading up to. I had this whole speech planned and everything."

"It means we can talk about it once I've had a chance to look over your numbers, okay?" Her tone is totally neutral and gives nothing away, but at least she's not immediately saying no.

"Okay." I turn back to the bed and my shirt piles and sigh, because nothing looks right.

"This dinner tonight," Mom says. "It's with the boy you've been tutoring, right?"

"It's not really tutoring, Mom. But yes."

"Hmm. Is it like a date?"

"I don't know," I say, going over to my closet and pulling out a green top. I stare at it for a second, decide it's too Christmas tree, and toss it onto the floor. "It's dinner with his parents and sister and her girlfriend."

"That sounds like a date to me." Mom comes over to join me and grabs a purple long-sleeved shirt with a cool detail around the neckline out of my closet. After studying it for a second, she holds it out to me. "Wear this. It looks pretty with your eyes."

She's right, it does. So I put it on and offer her another smile. "Thanks."

twenty-four

Jordan rings the doorbell at six thirty on the nose. Kevin gets to it before I can, even though I practically sprint down the stairs, almost tripping over Buffy in the process. I hear Jordan saying, "Hey, Mr. Henning," right as I make it to the landing. "Is Amber ready to go?"

"I'm right here," I say, skidding to a stop behind Kevin, shoes, coat, and purse in hand. I fumble with them, trying not to drop anything and also to catch my breath. I look up and see Jordan watching me over Kevin's shoulder and the whole breathing thing goes out the window for a second. He's smiling at me, and he looks nervous and excited and so happy, all rolled into one. He looks how I feel.

I want to kiss him. Because I can do that now.

"You must be Jordan," Mom says, coming up to stand beside me. She reaches out a hand to Jordan, and he takes it without a moment of hesitation. "I'm Claire. It's nice to meet you."

"Likewise," Jordan says, his gaze straying to me again. But then Buffy comes up to nudge him, and he breaks eye contact with me to bend down and rub her face.

"I've got some dessert to send with you two," Mom says, surprising me. "Give me a second to grab it, okay?"

She heads for the kitchen without waiting for a response.

"Good game Friday night, kid," Kevin says to Jordan, stepping to the side so that he's not between us anymore. "That was a season's best in points for you, wasn't it?"

Jordan nods, and his smile goes sheepish for a second. "And assists."

Kevin grins. "A good night to have that happen, don't you think?"

"Yeah," Jordan says, his smile fading a little as he looks from me to Kevin and back again.

Before I can figure out this strange reaction, Mom comes back, this time with a cupcake Tupperware in hand. She and Kevin exchange wary glances, but that's the only sign of awkwardness before she gives Jordan a bright smile and hands the cupcakes over to him.

"Wow." His eyes light up. "What are these?"

"Oh, nothing too special. It's this new chocolate cupcake recipe I've been working on. I like to try things out here before I go public with them at the bakery." Much to Kevin's dismay, though he hasn't been complaining about it much lately. I wonder if that will change after their fight. But no. I can't think like that. Not right now. "I think I've gotten this one perfected, so I figured it'd be a good one to send for dessert."

"Thanks, Mom," I say.

"Yeah, seriously, thank you," Jordan says at almost exactly the same moment. We exchange goofy grins, and then he turns to my mom and adds, "If you ever need someone else to test things out on, let me know."

Mom beams at him. "I will, for sure." She leans over to give me a quick hug and whispers, "He's cute," so only I can hear. "I like him." Louder, she adds, "You'll have her home by ten? I know there are only four days left before winter break, but it *is* still a school night."

"Yes, ma'am," Jordan says.

"Good. It was so nice to meet you," she says, and then she hurries back to the kitchen, leaving me and Jordan and Kevin alone again.

"Well, kids," Kevin says, "you'd better get going. Amber, you can probably swing ten thirty if you need to, all right? Just *call* if you're going to be late."

I look at Kevin, surprised, because my curfew is usually non-negotiable on school nights unless it's a special occasion. Kevin doesn't say anything though. He just winks and waves us toward the door.

"You've been holding out on me," Jordan says as he leads me to the car. "Did you not want to share your secret baked-good stash?" We're to the Jeep now and he stops at the passenger side, one hand holding mine, the other reaching up to set the cupcakes on the roof of the car.

"It's not that," I say. "Sometimes Mom's experiments are weird." They're never bad, but pineapple upside-down brownies are not something I ever needed to eat.

"I'm willing to risk it."

"Noted. Next time I come over, I will bring cookies. Or brownies. Or would you rather have more cake?" I realize I'm babbling, but I can't seem to stop. "Or—"

He kisses me, soft and lingering, and I sigh against his lips and breathe him in. He searches my face when he pulls away, and when I smile, he smiles back. "Any of that," he says. "All of it. All good."

"Okay," I whisper, and he kisses me one more time before he reaches around me to open my door.

*

The drive to Jordan's house lasts about two minutes even in the snow, and my chest is tight with nerves again by the time I'm following him through his garage door.

Just like on Thanksgiving, Jordan's family is all in the kitchen when we walk in. His mom and sister and a petite girl with dark hair—Tasha's girlfriend, I assume—are all sitting at the bar stools along the kitchen island, while his dad is fussing with something on the stove. Everyone turns around when we come into the room, and they all immediately flash warm smiles in my direction.

"Hi, Amber," Jordan's mom says. "It's so good to see you again."

I clear my throat and move myself closer to Jordan as he sets the cupcakes down on the counter. "You too."

"This is my girlfriend, Katie," Tasha says, and the dark-haired girl smiles and waves. I smile back, but before I have a chance to say hello or tell her it's nice to meet her, Tasha is pointing to the cupcakes. "What are *those*?"

"Homemade cupcakes." Jordan grins at me over his shoulder.

"My mom has a bakery," I explain. "Claire's Cakes and Confections, over in Waverley Square?"

"Oh man, I love that place," Tasha says. In a stage whisper, she adds, "Keep her forever, J, okay?"

Laughter fills the kitchen in response to this, and I can feel myself blushing. But then Jordan reaches back to grab my hand, and suddenly I'm not so embarrassed anymore.

We eat wings for dinner, and I mostly listen as Tasha and Katie chatter about finals and their plans to see one of their favorite bands when they go back to Iowa in January. Jordan's dad mentions something about skiing, and I must look confused because Jordan says, "We're leaving for Colorado on Thursday night. My aunt and uncle live outside of Denver, so we usually spend Christmas with them."

"Oh, that sounds fun," I say.

"Yes," Tasha says, "especially since our grandparents have been uninvited this year."

I cough on the sip of water I just took, surprised at her bluntness.

"Tasha," Jordan's dad says with a sigh, as Katie snorts into her plate. "Let's not, okay?"

"Fine." Tasha rolls her eyes. "Tell us about the game on Friday then, J. I'm sorry I had to miss it. Stupid Friday finals."

Jordan hesitates, glancing in my direction. "It's not a big deal, Tash. The game was fine."

"It was great," I say, not sure why he's trying to downplay it again. First with Kevin, and now with his own family? So weird. "Season's best for points and assists, right?"

"That's right," Jordan's mom says with a warm smile at me. "And the scouts that were there definitely took notice. At least according to Coach Miles."

"Scouts?" I ask, looking over at Jordan, who now has an oddly strained smile on his face.

"Um, yeah," he says, glancing around the table and then dipping his gaze to his plate. "There were a couple of scouts there from Wichita State to watch me play. Coach said after the night I had, he's pretty sure they'll be back again after the break."

I drop my fork; it lands on my plate with a clatter. "Are you serious?"

"Yeah."

"I—wow—that's awesome!" I splutter.

"We're pretty excited about it," his mom says, beaming at him. "Keep your fingers crossed for him."

"I will," I promise, even though my gut is twisting at the thought of Jordan staying here next year when I'm doing everything I can to make sure I'm in Lawrence.

❋

After dinner and the cupcakes, which only last about five minutes after Tasha opens the carrier, Tasha and Katie leave to meet up with some friends and Jordan's parents wave off our attempts to help them clean up the kitchen.

"You want to watch something?" Jordan asks. I nod, so he takes my hand to help me up and leads me downstairs.

We settle on the couch in the family room and Jordan pulls up Netflix, picking a movie at random when I tell him I don't care what he puts on. As the opening credits start rolling, he loops his arm around my waist and pulls me closer to him, so that my head fits under his chin. It's such a small gesture, but somehow it feels even more intimate than all the making out we did last night, and I have to close my eyes and take a deep breath because my heart is racing at his nearness.

We're quiet for a while, watching the movie, but then out of the blue Jordan says, "The scouts probably aren't a big deal. In case you were worried about it."

I twist around so I can see his face. He's studying me with a serious expression, but there's something else underneath that. Uncertainty. Wanting. And I realize he's not only downplaying this for me. He's doing it for himself, too.

"Are *you* worried about it?" I ask, watching him closely.

He blows out a breath and looks down at his hand, which is now resting on my hip. "A little bit."

"Why?"

"Because," he says slowly, fiddling with one of the belt loops on my jeans, "playing D-One has always been my dream, but this seems like it's too good to be true. I'm worried that if I let myself get my hopes up about this, I'll jinx it."

"I get that," I say, nodding. "But remember how you said Buffy's tricks were like magic, that first night I was over here?"

The corners of his mouth tug up in a smile. "The second night," he corrects, "but yes."

Warmth pools in my stomach and spreads out all over me, and I know I'm blushing but I don't look away. "Right, well. Magic. That's how I feel when I watch you play."

He goes still, eyes searching my face. "I think you might be biased."

I laugh. "Maybe a little. But you're the real thing, and if those coaches can't see it, they need to get their vision checked."

He blinks at me for a second, then tugs me forward and kisses me, running his hands up and down my back. I shiver at his touch and shift even closer to him, and the next thing I know we've been making out for so long that his mom is yelling down the stairs that it's time for him to take me home.

We're mostly quiet on the drive, both of us still trying to catch our breath, and when he pulls into my driveway I lean in to kiss him again instead of getting out of the car.

"You know," Jordan says when we finally break apart, his voice low, "there's another reason I'm worried about those scouts."

"What's that?" I ask, but I have a feeling I already know.

"You," he says. "And what it would mean for this. What we're doing."

I nod, because I'm worried about that too. But I made my choice when it comes to him last night, and even though I don't know what I'd want to do if we end up at different schools next year, I do know one thing for certain. "I promise, no more running. Whatever happens with college, we'll talk about it. Okay?"

"Okay," he says, watching me for a long moment before cutting the engine. "Come on. I'll walk you to the door."

twenty-five

On Christmas morning when I wake up, the whole house smells like baking chocolate and Mannheim Steamroller Christmas music is playing. For a moment I lie in bed soaking up that smell and those sounds, trying to decide if it's cookies or cake and humming along to "God Rest Ye Merry, Gentlemen." Things have still been a little tense around here for the past week, but I'm choosing to take "God Rest Ye Merry, Gentlemen" as a good sign. If Mom was really upset or in a bad mood, she wouldn't have gone for something so upbeat. Feeling good, I pat the bed beside me to invite Buffy up for Christmas cuddles.

My phone buzzes and I grab it to find a text from Jordan. **Merry Christmas. Call you later?**

I grin and text him back. **Yes, please. Merry Christmas. I'll save some cookies for you for Thursday.**

I stopped by his house last Thursday to say goodbye before he and his family left on their trip, and we made plans to hang out next Thursday, which just so happens to be the day they get back. "So we don't have to miss one," he'd said when he asked me. Heat rushes to my face just thinking about it.

After a moment, my phone buzzes again. **When you give**

them to me and watch me eat them in two bites, remember that I liked you before I knew your mom had a bakery.

Laughing, I rub Buffy's ears one more time, text back, **Will do**, and roll out of bed.

When Buffy and I get to the kitchen we find Mom at the island, her special Christmas mixing bowl in front of her and whisk in hand. She grins when she sees me. "I did the brownies already. I couldn't wait."

"That's okay," I say slowly, studying her face. Other than when she met Jordan last Sunday, she's had a sort of guarded expression all week. Like she was stuck deep inside her own head. She's been so quiet that I haven't even bugged her about my Lawrence folder, which we still need to discuss. But today she looks normal, totally fine. Like the fight last weekend and the weirdness since then never happened at all. "What are you doing now?"

"Chocolate chip cookies. Do you want to help?"

"Okay."

Mom's mouth drops open in surprise for a second, and I can't really blame her since I'm surprised myself—I haven't helped with the Christmas cookies in a few years. Then she beams at me, whips open a drawer next to her, and pulls out an apron, one that's covered in little sponge-paint snow people and has my name scrawled across the top in six-year-old-me's handwriting.

"Here," she says, holding it out to me. "I found it when I was unpacking the Christmas ornaments."

I only hesitate for a moment before I take it and put it on. Mom looks a little misty-eyed, so I hurry to reach for the bag of chocolate chips. "When you say help, you mean help you eat these, right?"

That does the trick. Laughing, she swats my hand away and shows me what she needs me to do.

Kevin comes to join us after a little while, and I eye him and my mother as he comes over to plant a kiss on her cheek. Kevin's PDAs haven't gone over well since that fight I overheard, so I'm interested to see what happens. Sure enough, Mom pulls away from him a little, but weirdly he doesn't seem bothered. In fact, the corners of his eyes crinkle as he smiles and leans in to whisper something to her.

Strange.

For a moment nothing changes, and Mom keeps mixing the dough she's been working on. But then she softens and turns to look at him, a hint of a smile on her face. They watch each other for a moment that stretches into sappy territory, and, when I recover from my shock, I clear my throat loudly to remind them I'm here. They jump a little and look over at me, Mom with a blush on her face and Kevin with a sheepish expression on his.

"Merry Christmas, Amber," he says, coming over to me. Before I know what's happening he's pulling me into a hug, and I'm so surprised that I let him do it. Over his shoulder I see Mom watching us; her eyes get bright like she might cry.

"You too, Kevin." I pull back a little so he'll let me go. I need to salvage this situation before we start talking feelings and holding hands and stuff. I look at Mom. "All right, are we gonna do presents now that he's up?"

Just like that the disbelief and wobbly look to her face disappear and she's scowling at me, in a good-natured sort of way. "Not until Cammie gets here. We'll open presents together. It's only fair."

"She could do one, Claire," Kevin says, surprising me yet again. "Cam would understand."

"It's okay." I glance over at Mom again, who looks like she has a lot more things to say about why we're not doing presents now. "I don't mind waiting. Gives us plenty of time to make cookies beforehand. Kevin, do you want to help?"

He beams at me. "Of course!"

We make chocolate chip cookies and snickerdoodles, then gingerbread and sugar cookies. We decorate the last two; I give the plain circles crazy patterns and swimsuits to the little snow people, which cracks Kevin up and even gets Mom laughing too. The whole thing is fun, and it feels like we've been doing this for a million years, which is very surreal and probably breaks more than half my rules. But right now I don't care, because I can't remember the last time I had a Christmas that felt so normal. I decide to just go with it.

I focus on decorating the cookies—and trying to keep Kevin from eating them before they cool enough for me to frost—and picking out a few of my favorites to save for Jordan. I even set aside a few plain cookies for Cammie, in case she wants to decorate some too.

Cammie shows up a little after lunch, stumbling into the kitchen with her arms full of presents. I'm the only one in here— Mom and Kevin are in the living room, making googly eyes at each other and the tree—so I rush to get up and help her before she slips in the snow she's getting everywhere.

"Whoa," I say. "Did you buy an entire store?"

"No. Dad had me hide stuff for you and your mom in my car."

My eyebrows go up. "That's actually pretty smart."

"Yeah," Cammie says, smiling now, "he's super into gift giving. He says it's like an art."

I laugh. "If he says so. Hey, before we take these into the living room, do you want a cookie? They're fresh."

"Um, yes." She comes over to join me and reaches for a snickerdoodle. "You know, you and your mom are bad influences when it comes to dessert."

I smile and pat her arm. "We do our best."

We each eat a cookie and then decide to load up a plate and take it into the living room where Mom and Kevin are waiting. At the sight of us with cookies in hand, Kevin gets up and says, "Cam, did you bring the presents?"

Before we can answer he's already heading for the kitchen to bring them in.

Once we get all the presents in the living room, I settle onto the floor with Buffy and Cammie sits on the couch with Mom and Kevin. We all wish each other Merry Christmas—which got forgotten in the midst of Kevin's present excitement—and then we finally get down to business and start talking gifts. I give Buffy hers first so she can look cute in her new collar and munch on her giant bully stick while all the unwrapping is going on. She's not a fan of the collar exchange but the treat wins her over, and she starts gnawing on it happily as I look to Kevin for further instructions.

He starts passing out presents, telling us all to wait until he's gotten everything divided up before we unwrap anything. "Okay," he says once he's done, already reaching for a little bag that's labeled for him and Mom. "Open everything except your biggest box. Most presents are boring to watch people unwrap, so we only do one big present to take turns."

I decide I like this method, though I do go slower than everyone else at opening my gifts. Mostly I get gift cards—to my favorite bookstore and this little boutique in New Market that always has the cutest clothes—but I get a few practical fun things too. Fuzzy socks. Christmas pajamas with reindeer on them. And a toothbrush with my name on the handle that's my favorite color blue. I look up in time to catch Kevin's wink, and to see that Mom and Cammie each got an embossed toothbrush too.

Finally it's down to the big boxes. "Oldest first," Mom says. She nudges Kevin, who gives a good-natured groan, and hands him his last present. I notice as she does this that she's got my present to her—a framed picture of the two of us in our Christmas pajamas last year—cradled in her lap. She sees me looking and smiles at me, and I am so glad that I made that last-minute trip to Target with Hannah and Jordan after work on Wednesday night. I changed my mind about a million times about what to get my mom. Looks like I picked the right thing.

Kevin does his big present (a signed boxed set of cookbooks by his favorite Food Network chef), and Mom unwraps hers (a diamond necklace and earrings set that is understated and beautiful and probably very expensive), and then Cammie goes next since she's next in the circle (she gets a necklace that was apparently her grandma's that makes her cry). Once Cammie has calmed down, it's my turn. I pull my last box toward me, surprised by how light it is, and start pulling off the ribbons and wrapping paper. When I open it up there's another box inside. Then another, and another.

"Oh my God, Dad," Cammie says. "How many did you do?"

Kevin grins. "Just a few."

"More than a few," Mom says. Her tone is very dry, but I can tell part of her is loving this. She hasn't done the box inside a box trick since I was a little kid.

In all, there are seven boxes. When I finally get to the last one, I really have no idea what to expect. I shake it to see if I can hear anything, and it sounds like thick paper sliding around in there. My heart sinks. Another gift card, maybe, or a check. But is that really worthy of a giant box-in-a-box trick?

I look at my mom to find her watching me, a strange look on her face. "Open it," she says, nodding toward me. "Go on."

I slip my fingernail under the tape holding down the lid until it breaks, and then I pull out what's inside.

It's KU basketball tickets. Four of them. For the game against K-State in February. I stare at the tickets for a long time, not understanding. Thinking there must be some kind of mistake, because this game is in Lawrence and I still haven't gotten permission to go there, even for a campus tour. Then I look up and see Mom's and Kevin's and Cammie's faces and I realize this is true.

"I thought you didn't do the tickets with the Kleins and your other friend anymore," I say finally, because I can't keep sitting here with all of them staring at me.

"I don't," Kevin says. "We bought these for you."

"We?"

"We." He glances at my mom, who gives me a hesitant smile.

"Are you serious?" I ask.

Kevin smiles wide. "As a heart attack."

Mom nods. "We've got it all worked out with Hannah's family."

"With Hannah's family?" I echo.

"Yes," Mom says. "The game isn't until seven and won't be over until late. We don't want you driving back in the dark, so you'll need a place to stay. Her brother has space at his apartment for you two, and whoever else you want to bring. Like we talked about earlier this year."

"Like we talked about," I parrot, because I'm still having a hard time wrapping my head around this.

"Yes. So two of the tickets are accounted for," Kevin says. "The other two spots are up to you."

I look over to find Cammie raising an eyebrow at me, and somehow I know exactly what she's thinking. Hurriedly I snap my attention back to Mom and Kevin.

"Okay," I say faintly.

They exchange a glance. Then, after a beat, Mom says, "We also thought . . . that you could set up a campus visit for while you're there. And that you and I should sit down after the new year and update your FAFSA information. To see if that will help with your aid package."

A campus visit. Like me going to KU next year is an actual thing. That's the real point of this present, I know it in my bones. Suddenly I understand why Mom wanted to wait to talk to me about my folder full of budgets and screenshots and all the details

I could think of to get her to say yes. They had this planned already. Or, I realize suddenly, remembering the snippets I heard of their fight, at least Kevin did. This is the thing he did without asking Mom first. I'd bet money on it. Something for me.

Fighting back tears, I jump to my feet and go to hug them. Mom first, and I say, "Thank you!" out loud as I do. But when I hug Kevin, I say it again, quieter this time so only he can hear. I can tell by the way he awkwardly pats my back that he understands what I mean.

twenty-six

Later that night Mom and Kevin leave to go to some fancy dinner at The Castle that Cammie and I weren't invited to, thankfully. Cammie helps me clean up the wrapping paper after they leave, and when we're done, I settle in the living room, fresh plate of cookies in hand. Cammie joins me, parking herself at the opposite end of the couch and reaching for a gingerbread man in a frosting beach towel. She bites off his head, then says, "I'm gonna crash here tonight, I think."

I look at her in surprise. She hasn't stayed over since the girls' night. I wonder why she stayed that night, why she wants to stay now, but maybe it doesn't matter. "Cool. We should pick something to watch. Something good and Christmassy."

"Christmassy?" She laughs. "Okay."

We go downstairs to pick a movie, Buffy following at our heels. She follows Cammie when she goes to get the remote, and nudges her with her nose. I start to call her over to me, but then Cammie reaches down and rubs one of her ears between her fingers. I think I might be hallucinating, but then Cammie does it again and I know I'm not.

Cammie and I are halfway through *How the Grinch Stole*

Christmas when I say, out of the blue, "Why don't you and Jordan ever hang out at school?"

She pauses the movie and glances over at me, raising her eyebrows.

"What?" I say, a note of defensiveness creeping into my tone. "I've just been wondering."

"I know you have," she says. "I can't believe you haven't asked either one of us this yet."

"Well I'm asking you now, but you don't have to answer. I get it if it's too personal or something."

"It's really not," she says, shaking her head. "I just don't want you to take the answer the wrong way."

I eye her warily. "Okay . . ."

She sighs. "So, you know J and I have known each other since we were in diapers, right?" I nod. "We hung out all the time when we were little kids, since our moms were best friends. We're actually only a few months apart. His birthday is in July, and mine is in September. We ended up in different grades because of the cutoff."

"None of this is weirding me out," I say. "It sounds like me and Hannah, honestly. Minus the moms being BFFs thing."

She crosses her eyes at me, and I laugh.

"For a long time, it was like that," Cammie says, fiddling with the remote. "But then we hit middle school and all the crushes and stuff that come with it, and every time my mom asked me if I liked anybody, she brought up J."

"Ah." I can see where this is going.

"Yeah," Cammie says, sighing again. "I think she thought it

would be, like, precious if we ended up together. But we thought it would be weird. Neither of my parents have big families, and I don't have any cousins at all on my mom's side. So Tasha and Jordan were like surrogate cousins to me."

"I can see that."

"His parents did too. But my mom couldn't let it go. Still can't, actually. So we stopped hanging out together outside of school, and then that turned into not hanging out when we were *at* school either. We actually weren't talking much at all anymore until last year when . . . well, you know that part."

When her parents split. When Kevin started dating my mom.

"Anyway," Cammie says after a long moment. "That's why we don't hang out at school still. We have separate worlds there, you know?"

"Yeah."

We lapse into silence, and eventually Cammie hits play on the movie again. But when it gets to the part where the Grinch brings back everyone's presents because his heart grew three sizes, I realize there's one more thing I need to ask Cammie tonight.

"Hey," I say, looking over at her again. "Do you want to come to Lawrence for the game?"

"Seriously?" she asks.

"Yeah." The first two tickets are obviously for Hannah and Jordan, and I thought about maybe offering the fourth spot to Ryan. But at some point today it occurred to me that I should ask Cammie. And not just to be nice. Because I actually want her to go.

She takes a long time to answer. Then, finally, she shakes her head. "Take J and Hannah and her boyfriend. Make it like an epic double date."

218

"I already asked Hannah and I'll ask Jordan when he calls me later, but the fourth spot is yours if you want it. And not just because Hannah already informed me that Elliot has his grandma's ninetieth birthday that week and all his family will be in town. I mean, you want to go to KU for college too, right?" I haven't forgotten Kevin mentioning this during that first, most awkward dinner.

"Yeah," Cammie says, blushing a little like she's remembering how she acted that night too, "but I've got another year before I get to that part. What about Ryan?"

I shake my head. "Ryan's a die-hard Mizzou fan. No way he wants to go to a KU game."

Cammie laughs, but she's still hesitating.

"Look, think about it, okay? You've got like a month to give me an answer."

"Okay," she says slowly. "But what if my answer is no?"

"Then I'll force Ryan to go."

She snorts, which turns into a full giggle, and then we're both laughing and it takes us a while to calm down. We have to rewind the movie so that we don't miss the ending, but I don't think either one of us minds.

Jordan calls a while later, when Cammie's upstairs making popcorn. We're watching *A Charlie Brown Christmas* next. When I told Cammie I'd never seen it she screeched at me and told me I hadn't lived. So dramatic.

"Hey you," I say when I answer. "Merry Christmas. How were the slopes today?"

"Merry Christmas," he says, and then he yawns. "Tasha and I gave up after two runs and came back to binge movies and gorge ourselves at the buffet, but I'm still beat. She says hi, by the way."

I curl up into a ball on the couch, pressing the phone tighter to my ear. "Tell her hi back, and tell your whole family Merry Christmas from me. Did you get any good presents?"

"These awesome new basketball shoes. You?"

"Tickets to the KU versus K-State game in February."

"Are you serious?" He sounds more alert now.

"Yeah, four of them." I explain about the campus tour and staying with Matt. "And I was thinking one of those tickets should be for you." I pause to swallow the ball of nerves that's suddenly in my throat. I'm not sure if it's normal to invite a boy you've been dating for like a week on a trip like this, but I can't not invite him. Not when I know how much he loves basketball. "I mean, if you'd want to come."

"Of course I'll come."

I laugh. "Don't you have to ask first?"

"Well, yeah. But I know my parents will say yes. They love KU basketball almost as much as I do."

Right then Cammie comes down the stairs, popcorn in hand. When she sees that I'm on the phone, she immediately starts making a kissy face at me. It makes her look like a fish.

"Okay," I say, "ask them and let me know."

"I'll ask them tonight. You don't mind if I say good night, do you? I'm having a hard time keeping my eyes open."

"No, it's fine. Cammie and I are gonna watch *Charlie Brown Christmas* and she just came back with the popcorn."

"You're hanging out with Cam?" Jordan asks, and I can hear the smile in his voice.

"Yeah."

"Good."

✳

The day before school starts back up, Jordan comes to visit me at work. "So I can see where the magic happens," he tells me, and I wonder how I kept myself away from him for so long.

I'm starting a new puppy class this afternoon, for all the people who got fur babies for Christmas. Everyone is in good moods and all of the puppies are fascinated by Buffy, who I brought along to be my helper and who is lounging in the center of the room like a queen among her subjects. She helps me demonstrate sit and down, the basics of the basics, and it's a good thing I brought her because a couple of the new owners need the reassurance of practicing on an already trained dog.

"She started like all of you guys," I tell the class, glancing over my shoulder to where Jordan is watching at the window, "so don't worry. You'll get there. You'll have them chilling in no time."

"What's 'chill'?" one lady asks, and behind me Jordan laughs.

"We'll get there," I tell her, smiling. "Let's try that sit again."

At the end of the lesson, I let my students know that if they're comfortable with it, they can let their pups off their leashes to come and play with Buffy. Everyone lets their puppies off the leash, and in a matter of seconds Buffy is swarmed by wriggly bodies. They crawl all over her and she just lies there. A queen among her subjects indeed. I glance back at Jordan again to find him grinning at me. *See?* he mouths. *Magic.*

After the lesson is over and everyone's gone, I take Jordan back to Stephanie's office to introduce him. She throws me a wink when he's not looking. "Looks like everything's good with you, huh, kid?"

"Yeah," I say, smiling as Jordan slips Buffy a treat from Steph's stash. "It was a good Christmas." My phone vibrates in my pocket and I take it out, going still when I see that it's a Lawrence area code. "Hey, I think I need to get this."

"Go ahead," Stephanie says. "I'll take these two to check out the baby guinea pigs we have in the back."

"Nice." Jordan follows her out of the room, Buffy stuck to his side like Velcro. He smiles at me over his shoulder as the door closes behind them.

I swipe my phone to answer the call, and say hello in the most professional voice I can manage.

"Is this Amber Richter?" a woman's voice says.

"Yes," I say in a rush. "This is she."

"Hi, Amber. I'm Carol Nguyen, the owner of Pet Universe. We got your application for a position as one of our animal associates this fall and love the look of your résumé. Would you be available to set up a Skype interview sometime in the next few weeks? Those tend to be easier for incoming freshmen."

Holy. Shit.

I take a deep breath to steady myself. "Yes, definitely!"

"Great!" Carol says, her voice warm and welcoming. "What about the first week of February? I know it's a little ways out, but we try to do all of our fall hiring interviews then to help with the decision-making process."

"I could make that work. But, um, actually, I'll be in town for a couple of days that week to do a campus tour. I could set aside time to come for an interview in person, if that would be helpful?" I was already planning on stopping by to check out the store, but it would be even more exciting to get to do it in an official capacity.

"That would be wonderful!" Carol says. "Tell me the dates and we can look at the calendar to get something scheduled."

When Jordan and Stephanie and Buffy come back a few minutes later, I'm squealing and spinning circles in Stephanie's desk chair.

"Whoa," Jordan says, as I skid to a stop facing him. "I'm taking it that was a good call?"

"The best." I beam up at him. I'm a little dizzy so I cling to his arms as I get to my feet. "That was this pet store I applied to in Lawrence."

"Pet Universe?" Stephanie asks, her face lighting up.

"Yeah. They want me to do an interview when we're in town."

"What?" Jordan tugs me into a hug. "That's awesome! Let's go celebrate when you're done with your shift. Dessert from wherever you want, on me."

Stephanie is beaming at me when Jordan lets me go. "I'll let you know when they call in that reference."

"Don't you mean *if*?"

"*When*," she says, shaking her head and waving us out of her office.

twenty-seven

Jordan and I end up meeting Hannah, Elliot, and Ryan at Hannah's house to eat Emperor's takeout and celebrate my interview, so it's later than I planned when Buffy and I make it back to the house. When we walk into the kitchen, I stop short at the sight of my mother, who is sitting at the kitchen island, laptop open in front of her and reading glasses poised on the end of her nose. She's got papers spread out all around her and her jaw is so tense that it makes me nervous.

"Oh, good," she says, looking up at me as I kick the door closed with my foot. "You're home."

"Yeah." I lean down to unclip Buffy's leash. "What are you doing?"

She nods toward the laptop. "I got my preliminary tax documents back from the accountant for last year, which means we can update the information we filled out for the FAFSA. The numbers are a little lower than I was estimating when we first submitted back in October, so that might help with your aid package."

"Oh." I'm not sure how to respond to this, because me getting a bigger aid package would be nice, but it also worries me that Mom's income wasn't as high as she thought it'd be. "Um, okay."

She watches me for a beat with a strange look on her face, and then she gives her head a tiny shake. "Anyway, are you okay with doing this now? I know it's getting a little late and you have school tomorrow, but I'd like to get a jump on things. If we get this submitted tonight we might hear back on any updates from the school before your visit in a few weeks. Which would be nice, don't you think?"

"Definitely," I say, coming over to sit next to her quickly before she changes her mind. "What do you need me to do?"

"Log in to your account," Mom says, a tight smile spreading over her face. "I couldn't remember the password we made the first time."

It takes us over an hour to go through the form again and update all the numbers from Mom's stack of paperwork, and the further we get into the process the more anxious I start to feel about Mom's financial situation. The numbers she has me enter for gross income and net income are smaller than what we estimated last year by a lot more than I thought they'd be, and when I look at the comparison I start to understand better why she's been freaking out so much about money. But when I try to ask her about this she waves me off. "We're fine, Amber. The money part is for me to worry about, not you."

When we're finally done, I don't get up right away even though I keep yawning. This is the first time she's really seemed open to talking to me about my plans for next year, and there's no way I'm not going to take advantage of this moment now that it's here. "Did you have a chance to look over that list of apartments I gave you?"

"I did, actually," she says, reaching for a stack of papers on the counter. She sifts through them for a moment and pulls out the folder I gave her. After a moment of hesitation, she hands it back to me. "I made some notes and crossed off a couple based on some Googling I did. Hopefully this will narrow down what you need to look at while you're in town."

I flip open the folder and sift through the contents, a lump rising in my throat as I realize she hasn't just made a few notes. She's written detailed thoughts and comments on every single page.

"Wow, Mom," I say finally, flipping the folder closed again. "This is great. Thank you so much."

"It's nothing," she says.

But I shake my head, because it's not nothing. "Mom, come on. This is really helpful. It's almost better than the tickets."

"Almost?" she says, her voice dry. But her eyes are suspiciously shiny, and she reaches up to swipe at them before she snaps her laptop shut.

"Only because the tickets were the first time you said yes to Lawrence instead of no or maybe later. Kind of hard to top that."

"Oh. Well, good."

She starts gathering up her stuff, so I get to my feet and slowly make my way toward the doorway. But at the last second, I turn back. "Mom?"

"What, baby?" she asks, in the exact same way she's been doing my whole life.

"Why did you finally change your mind? About Lawrence, I mean."

She studies me for a long moment, her expression unreadable. Then she says, "It really will be easier if you stay here and live at home, and part of me is having a hard time letting that go. But then you gave me that folder, and when I read it . . ." She shakes her head. "This is your dream. I want to do what I can to help you get it, not stand in your way just because it will be harder."

I can't help wondering if Kevin has something to do with this change of heart, but I don't ask her if he does, because I'm not sure it matters anymore. I rush over to her and hug her tight. When I pull away she reaches out to touch my face and smiles.

"Go get some sleep."

The next few weeks fly by. Hannah and Elliot are painfully adorable, and Elliot starts having actual, full-fledged conversations with me and Ryan. Jordan's friends start sitting at the table next to ours in the mornings and at lunch so that he and I can swap where we sit without having to miss out on time with our usual people. Cammie even stops by to sit with us sometimes, which I can tell makes Jordan happy. And things at home are back to how they were before Mom and Kevin's fight. No more tension that I can detect, and no more fights.

It's really freaking nice.

The week before our trip to Lawrence, Jordan comes over on Tuesday night for family dinner. Mom and Kevin pepper us with questions about our plans for while we're there. Mom is focused on the timing of things and wants to make sure our campus tour will be over in time for me to make it to my interview at Pet

Universe, but Kevin keeps mentioning other places we need to check out. Mass Street and Johnny's Tavern and the museum at Allen Fieldhouse and a bunch more things I know I'll never remember. He's so enthusiastic about it all that I can't help smiling and nodding along. Even Mom is fighting a grin by the time we finally get him to change the subject.

Then suddenly he gets stern and asks about the sleeping arrangements at Matt's apartment. I spit out the bite of broccoli I just took, and Jordan chokes on a drink of water.

"Actually," Cammie says, speaking up for the first time in a while, "I've been meaning to ask about that too."

Jordan widens his eyes at her like she's some kind of traitor, but she gives her head a tiny shake and keeps talking.

"Amber," she says, turning to me, "did you ever find someone to take that fourth ticket?"

"No." We haven't talked about this since Christmas, but I was planning to double-check with her about it tonight before I corner Ryan tomorrow and guilt-trip him into coming with us.

"Oh," Cammie says, sounding surprised and a little pleased. Jordan glances between us, his expression cautiously optimistic. He knows I asked Cammie to go with us, but I don't think he was really expecting her to say yes. "Um, I'd like to go, then. If the offer still stands. And if that's okay with you, Dad," she adds, turning back to Kevin.

"It does," I say, at the exact moment Kevin says, "Honey, of *course* that's okay with me."

"Cool," Cammie says, looking down at her plate. "Can you talk to Mom about it for me though?"

"Of course," Kevin says, his brow furrowing a little.

"Thanks. Do we have dessert planned, or can we walk to the bakery to get one of those cheesecake things you made last week, Claire? They were really good."

It's the best tactic she could have used to change the subject, because this suggestion makes both Jordan's and my mom's eyes light up. Mom immediately says yes and starts clearing plates off the table.

✳

Before we leave for the bakery, I let Buffy out in the backyard and then take Jordan upstairs to show him my room. He takes in my bookshelves—lined with a mixture of romance novels and books on animal behavior—the photo collage on my closet door, my sloppily made bed, and then stops in front of the shelf with all my bobbleheads. He reaches out to nudge the Jayhawk one, then the Wildcat and the Shocker on either side of it, then shakes his head and turns to me, smiling.

"What?" I ask, even though I already know.

"Nothing. Just, if I'd had to choose, I'd've figured you'd collect stuffed dogs or something. Not bobbleheads."

"Bobbleheads are where it's at," I say.

He grins and bends down to kiss me. "I won't forget."

"You better not."

"Never," he says. "Promise."

We grin at each other for a second, but we're interrupted by a knock at my door. When I turn to look, Cammie is lingering in the hallway, her expression uncertain as she watches us together.

"Hey," I say, motioning for her to come in.

"Hey." She takes a tentative step into my room. "I hope what I said downstairs is okay. About coming on the trip, I mean. It seemed like the easiest way to get Dad to stop talking about the whole shared-bed thing."

"Of course it's okay," I say, exchanging a look with Jordan. "Seriously. I was going to ask you about Lawrence tonight since we hadn't talked about it again, but you beat me to it."

"Oh," she says, relaxing a little. "Okay then." She looks between me and Jordan again. "Was I interrupting something or can we go get cake now? Because I have seriously been thinking about them for a week, and I might die a little if I don't get my hands on another one soon."

I laugh and motion toward the door. "Cake now is good."

"Sweet," Jordan says, moving closer to me and leaning down to press a quick kiss to my mouth. He grins at me, and then at Cammie, and adds in a stage whisper, "First one out the door gets dibs on the blondie bars."

Then he bolts from my room, leaving me and Cammie blinking after him in surprise for a second before we burst out laughing and hurry to follow him.

twenty-eight

Cammie and Hannah both stay over the night before we leave for Lawrence since we have to hit the road at the crack of dawn to make our campus tour on time. We plan to go to bed early, but end up staying up way too late watching movies in the basement. I fall asleep on the couch and don't wake up until Kevin comes downstairs around midnight to turn off the TV and make sure we get up to our rooms.

It's still dark outside when we come trooping downstairs the next morning. Kevin is already at work—twice a week he and Oscar have early-start days so that they can accommodate some appointments before people have to be at work or school—but I am beyond glad to find Mom waiting for us in the kitchen with muffins, bacon, and an assortment of caffeinated beverages. She loads us up with food and drinks and a cooler for the road, then shoos us toward the door right as Jordan knocks on it.

"Hey," he says, leaning in for a quick kiss as he steps inside. He looks a little rumpled, but still way more awake than Hannah or Cammie or I do, which is good since he's the one doing the driving. "You guys ready to go?"

"Just about," I say, turning back to go give Buffy some love before we leave.

"Good morning, Jordan," Mom says behind me. "I packed some breakfast for you, but you might want to get to it now before the girls eat it all."

"Oh, awesome." I glance over my shoulder in time to catch the wide grin he's giving my mom. "Thank you so much."

Mom waves off his thanks, but I'm pretty sure she's blushing.

We say our goodbyes—Mom hugs me a little tighter than usual—and then load up the car. Jordan backs out of the driveway right as the horizon is starting to lighten up.

Hannah and Cammie fall asleep in the backseat pretty much the second the food is gone, so it's just me and Jordan up front, him driving, me navigating. The turnpike is so empty that sometimes it feels like we're the only people awake in the world.

"You nervous?" he asks me after a while, and I know he means about my interview. It's set for four thirty this afternoon, which should give me time to look at most of the apartments on my list after the campus and dorm tour we're doing this morning.

"A little." I could always get a campus job since I got work study as part of my aid package, but this is so much more in line with what I want to do. And it pays more too.

"You'll be great." He reaches over to tap my thigh. "Seriously. I have no doubt you'll get it."

"We'll see," I say, but I'm smiling. "Are *you* nervous about today?"

While Hannah and Cammie and I do the campus and dorm tours and check out apartments with Matt, Jordan is heading to Kansas City for an unofficial visit to Rockhurst. He hasn't heard anything more from Wichita State yet on whether they're interested in him for next year, so he figured today would be a good chance to take another look at the school that's been most actively recruiting him. One of his old teammates plays for Rockhurst, so he agreed to show Jordan around.

"Not really." He glances over at me. "It'll just be me and Mateo checking out campus and the basketball setup. I did an official visit last year and that one had me anxious, but this is a lot less pressure."

"That makes sense." We're quiet for a beat and then I finally ask the question that's been weighing on me since the night he told me the Wichita State scouts came to watch him play. "Will you be disappointed if that's where you end up? At Rockhurst, I mean."

"I don't know," Jordan says slowly. "I don't think so. I want to play next year, and they have a great program. I've felt really comfortable with them every time I've gone to check them out, and I'd be proud to play for them." He looks over at me again and smiles slightly. "But if Wichita State offered me a spot? I'd take it. No question. Playing Division-One ball in my hometown, for a team that plays in March Madness every year? That's like my ultimate dream."

I nod, not at all surprised by this answer even though it makes my gut twist with worry. "It would be pretty amazing, wouldn't it?"

"Completely. But I'm trying not to think about it too much, because it might not happen." He grips the steering wheel tighter for a second. "And there are other reasons besides basketball that Rockhurst is appealing."

Heat rushes to my face, because I know he means being closer to me. But before I can figure out what to say in response to this, there's stirring from the backseat and Cammie's groggy voice says, "Are we there yet?"

"A little less than halfway," Jordan tells her, and she groans.

"Lame. Can we play games or something to kill time? I don't think I can go back to sleep. Also, don't hate me, but I really need to pee."

"There's a rest stop in ten miles," Jordan says, laughing. "So you have that long to figure out the game situation, okay?"

"Sweet."

We stop at a rest stop a few miles past Emporia to use the bathrooms and get more snacks and drinks, and Cammie decides we should play something called the cow game, where we get points based on how many cows we see walking or running along the highway. I'm skeptical at first because it seems kind of silly, but it ends up being a lot of fun. Hannah and Jordan are tied when we finally get to the exit we need for Lawrence. She leans forward so her head is between our seats and says, in a deadly serious voice, "This isn't over, Baugh. Round two tomorrow on the drive home. Winner takes all."

"You're on," he says, equally serious, and Cammie and I just about die laughing.

We calm down as we pull off the highway and head into town, and I peer out the window as we drive toward campus, wanting to take everything in.

"I think this is your stop," Jordan says when we pull into the parking lot of the Visitor Center, which is on the first floor of one of the dorms.

"Yup," Hannah says. "Matt said he can pick us up, so don't worry about rushing back from KC, okay? He'll give Amber a ride to her interview if you're still busy."

"Got it," Jordan says, looking back at her and Cammie. "Tell him thank you for me. See you guys later." They both say bye to him and he gives them a little wave as they get out of the car. Then he turns to me. "I'll call you when I'm done. And I know Hannah said not to rush back, but I'll make sure I'm here in time to take you to your interview, okay?"

"Okay." I lean in to kiss him and fight the sudden rush of anxiety I get at the thought of him leaving me here. It feels like a preview of what next year will be like if he—but no. Jordan said he wasn't going to think about that, so I'm not either.

He smiles at me when we pull apart. "Have fun."

"You too," I tell him, and then I get out of the car and join Hannah and Cammie on the sidewalk.

"C'mon," Hannah says gently, tugging my arm. "We've got exploring to do."

I let her pull me forward and link our arms together as we head into the building. I only look back at Jordan once as he drives away.

❊

Three hours later, I am convinced of two things. First, that I absolutely love this campus and will do everything I can to make sure I get to be here next year. And second, that I'm either going to be living on my own next year, or I'll need to find another roommate.

Hannah tries to act cool and disinterested during the dorm

tour, but I know her way too well for her to fool me. She's practically glowing with excitement by the time we get done touring the sample rooms they have set up. The last one we look at, a traditional dorm instead of a suite, has lofted beds that make her eyes light up.

Cammie has to stop at the bathrooms in the Visitor Center once we're done with the tour, but the line is so long that she tells me and Hannah to go wait for her outside. So we find an empty bench within view of the door and sit down so Hannah can text Matt to come pick us up. When she's done with that Cammie still hasn't come to find us yet and Hannah won't meet my eyes.

"We should talk about it," I say finally, because I'm tired of the awkward silence.

"Talk about what?" Hannah says.

"The dorms and the fact that you're in love with them."

"I am not," she says, getting to her feet. "I mean, I guess they're okay, but like, I'm not in *love* with them."

"Hannah." I roll my eyes at her. "Come on."

She tips her head to the side and studies me closely for a second, then takes a deep breath and blurts out, *"Yesokayyou'reright."*

"Then that's where you should live next year, Han," I tell her, standing so I can link my arm through hers.

"But what about you? Can you really afford to live on your own?"

"I have my list of places," I remind her, "and Mom made some notes on the budgets I did. I'll figure it out."

"Are you sure?"

"Yes," I tell her, even though I'm not.

"Hey," Cammie says from behind us, and we both spin around to face her. "Is your brother on his way?"

"Yeah," Hannah says, disentangling herself from me and taking a step closer to the curb so she can squint at the entrance to the parking lot. "Actually, I think I see his car now."

She's right, and a minute later Matt is opening his door for us with a wide smile. He goes for Hannah first, giving her a hug and ruffling her hair. I get the same treatment as Hannah, but he hesitates with Cammie, who is hanging back, a strange, almost shy look on her face.

"Hey," he says after a beat, sticking out a hand for her to shake.

"Oh my God, are you middle-aged or something?" Hannah asks, batting his hand away. "Cammie, this is my brother Matt. Matt, this is Cammie. He would have been a senior when you were a freshman, so I'm sure you've seen each other around before."

Cammie clears her throat a little and gives him a small smile. "Hi."

They watch each other for a beat longer. Then Matt jingles his keys and says, "Let's go get some lunch."

twenty-nine

Matt takes us to a Greek restaurant on Mass Street, where the food is amazing. Hannah and Matt chatter at each other as we eat, and Cammie asks the occasional question, but I mostly stay quiet. Between my worry about finding a place to live next year and my interview this afternoon, I've got a lot on my mind. I also can't stop checking my phone to see if Jordan's called yet, even though I know he hasn't and probably won't for a while.

"All right," Matt says, when we're finished eating. "Hannah said you wanted to look at some apartment complexes today, right?"

"Yeah," I say, snapping my attention away from my phone and focusing it on him. "I made a list of places I want to check out. Here." I dig the revised version of my list out of my purse and hand it over. He takes it and starts skimming it, nodding his head a little as he reads. "Mom and I came up with this via some Google research, but can you think of anywhere else we should look? We need places that allow big dogs."

"German shepherds," Hannah adds.

"Right," I say. "But the rent can't be too crazy. I'm on a tight budget next year, especially if I can't find a roommate."

Matt looks from me to Hannah and flashes his sister a warm smile. "So you finally decided, huh?"

"Yeah," she says, grinning at him. Then she shoots a guilty look in my direction. "I still feel bad about it though."

"Stop," I tell her. Then I turn back to Matt and nod at my list. "Well?"

"This is a good start," he says. "We'll go to this one first," he adds, holding the list out to me and pointing at one of the names in the middle of the page. "C'mon."

He gets up and Hannah and I do too, but Cammie stays in her seat. "Wait," she says, shooting a confused look my way. "We're looking at apartments?"

Hannah and I exchange a glance. "Yeah," I say. "I can't live on campus next year with Buffy."

"Right," Cammie says slowly, getting to her feet. She still looks confused, and she stays quiet as we get back in the car and go over to the first complex Matt wants us to check out.

The fun of apartment hunting ends pretty quickly, because everything is either gross or way too expensive for me to afford a one-bedroom on my own.

"I think I'll have to get a roommate," I say between the third and fourth complexes on our list.

"I can ask around," Matt says, catching my eye in the rearview mirror. "See if anyone I know is looking for a roommate for next year."

"Thanks."

"That first place we looked at seemed like it might be an option," Hannah says, twisting around to look back at me. "They rented by the room, right? So you could pay for a room in a four-bedroom and see what roommates you get based on the lottery they do."

"Yeah, maybe," I tell her, because I know that's what she needs to hear so she doesn't feel guilty. I don't have the heart to tell her that even a room in a four-bedroom at that place would be really stretching my budget.

"It might be worth it to look at something in the state streets like what my roommate and I found," Matt says. "The one-bedrooms down there are pretty tiny, but they aren't as expensive either. I could hook you up with our landlord. See if she has anything that could work."

"That would be amazing," I say. "Let me know what you find out."

At the last place we visit, Hannah pulls me aside. "What is Cammie's deal?"

I glance over at Cammie, who is frowning and opening the kitchen cabinets like she doesn't even see them, which is pretty much how she's been acting this whole time. "I don't know. She's bored, maybe?"

Hannah shakes her head. "I don't think so. You should talk to her."

"You think?"

"Yeah."

"Okay. But—" My phone vibrates in my purse and I hurry to dig it out. "It's Jordan!" I say. Quickly I swipe to answer and press the phone to my face. "Hey you. How'd it go?"

"Good, I think. It was good to see Mateo again, and I got to meet a few more guys on the team."

"Oh, awesome," I say.

"Yeah, it was. Where are you?"

Matt emerges from one of the bathrooms in this place and I wave him over. "We're looking at apartments, but we're getting ready to head back to Matt's now. I have to be at my interview in an hour."

"That's perfect," he says. "GPS says I'll be at Matt's apartment in thirty minutes."

Relief floods my chest. "That's great. See you soon, then?"

"Definitely."

*

We end up getting back to Matt's apartment right as Jordan is parking in the tiny lot behind it. I run over to hug him. He buries his face in my neck, then loosens his hold on me enough to study my face. "You ready to kick some ass at your interview?"

"Mostly," I say, getting up on my tiptoes and kissing him. I mean to make it quick, but I have a hard time letting him go.

"Whoa, whoa," Hannah says. "This is a public space, you two."

We break apart and I look over and see Matt, Hannah, and Cammie all watching us, smiling. My face gets hot and I look over at Jordan to see he's blushing too, a goofy grin on his face.

"Sorry," he says. But he reaches a hand out and traces a finger down my arm, which tells me he's really not.

Matt lives in the state streets between Mass Street and campus, where the houses are all old and beautiful, with big front porches and huge trees in the front yards. His place is actually a house that's been divided up into three apartments. The front porch sags on the left and the boards creak at the slightest movement as we wait for Matt to find his house key. These are things that would probably bother me anywhere else, but here they seem to fit. I'm even excited by the rickety staircase we have to take to get to Matt's front door. It's so narrow that my purse bangs into the wall with every step, no matter how many times I adjust it.

"It's not much," Matt says, as we follow him into the main room, which is a kitchen/dining/living combo, "but it gets the job done. And it's a great location. Within walking distance to campus. I figured we'd walk to the game tonight. On game nights parking on campus is always a bitch."

We all nod and follow him further into the room. He goes over to the back wall and opens the three doors there one by one.

"My room," he says at the first one. From what I can see, his entire floor is covered in dirty clothes. Typical. "Bathroom," he adds, opening the second door and pointing at the toilet. "And my roommate's room. He's crashing at his girlfriend's house tonight so you guys have a place to sleep. Han, I figured you and the girls can take his bed. And you," he says, rounding on Jordan and narrowing his eyes, "can sleep out here. The couch is very comfortable."

Jordan nods agreement, his expression serious, and Matt looks relieved.

I'm half-relieved, half-disappointed about these sleeping arrangements, but it doesn't take long before the disappointment starts winning.

We have just enough time to drop off our stuff before we have to turn around and leave again so that I can go to my interview.

Matt drives since he actually knows where we're going, and while Hannah rides shotgun, I sit in the back between Jordan and Cammie. Luckily we don't have far to go: It feels like we've barely been in the car five minutes when Matt pulls us into a shopping center that looks like it's seen better days, swings his car around to the very edge of the lot, and parks in front of a building that's set off on its own in the lot. Pet Universe.

"Your stop, Amb," Matt says.

"Thanks," I say. Beside me Jordan leans in, reaching a hand over to squeeze my knee. "Are you guys coming in?"

"We can," Matt says, "but I figured you'd rather go in alone, right?" I nod and he grins. "Cool. There's a thrift store at the other end of the strip mall that's pretty sweet. We'll go check that out while you do your thing."

"Sounds good," I say, and we all unbuckle and get out of the car.

Jordan gives me a quick kiss once we're on the pavement, and Hannah and Matt both give me reassuring smiles. Cammie's still looking a little stiff, but she sounds sincere as she says, "Good luck."

"Thanks."

"You've got this," Hannah says. "Text us when you're done, okay?"

"I will," I say, and then I take a deep breath and turn to head into the store.

The first thing I notice when I walk inside Pet Universe is how bright and open everything is. They've got the small mammals up front in glass enclosures, a beautiful parrot on a perch in the center of the room, and tanks full of colorful fish lining the back wall. It's busy too, even on a weeknight, and I see at least a dozen employees spread throughout the room helping customers. I mentally cross all of my appendages that this job works out. I can already tell that I would love it.

After a second of absorbing everything, I go over to the registers to let them know I'm here for an interview. The girl behind the counter, who looks maybe a year or two older than me, gives me a friendly grin and tells me she'll let the owner know I'm here. I only have to wait a few minutes before a short woman with a wide smile comes bustling out of the fish area.

"You must be Amber." She sticks her hand out for me to shake as soon as I'm within her reach.

"I am," I say, shaking her hand. "And you're Carol?"

"That's me." Her smile widens. "Come on with me and let's do this thing."

Carol's version of an interview ends up being more of a store tour full of questions for me. She takes me around each section of the place and gets me to tell her about my work and training experience as we walk. At one point the parrot, who she introduces as Boomer, hops off her perch and onto Carol's shoulder. Boomer stares at me as I tell Carol about the early stages of working with Buffy, and to be honest I feel like I'm being judged more harshly by the bird than I am by the woman who will hopefully be my boss.

The whole thing only takes about half an hour, which isn't as long as I was expecting, but Carol is beaming at me by the time we're done. She takes me back up to the front of the door, gives me her card and another firm handshake, and says, "I'll be in touch," in a way that gets every single one of my hopes up. I wait until she's disappeared through the door in the fish area before I head back outside and send a group text to let everyone know that I'm done.

"How'd it go?" Hannah demands a minute later, when I meet everyone back at the car.

"Good," I say, unable to hide my grin. "I mean, obviously I don't know for sure yet. But I have a good feeling."

thirty

We take the car back to Matt's place and then walk down to Mass Street for dinner. Matt points out all the restaurants we need to try eventually, and also all the bars that aren't strict about carding. Hannah finds it hilarious that he's being so strict about Jordan sleeping on the couch tonight but is okay with pointing out places for us to get smashed illegally next year. We get pad thai and toast Jordan's campus visit and my hopefully successful interview. Then we walk over to the game, joining the streams of students who live near and on campus flooding into Allen Fieldhouse.

I've heard stories about what it's like to watch basketball in Allen Fieldhouse, but even the stories couldn't prepare me for this. The crowd is already at a low rumble when we come in and head for the student section, and the entire place is a sea of blue and red.

"Where did you guys used to sit when you came with the Kleins?" I ask Cammie, raising my voice so she can hear me over all the commotion.

"Near half-court, a few rows back," she says, nodding toward a section that hasn't filled up as much as the others yet.

"Nice," Hannah says. "Best view in the house, right?"

Matt shakes his head. "It may be a better view, but the student section is more fun. You'll see. Come on!"

We find seats next to Matt's roommate and some of their other friends about halfway up the stands. A couple of them went to our high school and recognize Jordan thanks to his basketball stats; they pepper him with questions about his season and his college plans as we wait for tip-off. The whole time he's talking to them he keeps an arm draped loosely around my back.

When the teams finally come out onto the court, the noise in the building cranks up about ten notches. And when it's finally time for the tip-off and the Jayhawks get the ball, it becomes a full-on roar. It's electric, being a part of this, and as I steal glances at Jordan and the others, I know I'm not the only one who's feeling like that.

Matt is right: Sitting in the student section is a *lot* of fun. We cheer when our team makes a basket and hold up newspapers to show our boredom when the other team goes to the free-throw line. I've watched a lot of KU games on TV over the years, but this is by far the most fun I've ever had watching one. And when we win by ten points and the whole Fieldhouse starts doing the Rock Chalk chant, I get goose bumps at the beauty of it.

After the game we go back to Matt's, all talking and laughing over each other as we discuss the highlights. We stay up late, later than I know we should, and it's a long time before Matt finally gets up, stretches, and says he's going to bed.

Matt's only been in his room for a few minutes when Hannah gets to her feet. "You know what? I'm tired too."

She gives Cammie a pointed look, and Cammie clears her throat. "Right, yeah, same."

Jordan is next to me on the couch, and I can feel him watching me, waiting to see what I'll do about this obvious setup. Careful to keep my voice neutral, I say, "Okay. You guys go ahead. I'll be there in a little bit."

Hannah doesn't bother to hide her gleeful smile. "Okay."

She beckons for Cammie to follow her, and with a quick "Night!" from Hannah and a good-natured eye roll from Cammie, the two of them disappear into Matt's roommate's bedroom, leaving me and Jordan alone.

"So," Jordan says slowly, in the same kind of neutral tone I just used. "You wanna watch a movie or something?"

"Yeah." I trace one of the whorls on the couch cushion. "You pick."

He grabs the remote off the coffee table and pulls up Netflix, and we spend a few minutes scrolling through the selections, trying to find something to watch.

"What about this one?" Jordan asks, stopping on a rom-com that came out a few years ago.

"Sure," I say, because while I like this movie, it's one that I don't mind having on as background noise. Which I'm pretty sure is all it's going to be, if I'm reading the signs right.

He hits play and leans back on the couch, reaching out to tug me closer after a beat of silence. We shift around a bit to get comfortable and end up with him up against the back and me in front of him, pressed into his side. I focus on the rise and fall of his chest behind me as the opening credits start to play.

"Is this okay?" he asks quietly, his breath warm on my neck.

In answer I nod and settle in even closer to him, blowing out a breath when he cautiously loops his arm around my waist and splays his fingers out over my stomach.

For the next twenty minutes or so we actually watch the movie. At least, I think Jordan does. I mostly stare at the screen and focus on the feel of his hands on me. At some point he starts tracing designs on my hip bone, which is very, very distracting. Slowly I move from my side to my back. Then from my back to my other side, so that we're facing each other. And that's when I see that Jordan's not watching the movie either. He's watching me.

"Hey," he says, his voice low.

"Hi," I whisper back.

He reaches a hand out and tucks my hair behind my ear, then trails his fingers down the side of my face. My skin feels like it's on fire where he touches me, and I want him closer. I grab his head and pull it down so I can kiss him. He kisses me back, deeply, and I pull away from him, breathing hard.

His eyes search my face. "What?" he asks. "Too much?"

"I think," I say slowly, "that I'm ready to not go as slow. Not to go fast, just—just to not go as slow." I take a deep breath to calm the ball of nerves that's rising in my throat and study his face. "Does that . . . does that sound okay?"

He gives a little *ha* of laughter that somehow sets me at ease. "That sounds more than okay. But I mean, I don't expect—you don't have to—" He stops and shakes his head.

I reach down to tug at his shirt. His muscles flex as I run my hands up his stomach, and he pulls back enough to help me slip his shirt over his head. "I know I don't have to," I say, tracing patterns on his skin now. He shivers at my touch and I get this thrill that I can make him react like that. "I want to."

I want to be as close to him as I can. I want to see him. I want to let him see me. So I sit up and tug my own shirt over my head. And then I take my bra off too.

Jordan's eyes go wide and he studies me, letting his gaze linger. Then he pulls me back down next to him, so we're pressed together, skin to skin. "Whatever you're ready for," he says, leaning in so our lips are almost touching, "that's what we'll do."

"Okay," I whisper, and kiss him again.

After that we aren't talking with words.

Hannah corners me in the bathroom the next morning. Or actually early the next afternoon, because we sleep in way late. "So," she says. "How was it?"

I look at her in the mirror, yank the toothbrush out of my mouth, and spit into the sink. "How was what?"

"Whatever you and Jordan were doing until four o'clock this morning," she says, glancing over her shoulder at the closed bathroom door, as if she's afraid someone else might be listening at the door. She turns back to me and grins. "You thought I didn't wake up when you came in, but I totally did."

I can feel my face flushing as I think about last night, how Jordan and I kissed and kissed and how we peeled each other's clothes off slowly. How I let him see more of me than anyone has, ever. How I let him touch me in some of those places too.

"It was . . . good," I say, my voice low, and Hannah squeals. "You really like him, don't you?"

Like doesn't feel like a big enough word anymore, but I'm not ready to think about what comes after that. Not when everything about next year is so up in the air. "Yeah, I do."

"I'm glad." She studies me for a second. "Did you have sex with him?"

I shake my head. "I'm not ready for that yet. And even if I was, we didn't have a condom, so it wouldn't have been safe."

We did talk about it, and I think it might happen soon. But I want to keep that to myself for a little while. Enjoy it.

"And he was good with that?" she asks. I nod and she beams. "Good. I knew he was a keeper, but I just wanted to make sure."

Hannah and I finish getting ready—which mostly involves Hannah brushing her teeth and doing more beaming at me in the mirror—and then we go back out into the living room so that Cammie and Jordan can have their turns in the bathroom. Cammie goes first, and while she's in there and Hannah's in her brother's room—trying to wake him up to tell him we're getting ready to leave and that he needs to go to class—Jordan and I are left alone in the living room again. He smiles at me shyly, and I smile back, glad I'm not the only one who's feeling a little nervous this morning.

I go over to him and twine our fingers together, tipping my head back so I can see his face. He's studying me intently, his eyes going back and forth between mine like he's trying to make sure I'm okay. I lift up on my tiptoes to kiss him; he's much more relaxed when I pull away.

"Did you get into the room okay last night?" he asks, rubbing his thumb across my knuckles.

I nod. "Hannah left a space for me."

"That's good," he murmurs, leaning down to kiss me again.

Before he makes contact a voice says, "J, you're up," and I look over to see Cammie smirking at us from the bathroom doorway.

Jordan goes to take his turn in the bathroom, and by the time he comes back out the rest of us, Matt included, are assembled in the living room. Matt walks us down to the car, barefoot and bleary-eyed, tells Cammie and Jordan it was nice to see them, and hugs me and Hannah goodbye.

"I feel a lot better about you guys being here in August after seeing how well you behaved yourselves last night," he says when he lets me go. That earns him a punch in the arm from Hannah, but I just laugh and get in the car.

thirty-one

We get back to town right around dinnertime, and after brief hellos to my mom and Kevin, Cammie leaves for her mom's place. We're having leftovers from last night's dinner, so Mom decides we should eat at the kitchen island instead of in the dining room. Buffy, who's been stuck to me like glue since I walked in the door, manages to wedge herself under my barstool. Her head rests on my foot while I tell Mom and Kevin about the trip.

"How'd you like the state streets?" Kevin asks, after I tell them about Matt's apartment.

"So cool," I say. I pause to take a bite of my food, Kevin's latest tofu concoction, which isn't half bad. When I'm finished chewing, I add, "All the apartments down there sound so expensive though. Matt said he'd put me in touch with his landlord, but I don't know if I'd be able to afford any of them without a roommate. Which I no longer have since Hannah wants to live in the dorms."

Kevin frowns and Mom clinks her fork hard on her plate and I realize I've said something wrong.

"Apartments?" Kevin asks. Buffy's head lifts off my foot at the tone of his voice.

I look from him to my mom, to see if Mom will give me some kind of clue here. But she's got her eyes closed like she doesn't want to hear what happens next, which leaves me on my own. "Um, yeah. Since I want to take Buffy with me next year, I can't live in the dorms."

"Right," Kevin says, his voice hollow and forced. He pushes his stool back from the counter and sets his napkin beside his place. "Excuse me, Amber. Bathroom." He leaves without another word and I listen as his footsteps echo through the living room and turn down the hall.

"Mom?" I ask, turning to look at her, "What—?"

But she doesn't answer. She's already pushing her stool back and leaving the room too.

I follow her, trying to catch my brain up with what just happened. Why would Kevin freak out about me looking at apartments in Lawrence? Did Mom not tell him, maybe? But that shouldn't matter. It's not like how I afford college or where I live next year has anything to do with Kevin.

I stop at the end of the hallway, like I did the night before the dance. This time I don't have to strain to hear them, because Mom left the door open a crack in her rush to go after him.

"—talked about this, Claire," Kevin is saying. "I told Cammie about it, to make sure she was okay with everything. Why didn't you tell Amber?"

"You know why," Mom says, her tone frustrated. "She wouldn't like it. She'd get upset with both of us. Amber doesn't want handouts for things like this, especially not from someone I'm dating."

There is a long pause after this and a hot, uncomfortable feeling swoops through me. I crouch down and wrap an arm around Buffy's neck to steady myself and she leans into me, holding me up.

Finally, Kevin says, "Is that all I am? Someone you're dating?"

"*No*," Mom says. "But I've told you how Amber feels about—about my past. She'd think . . . she'd think I'm trying to force you on her. I don't want to do that to her again."

"Telling her about the house isn't forcing her to like me, Claire."

House? What house?

"It's giving her a choice. I thought we agreed she deserves that."

"We did," Mom says, her voice breaking. "I just don't think that's how she'd see it."

"I see. So you lied." The way Kevin says *lied* is like being doused with icy water. I can tell without seeing his face that lying, to him, is unforgivable. I don't blame him—I hate lying too. But I hate it even more that Mom lied because of me. And that I understand why she did it.

"That's not—I didn't—I was going to talk to her about it after her trip. I wanted her to visit, get a feel for the city, and get a chance to look at all the apartments *she* picked. If we told her about the house first, she'd feel obligated to live there. I know she would. And that wouldn't be fair. What are you doing?"

I hear the sound of drawers opening and closing. "I'm changing," he says. "I need to go for a walk or a run or something. I understand why you didn't tell her about this, but I wish . . . you know how much this hurts me, Claire. And you know why. I need some time to cool my head."

Mom says something back, but I don't hear what it is. I'm too busy backing out of the hallway and into the living room, where I trip over one of Buffy's toys and fall backward onto the couch. I pull my knees up to my chest and I stay there until the sound of footsteps makes me look up and there's Kevin, decked out in sweats with running shoes in hand, standing in front of me.

"Amber," he says, a stricken expression on his face. "How much did you hear?"

"All of it."

"I'm sorry," he says, and he sounds like he really means it. "I have to go, I—" He stops, looks at the front door, and sighs. "You should talk to your mom."

"Okay," I whisper.

"Okay," he says, nodding. "I'm sorry," he says again. Then he leaves and Buffy goes over and paws at the door, whining, like she wants him to come back.

After a minute, I get up and go back to find my mother. She's sitting on the bed in their room, tears in her eyes, looking around like she doesn't know what to do.

"Mom?"

She jumps at the sound of my voice and swipes quickly at her face. "Oh hi, honey. Kevin had to run to the office for—"

"I heard you."

Her hand drops and she looks down at her lap. "Oh."

I steel myself and go over to her, settling myself in beside her on the bed. It's the first time in a long time that I've been in her room, and I look around at the mix of her things and Kevin's, thinking how well they go together and wondering if that's all just been ruined because of me.

"I want to know what that was about," I say, and she sighs and takes my hand.

"Kevin has a friend who lives in Lawrence and owns a management company. He mostly has commercial properties, but he's bought a few houses near campus over the years and rents them out to students."

"Okay," I say slowly. "So what does that have to do with me?"

"Jeff—Kevin's friend—promised Kevin a few years ago that when Cammie goes to school in Lawrence, he'd cut him a deal on renting a place for her off campus. With a roommate and the discounted rate, it will cost significantly less than if she lives in the dorms." Mom stops and looks at me for a second, like she's deciding something. Then she nods and says, "So when Kevin found out that you want to go to school in Lawrence, he asked Jeff if he could have the same deal for you."

My heart is racing and I feel shaky all of a sudden. "Why would he do that?"

Mom shakes her head and sniffs loudly. "Because that's what Kevin does, honey. That's the kind of man he is. He thinks of you as his family, and he knows you haven't had the most . . . stable life. That it's been hard for us, and especially you, a lot of the time. He didn't think it would be fair for you to struggle to find somewhere to live with Buffy and then watch Cammie have a ready-made place to stay a year later. He wanted to give this to you too." She clears her throat and adds, "He said Jeff has the perfect place for you. A little house right off campus. They're holding it until you decide what to do. And . . . and Kevin wants to pay. For your portion of the rent. Since that's what he'll do for Cammie, and since he knows I can't."

Kevin wants to pay for me to have a place off campus to live next year? Somewhere I can keep Buffy with me while I'm at my dream school? I can't even wrap my head around that.

"Why didn't you tell me?" I ask, snatching my hand out of Mom's and scooting away from her on the bed. I'm having trouble processing everything, but her lie makes me angry, so I grab on to the anger and hold tight. "Were you ever going to?"

"Yes," she says, looking at me steadily, "I was going to a few weeks ago, even though I was worried about what you'd say since you were so resistant to using a friend of his to fix your car. But then I found your list."

I go still. "What?"

"Your list," she says, looking away from me now. "Your rules. I couldn't find the password for the FAFSA account, and I remembered you wrote it down. So I looked for it. In your desk. So that I would be ready when you got home from work."

The rules. She found the *rules*. Oh my God, I'm going to be sick. "Mom," I say, "I'm—those aren't—"

"You don't have to explain," she says, her voice thick. She's crying. And I hate it. "After I found them, I didn't think—I didn't think you'd *want* to hear about the house. So I decided to wait until after your trip. I wanted you to look at the apartments we picked and get an idea of your options before I added this one."

"You could've told me before I went," I tell her, even though I know it isn't true.

"No," she says. "You would have felt obligated, and I didn't want that."

"Mom," I say, but I don't know what else to add, because she's right.

She brushes the tears off her face and gets to her feet. "You know, I read that list and I understood every rule, honey. Every single one."

Then she starts toward the bathroom, mumbling something about her makeup getting in her eyes.

I used to imagine this moment. Years down the line, telling my mom how hard all of her relationships have been for me. How much it hurt to get comfortable with someone right as she was ready to move on. I thought it would feel good for her to know those things, but it doesn't.

It feels like shit.

thirty-two

I find Hannah first thing the next morning at school at our usual table with Elliot and Ryan. She takes one look at my face, disentangles herself from Elliot, and comes over to loop a protective arm around my shoulders.

"Get cookies," she tells the boys, and then she drags me to the accessible stall in the bathroom by the gym, where no one ever goes.

"What happened?" she asks, and it all comes out in a rush. Kevin leaving for the world's longest run, the rules, how Mom left not long after Kevin came home and didn't come back until late. By the time I'm done talking I'm half laughing, half crying, and Hannah is rubbing my back and making soothing noises to calm me down.

"Okay," she says, once my breathing is somewhat back to normal. "It does sound bad. But I have to remind you that fights do happen in grown-up relationships, so maybe it's not as bad as you think."

"I don't think he slept at home last night. Or if he did, he left again really early this morning."

Hannah bites her lip and hands me a wad of toilet paper so I can wipe the mascara under my eyes. "Yeah, that's not good . . . Have you talked to Cammie yet? Or Jordan?"

I shake my head. I've been thinking about, and dreading, both of those conversations since last night. "Jordan asked me to come over after dinner last night but I said no. I haven't heard from Cammie. I don't even know if she knows what happened."

"You should talk to her. To both of them."

"I don't know," I say, because I'm afraid of what they'll say.

The first bell rings and we exchange a glance.

"We can stay here if you need to," Hannah offers.

I shake my head and unlock the stall door, pushing it open and going to check my makeup in the mirror before we go out to face the masses. My eyes are puffy and red, but otherwise it's not terrible. Hannah digs some concealer out of her purse and blots it on me to cover up the mascara that I can't quite wipe away.

Ryan is waiting for us outside the bathroom when we come out, and he wordlessly passes me the bag of cookies.

"Thanks," I mumble.

"Everything okay?" he asks.

I shake my head. "Not really."

"Sucks," he says, patting my shoulder.

"Tell me about it."

"Where'd Elliot go?" Hannah asks.

"He's taking your stuff to first period." Ryan hesitates for a second, then adds, "Cammie stopped by the table not long after you left. I'm assuming she has something to do with whatever happened, because she looked . . . mad."

I blow out a breath and shove a cookie into my mouth. Great.

The three of us go to my locker so I can dump my backpack and get my books for first period. I'm trying to find my mini stapler when there's a tap on my shoulder and I look over to see Cammie standing next to me.

"Hey," I say cautiously.

"Hi. Want to tell me why my dad slept at Oscar's last night?"

I take a step back at the sharpness of her tone and bang the back of my head into my locker door.

"Shit," I say, reaching up to press on the back of my head. Eyes watering, I grab the door and slam it closed.

"You okay, Amb?" Hannah asks from behind me.

"Yeah," I hiss, gritting my teeth in pain. I look back at Cammie, who is glowering now. "He and Mom had a fight."

"About?"

I hesitate for a second. "The apartment stuff. He didn't know we were gonna be looking at them."

Her eyes narrow. "Whose idea were the apartments? Yours?"

"I mean, yeah, but—"

"God, I can't believe you, Amber!" Cammie says, shaking her head. "My dad was so excited to do this for you. He said he wanted to make it fair, and at first I hated that because why does it need to be fair when you're not his kid? But he said he wants us all to be family for a long time, and the more I thought about that, the more I—" She cuts herself off with a huff, eyes on the floor. "I thought it would be nice. And then you shit all over it."

"I didn't," I blurt. "It's just—"

But she's backing away from me. "I don't want to hear it."

She turns and hurries off down the hall without another word, right as the warning bell rings.

A hand settles on my arm and I look over at Hannah and Ryan, who are both watching me with worried eyes.

"Bathroom?" Hannah asks.

"I can't miss. If I get upset, I'll blame it on my head."

Hannah looks like she wants to argue, but Ryan cuts her off with a shake of his head. So she sighs and says, "I know that wasn't a great conversation, but I think you should try talking to her again. Explain it all."

"I don't think she wants to hear it, Han."

"Maybe not," Hannah says, "but you know she needs to." And with that, she links her arm through mine and walks me to class.

✻

I still haven't seen Jordan by lunchtime, and when the bell rings I'm so nervous about running into him and having him be just as angry as Cammie was this morning that I feel like I might throw up.

To avoid finding out, I linger in the hallway off the commons and send Hannah in to get my food, which she does with a deep sigh and a roll of her eyes that she doesn't make much of an effort to hide. She's barely been gone five minutes—so not long enough to make it through the à la carte line—when I hear her voice and two pairs of footsteps coming toward me.

"Look who I found," she says, coming around the corner and gesturing to the person behind her.

Jordan.

"Hey," I mumble, narrowing my eyes at Hannah.

"Hey," Jordan says, his brow furrowed in worry.

Hannah shoots me a reassuring smile as Jordan comes around her and over to me. "I'll leave you guys alone. Ryan's getting your food, Amb, but I'll put it in your locker if you don't come in to lunch."

"Thanks." She goes and then I look at Jordan. He's watching me carefully, studying my face, and I can't tell if he's talked to Cammie about my alleged mooching or not. So I blurt, "Have you talked to Cammie today?" and then immediately snap my mouth closed and stare at my feet.

"No. I did see Kevin leaving the Kleins' house this morning in either sweats or pajamas though. You okay?"

"Oh. Yeah." A lump rises in my throat, but I do my best to swallow it. "He and my mom had a fight. And Cammie hates me now, just FYI."

"What?" Jordan asks, raising his eyebrows. He grabs hold of my hand and tugs me closer to him. "What are you talking about?"

I take a deep breath and open my mouth to tell him it's nothing, to forget I even said that. But what comes out instead is . . . everything. Mom and Kevin's fight, the rental house in Lawrence, and my encounter with Cammie this morning that could not have gone more wrong.

When I'm done, I hold my breath, waiting to see what he'll say.

"That explains why I couldn't find either one of you this morning," he says finally. "I looked for you everywhere. But you've been avoiding me."

"No," I say, which is only partly untrue. He raises an eyebrow and I sigh. "Maybe a little. I just worried that . . ." I can't finish the thought. It feels stupid to tell Jordan I worried he'd pick Cammie over me, even though it's the truth.

"Yeah, I think Cam had the same idea." He leans against the locker bay and reaches for me. I only hesitate for a second before

I let him pull me close. He presses his lips to my hair and says, "You don't have to worry about me. I'm not going anywhere. Okay?"

"Okay," I agree, getting up on my tiptoes to kiss him. He kisses me back, reaching both hands up to cup my face, and I grab onto him like a lifeline, glad that in the midst of all of this, I still have him.

At least for now.

＊

After school I stop at home to pick up Buffy and then walk to Jordan's house. We've kept up our Thursday night tradition even though Ms. Ulbrich has decided he no longer needs an official editor, and tonight I'm more grateful than ever for that. We eat dinner with his parents and play horse until my fingers are numb and then go inside to watch movies and steal kisses on his couch. I stay later than usual and somehow fall asleep with my head in his lap. I wake up to him gently shaking my shoulder and his parents smiling at us from across the living room.

"What time is it?" I ask, my voice thick and scratchy from sleep. Buffy's on the floor at our feet, and she lifts her head when she hears me. I reach down to rub her nose, trying to gauge how long I was out.

"Almost ten," his mom says, while Jordan brushes my hair out of my face.

"Oh shit," I mutter, pushing myself upright even though all I want to do is burrow myself closer to Jordan and stay there as long as possible. "I've gotta go so I don't miss curfew."

"I'll take you home," Jordan says, shifting to the edge of the couch and reaching for his shoes.

We hold hands the whole drive, Jordan absently rubbing my knuckles with his thumb. But when we turn onto my street the circles stop and his grip on me tightens. And I know exactly why: Kevin's car is in the driveway.

"Do you want me to come in with you?" Jordan asks as he pulls in and puts the Jeep into park.

I shake my head and take a deep breath. "It's okay. They're probably both asleep already and forgot about the lights."

"You sure?" Jordan asks, and I nod. "Okay," he says, leaning in to kiss me. "Text me if you need anything. No matter how late, okay?"

"Okay," I promise, kissing him again and lingering for a long moment before I pull away.

The house is dark and still when Buffy and I slip inside, so I'm careful to keep quiet as we head upstairs. At the top of the landing, though, I stop short, because the door to the guest room is open and I can see from the hallway that one of the bedside lamps is turned on. I take a step closer and peer inside to find Kevin, still in his scrubs, putting a stack of folded khakis into the dresser.

"What are you doing?" I ask, stopping in the doorway.

He looks up, startled, then relaxes when he realizes it's just me. "Amber. I'm, uh, going to be sleeping up here tonight. And maybe for a little while. But don't worry, I'll use the downstairs bathroom to get ready. I don't want you to have to share."

The fact that he thinks I care about bathroom sharing when

there's so much else wrong with this situation is totally ridiculous, and suddenly I am so, so *angry*. At him for leaving last night and at my mom for not telling me what he wanted to do and at the million other things that led to this moment.

But it's late and I'm tired and I don't want to make anything worse. So I say, "Whatever. Fine," and take Buffy to my room, shutting the door firmly behind us.

thirty-three

The next few days *suck*.

Kevin is still sleeping in the guest room. Cammie is avoiding me and won't respond to any of my texts. And Mom is putting in long hours at the bakery, allegedly since they have a bunch of weddings coming up the next two weekends. I don't buy that as an excuse though. I know the real reason is she doesn't want to be at home right now, and I can't say I blame her. I'm spending pretty much every moment I can either at Jordan's or at Hannah's, just to escape the awkwardness.

Saturday morning at work I force myself to dredge up enthusiasm when I tell Stephanie about the Lawrence trip and my interview with Pet Universe. She's pumped for me, as expected, and seems totally convinced that I'll get the job.

"They haven't called me yet, but I'm sure they will any day now," she says.

I smile gamely at her even though hearing that Carol hasn't started calling my references yet bums me out even more than I already have been.

Saturday night Buffy and I do a movie night at Hannah's. She's in full pep-talk mode, so I mostly just nod and smile when she tells me that Mom and Kevin are definitely going to make up, and that I just need to try talking to Cammie again to set the record straight. In the middle of movie number two of the evening and lecture number five million, I find myself wishing Ryan had come over for movie night instead of going to a party with Megan. I could use a dose of his quiet right now. And his ever-present chocolate stash, because I am definitely in the mood to eat my feelings.

On Sunday I go to Jordan's for lunch, and afterward we play a few games of horse in the weak sunlight. When we can't feel our fingers anymore we go inside and down to his room, where he curls up next to me on his bed and lets me be quiet. It's the most relaxed I've felt since we were in Lawrence, which I can't believe was only five days ago.

"Has she texted you back yet?" I ask him finally, the same question I've been asking him daily since everything went down. I'm not the only one Cammie has been avoiding for the last few days. She's been freezing Jordan out too, and the knowledge that she's cutting him off because he's with me is the hardest part of all of this.

He shakes his head. "I left her another message yesterday and texted again this morning, but I'm still getting radio silence."

I can hear the hurt in his voice and tears prick the backs of my eyes because this is all my fault. "I'm sorry," I whisper. "I didn't want you to get caught in the middle of this stuff."

"You have nothing to be sorry for," he says, reaching out to brush my hair off my face. "Cam's the one who stopped talking to me. You didn't make her do that."

"I think I did though," I say.

"Amber. Stop. Okay?"

"Sorry," I say, pushing myself upright and avoiding his eyes. "I'd better go. I need to let Buffy out."

"Hey," he says, his voice low. "Don't be like that."

"I'm not being like anything. I really do need to get her."

I can feel him watching me, and I stay still, waiting to see if he'll push me on this or let it go.

After a long moment, he sighs and sits up too. "Come on," he says, getting to his feet and holding out a hand to pull me up. "I'll walk you home."

❋

It's Valentine's Day week and the whole school has been decorated in pink and glitter and hearts on Monday morning. The pep club has a table set up during lunch every day where we can buy carnations to send to people on Thursday, and it seems like every conversation I overhear in the hallways is about what people are doing for the holiday. Even Hannah has been caught by the bug, though she does her best to curb her enthusiasm in front of me.

The last thing I want to do is celebrate a day of love, since I am apparently a love ruiner of all kinds, but when Jordan says, "You're still coming over Thursday night, right?" at lunch on Monday, I can't help feeling a little intrigued.

"Why?" I ask, looking up from my nachos and narrowing my eyes at him. "You don't have something cheesy planned, do you?"

He smiles at me easily, apparently not mad at me for bailing on him yesterday. "Maybe. You'll have to wait and see."

That night after work I run into Kevin in the bathroom. He's brushing his teeth, and hurries to spit when I come in the door.

"I'm sorry," he says, mouth full of foam. "Claire was in bed already and I didn't want to wake her up."

"It's okay," I say shortly. "I need to brush too."

"Oh, here." He scoots over so that I have room at the sink, and after a moment of hesitation I step up beside him and grab my toothbrush out of the holder.

"Thanks." I reach for the toothpaste but then I stop, watching Kevin's reflection in the mirror as he starts scrubbing at his teeth again and spits into the sink. He looks tired. And old. And sad. Mostly that. And maybe that's what makes me say, "Kevin? Do you love my mom?"

Slowly, he sets his toothbrush on the counter and stares at me. "Of course I do."

"Then why did you leave that night?" I ask, staring down at my toothbrush and running my fingers over the embossed letters of my name. "She was just trying not to hurt me."

He's quiet for a long, long moment. And then he says, "Yes, she explained that. And you are absolutely right. Leaving that night was the wrong thing to do, and I'm sorry. For hurting your mom . . . and for hurting you."

My breath catches and a lump rises in my throat at this frank acknowledgment.

"It's okay," I say, looking up. But he shakes his head.

"It's not, and you don't need to tell me that it is. Okay?"

I nod. And then, because I've been wondering about this for days now but haven't felt like I could ask until this moment, I say, "So . . . a house?"

He laughs and the sound is such a welcome break to the tension that I find myself smiling in response.

"Yes," he says, leaning against the counter. "It's by Nineteenth and Iowa. Not big or fancy, but it's close enough to walk to campus and it has a fenced-in yard. Jeff said the renters living there now are graduating this year, so it'll be open August first. I sent Oscar up to check it out for me in December, since I couldn't make the trip myself. He knew right away it was the one."

"How much?" I ask, once I've had a second to take everything in. "Because I've looked at some of the listings for rentals in that area and I know I can't afford them on my own."

"I think you could make this work with your budget," Kevin says, serious now, and then he rattles off a number that I commit to memory so that I can crunch it later. He studies me for a second, then adds, "But your mom told you that I would like to pay for your portion of the rent, right?"

I'm shaking my head before he even finishes this sentence. "No. I'm not your kid, and if for some reason you and Mom don't work out, I can't . . ." I take a deep breath and try again. "I just can't take your money, okay? I can't plan on having it for something that means so much to me when you could just take it away anytime you want."

"I would never do that," Kevin says slowly. "But I understand."

"Good." Something about his tone makes me suspect that he really *does* understand. That maybe Mom told him about my rules, and why everything about this is so hard. But I don't want

272

to talk to Kevin about those details before I talk to her, so for now, I keep my mouth shut.

"Are you open to looking at the house, though? Because I think it would be perfect for you and Buffy. And Hannah, if she changes her mind about the dorms."

"I don't know." I look down at the sink. "I'll have to think about it."

"Of course," he says. "Jeff said he'd hold it for us as long as we need for you to decide what works best for you. No obligation. Okay?"

I nod, fighting back tears. I have a lot to think about, but that part can come later. For now, I decide to tell Kevin the truth. "I'm glad you're home, even if you are sleeping in the guest room. Just so you know."

He smiles. "I'm glad too."

He turns to go out the door that leads to the guest room.

"Wait!"

He looks back at me.

"Mom loves Italian food," I say. "Especially from Ti Amo."

"Ti Amo," he repeats.

"Yeah."

"That could be good for Valentine's Day," he says slowly. "Don't you think?" I nod and he smiles again. "Okay. Good night, Amber."

"Good night." I finish brushing my teeth and I go back to my room and put on pajamas and crawl into bed, patting the space beside me so Buffy will hop up too. She curls into my side and I run my fingers through her fur.

For the first time in days, I don't have trouble falling asleep.

The next morning when I pull into the school parking lot, Cammie's little blue Honda is only a few cars ahead of mine. A day ago I would've driven as slow as possible to avoid her, but that was before I talked to Kevin. When I woke up this morning after the first good night of sleep I've had in a week, I decided that Hannah has been right this whole time: I do need to talk to Cammie and my mom. I wanted to catch Mom first, but she was already gone by the time I got downstairs. So seeing Cammie like this feels like a sign.

I make a careful note of the row she parks in and pull into the next row over. I scramble to gather up all of my stuff and slam the door behind me, hiking my backpack up onto one shoulder as I power-walk up the row of cars. As soon as Cammie is within earshot, I say, "Hey! Wait up!" and pick up my pace to a jog.

Cammie glances over her shoulder and scowls when she realizes I'm the one who yelled at her, but she doesn't turn and run. Instead she slows her pace enough for me to catch up to her, and even gives me a few seconds to catch my breath before she says in a cold voice, "What do you want?"

"I wanted to talk to you," I say, panting a little. "About Jordan."

She stops short and looks at me. "What about him?"

I hunch over a little and grab at a stitch in my side. "You need to stop this bullshit freezing-him-out thing," I say. "It's rude and it hurts him and he didn't do anything to deserve it."

Her eyes widen in surprise, then narrow into a glare. "Cute, Amber. Throwing my words back at me. But this isn't the same thing."

"Isn't it?" I ask. "You're avoiding him because you were so afraid he'd pick me over you after something went wrong with our parents that you didn't even wait to see what he'd do."

"That's not—" she starts.

"Yes, it is," I say straightening up. "And do you know how I know? Because it's what I was so worried about before he and I got together. That he'd pick you." I watch her carefully for a second. "Luckily someone came over and talked some sense into me though. I figured it was time for me to return the favor."

Cammie doesn't say a word in response to this, but her face flushes, so I know I've made my point.

"Look," I say, when it becomes clear that she's going to stay quiet, "I told you the truth that the apartments were my idea because they were. I didn't know about the house when we went, but it doesn't matter because I would have wanted to look at other options anyway. For reasons that don't have anything to do with you or your dad. At least not directly."

Still, she says nothing. She just lowers her gaze to the ground and fiddles with the strap of her bag.

I study her for a second, and then I take a deep breath and decide to go for broke. "You know what you said in the hall that day? About how it would be nice if we were family for a long time?"

She gives a jerky nod.

"Right, well. I think so too. Just so you know."

Then I turn and start marching up toward the school without waiting for her to say anything back.

thirty-four

I keep my conversations with Kevin and Cammie to myself for the next two days, because I'm afraid that if I tell anyone I'll somehow jinx them and the things I said to Kevin and Cammie won't matter at all.

I also keep quiet because I still have the toughest conversation to go: my mom. I try to catch her after school on Tuesday, but she works late again and I fall asleep before she gets home. On Wednesday she's gone early in the morning and I have to close at work. But on Thursday night before I leave for Jordan's and she goes to dinner with Kevin, I finally catch her sitting at the little vanity in the master bathroom. She's got her makeup done for evening and she's wearing a dark red dress that is equal parts understated and va-va-voom, but her expression is so uncertain as she studies herself in the mirror that I get another stab of guilt as I watch her.

"Mom?" I say, and she startles and twists to look at me. The dangly earrings she's got on make little swishing sounds and glitter in the light, adding to the whole effect of her outfit. "Wow. You look amazing."

Her expression softens and the corners of her mouth tug up in a smile. "Thank you, honey. Are you leaving for Jordan's now?"

"In a minute," I say, taking a deep breath, coming further into the room and sitting on the edge of the giant whirlpool tub. "I wanted to talk to you first."

"Of course. What about?"

"I wanted to say I'm sorry," I blurt, before I lose my nerve. "About my rules. I never meant to hurt you, and I *never* thought you'd read them, but I know that's no excuse so please don't hate me. You don't hate me, do you?"

Mom blinks at me in surprise and then gets to her feet in a rush, coming over to sit next to me and looping an arm around my shoulders to pull me close.

"Amber, honey, *no*. I don't hate you, and you have nothing to be sorry for. I love you always, forever, no matter what. And *I'm* sorry. For so many things, but mostly for putting you in situations that led to you needing that list in the first place. I'm not proud of how the choices I've made in my love life have affected you, but I'm trying to do better this time. With Kevin."

"I can tell," I say. "And I appreciate that."

She squeezes me even tighter, but after a second she loosens her hold on me and pulls back to study my face. "I'm sorry for going through your desk to get the password that day too. I promise I wasn't snooping intentionally, but it is your private space and I should have respected that."

"I know you weren't." I sniff, wiping sudden tears off my face. "And just so you know, lately I'm not feeling like I need the rules as much anymore."

She pulls back so she can peer into my face, and when I smile at her, she smiles back. "You don't have to get rid of them just because I know about them, you know. They're pretty good. And funny too. That holiday dinner one is because of Aunt Marin, right?"

"Yeah," I say, and Mom shudders.

"Ugh, that woman was the worst," she says, and for the first time in a long time we laugh together. It feels amazingly good.

I get to my feet and take a hesitant step toward the door. "I'd better go. Jordan has something cheesy planned, apparently."

"That sounds nice," Mom says, standing up too and reaching to fiddle with one of her bracelets. "Kevin won't tell me where we're going."

"Don't worry, you'll like it."

She raises her eyebrows at me. "You're in the loop, huh?"

"She told me where to go," Kevin says, and both of us turn to find him standing in the doorway. He smiles warmly at me for a brief second before turning his attention to my mom. "Wow. You look fantastic."

She blushes and ducks her head while I laugh and nudge her with my hip. "See? I told you so."

"Yes you did," she says, taking a step toward Kevin. "Have fun tonight, honey," she adds, glancing back at me. "Be home by ten thirty."

"Okay," I say, as Kevin takes her hand and winks at me from the door. They've already started out of the room when I say, "Hey, Mom?"

"Hey what?" she says, turning around.

I take a deep breath. "I love you always, forever, no matter what, too. Okay?"

Her eyes are suddenly, suspiciously shiny. But she keeps her voice steady and her smile doesn't waver when she says, "Okay."

✳

Jordan is waiting outside for me when I pull up to the curb in front of his house.

"Hey," he says, coming out to kiss me as I get out of the car. He pulls back for a second, studying my face. "You look happy."

"I am," I say. "It's been a good day so far."

"Yeah?" he says, smiling.

"Yeah."

He bends down and kisses me again, soft and light. "I'll try to keep the trend going. Come on."

He leads me up the sidewalk and through the front door. I freeze in the living room, staring around at everything. There are candles burning all over the place and a little table for two is set up in the middle of the room. "Is this for me?"

"Yeah," Jordan says, grinning. "Do you like it?"

"It's perfect." And it is.

"I made you dinner," he says, his voice proud. He leads me into the kitchen to show me what he's cooked, and I stop short when I see mac 'n' cheese.

"From the box?" I ask, turning to smile at him.

"Yup. Kraft. That's your favorite, right?"

I get up on my tiptoes and kiss him. "Right."

Dinner turns out to be completely cheese-themed, which makes me laugh when I think of asking him if he had something cheesy planned. Mac 'n' cheese, broccoli and cheese, Cheetos, and bagels and cream cheese. It's perfect, except for one thing. The longer we sit here eating, the more distracted Jordan gets. And I can't figure out why.

"You okay?" I ask, finally.

"Yeah," he says, giving himself a slight shake.

"Okay." I don't quite believe him, but I'm feeling so good about tonight that I choose to let it go.

When we're done eating, I start to take our dishes into the kitchen. But Jordan waves me off. "Part of the deal is that you don't have to clean this up."

"But I want to help you."

He comes up behind me and wraps an arm around my waist. "And I appreciate that," he whispers in my ear, "but here's the thing. I can take care of it later. Because right now, there are other things I'd rather be doing."

His voice sends a shiver up my spine. "Like what?" I ask, twisting around so we're face-to-face, so close we're almost kissing.

He kisses me lightly and pulls away, laughing, as I try to deepen it. "Like giving you your present."

I take a deep breath to slow my heartbeat. "I didn't think we were doing presents."

"I know," he says, "but I found this and knew I had to give it to you." He goes over to one of the bookshelves in the living room and pulls out a silver-wrapped package. "Here," he says, holding it out to me as he comes back over. He scoots his chair around and sits down next to me and adds, "For you."

I open the lid slowly and stare at what's inside. Then I crack up laughing. It's a custom bobblehead of Jordan wearing a basketball uniform from our middle school.

"Where did you get this?" I ask.

He grins. "One of the parents had them made for the whole team at the end-of-season banquet in eighth grade. I totally forgot about it until I saw your collection. Figured you'd appreciate it more than I did."

"Oh, I will," I say between giggles. "It's perfect. Thank you." I lean forward to kiss him, but before I make contact he pulls away from me. "Is something wrong?"

"Yes . . . no, I don't know." He leans forward so his elbows are on his knees. He's not looking at me. "I have to tell you something."

A heavy feeling settles over me. I set my bobblehead aside and pull my knees up to my chest. "Okay."

"I had a meeting with Coach yesterday. To talk about Wichita State."

Understanding hits me and I smile at him even as my eyes start to water and my throat gets scratchy and tight. "They offered you the spot, didn't they?"

"Yeah," he says, his voice cracking a little. There's a long pause where we just look at each other. "I'm gonna take it. I sign tomorrow."

I give this watery laugh and swipe at my eyes. "I'll have Mom frost some basketball cookies for me to bring. That'll really be—"

"Amber."

"—good. God, I'm so proud of you. I told you watching you play is like magic, didn't I? I'm glad they could see it. Do you think—"

"Amber. Stop." He reaches out and grabs my shoulders and I

281

stop, focusing my gaze on his face. "Actually, there was a second thing I wanted to tell you. And a third thing too."

"Is that all?" I squeak. I'm not sure I can handle two more things. Not after the first one. Not after the past week.

"Yeah. Promise."

"Okay. Hit me."

He looks at me for a second and then he gets up and holds out his hand. "All right. But first we have to go outside."

"Okay . . ." I say, following him out to the garage. I watch as he opens the garage door and rummages for the basketball. "What does this have to do with the next two things?"

"You'll see. Come on. You first."

I miss, so Jordan gets the ball. He takes a hard shot, harder than usual, and when I miss again, he says, "That's L."

"What?" I ask, chasing after the ball as it rolls down the driveway. "What kind of horse are you spelling?"

But he smiles and shakes his head. "Come on, Amber. Just play."

We play, and he gets an L, and then I get a second letter and he says, "That's O," and my breath catches because I think I know where this is going now. I miss again.

"That's V."

I let the ball roll into the street and go over to him.

"What are you spelling?" I ask, my heart pounding in my chest.

"What do you think?" He closes the space between us and reaches up to brush my hair out of my face.

"Love?" I whisper.

"Love," he says.

"Why?"

"Because I love you," he says.

"Really?"

He nods.

"I love you too."

Saying that to him feels like freedom. Like its own kind of magic.

He kisses me and I breathe him in and it is everything, this moment. But then he lets me go and I remember that he had one more thing to tell me.

"What's the third thing?" I ask.

He grins. "The third thing was really more of a question. How do you feel about long-distance relationships?"

"Scared," I say, and his grin fades. But I am scared, and I can't lie to him about that even with the best of intentions.

"Me too," he says. "But I don't see us breaking up before August, do you?" I shake my head. I definitely do not see that happening. "That's what I thought. And since that's the case, I want to try to stay together. Making it work long-distance is less scary than not being with you."

Warmth sparks in my chest and starts moving through my veins, hot and slow. I reach up and cup Jordan's face in my hands. "I like that plan."

He sags in relief. "Good."

I have so many things I want to say to him, but I can't seem to find the words. So I kiss him again and try to pour everything I'm feeling into it, and hope he understands.

thirty-five

The next morning when I wake up, I roll over and stare at my Valentine's Day present—my own Jordan to keep always—for a long time before I get out of bed. I get a text from my actual real Jordan right after I get out of the shower that makes me tear up. It says, **I thought you said you didn't get me a present** and is followed by a screenshot of his text conversation with Cammie. There are two new messages from her to him, dated this morning.

Sorry for being such a dick for the past week, the first one says.

And then, a minute after that one, **Tell Amber thank you for the reminder, okay?**

When Buffy and I come downstairs, Mom and Kevin are both in the kitchen, leaning into each other over coffee mugs at the island. I stop short when I see them and Mom turns to look at me.

"Good morning, honey," she says, her voice tentative but happy. Behind her, Kevin grins.

"Morning," I say. "How was Ti Amo?"

Mom holds a cinnamon roll out to me. "It was good. Wonderful, actually." She gives me a small smile. "Thank you for making that suggestion."

I shrug and look away. "I thought it might help."

"You were right. It did."

Kevin clears his throat, and Mom and I both turn to look at him. "Your mother and I thought," he starts, and then he stops to raise his eyebrows at her. She nods and he continues, "Your mother and I thought that, sometime this weekend, maybe tonight after you get home from school, we could sit down and talk about your living situation next year. Together."

"Like, as a family?"

Mom shoots me a worried look. "Well yes, but—"

"Okay."

"Okay?" she asks, like she doesn't quite believe me.

"Okay. But can I eat first?"

Kevin laughs, long and loud, and Buffy gives a happy bark in response. It sounds wonderful after all the quiet around here lately. "Of course."

❋

At school the principal gets on the announcements at the beginning of third period, to say that anyone who wants to see Jordan Baugh sign to play for Wichita State next year can now head to the commons. Half of my study hall class leaves with me, and I can't say I'm surprised. Spring semester is always full of signings like this, but it's not very often that one of our classmates goes D-1.

I let the rest of my class push their way toward the front of the crowd and hang back, waiting for Hannah at the end of the hall like we planned. She shows up after a minute with Elliot, Ryan, and Megan in tow. All of them smile at the surprised look on my face, and Hannah hooks her arm through mine and leads us down the hall.

After a few minutes of everyone milling around and talking, the principal gets up on a little platform at the edge of the tables up front where Jordan's sitting and asks everyone to quiet down. Then he starts in on his speech. We're so proud of this student, such a fine athlete and academic, so honored to have these choices, et cetera. Hannah and the boys and I are back by the dessert tables, so I grab one of the basketball sugar cookies Mom frosted at warp speed this morning and hold it up for Jordan to see. He grins.

There's a tap on my shoulder and I turn around to see Cammie standing behind me.

"Hi," she says warily, studying my face.

"Hi," I say, exchanging a glance with Hannah, who gives me a thumbs-up. "Are you coming over this weekend?"

"I don't know," Cammie says, the words halting and slow. "Maybe."

"You should. It's better." Not perfect, but better. And I've learned to take what I can get.

"I'll think about it."

"Good," I say, and then we turn and watch Jordan sign on for his dream. I do a wolf whistle and Cammie does a weird cat-call and the two of us look at each other and grin. But that's not the best part.

The best part is that when I look back up front, Jordan is looking right at me. Or really, at me and Cammie. And at the sight of both of us together, cheering him on, he beams.

*

Over spring break in March, Mom, Kevin, Cammie, and I go to Lawrence to take a second look at some of the apartments I checked out and so Cammie and I can see the rental house Kevin's friend set aside for us.

I finally hear back from KU on my updated FAFSA the week before we leave. My aid package has improved a little, but even with that, the outside scholarships I've gotten, and the job I finally got offered at Pet Universe in the fall, I still won't be able to afford the house on my own next year without taking out any loans. So we make a deal: If I love the house, Kevin will add his name to the lease and pay the difference to make it work for me.

"You really don't have to do that," I say, but he shakes his head and smiles.

"I already set aside that money, Amber," he said. "It's on the table whether you live in this house or not."

And even though I'm still having a hard time wrapping my head around his generosity, I agree.

For the most part, Mom hangs back while we look, letting Kevin and Cammie and me do the talking. I laugh when Kevin looks in the kitchen cabinets at every apartment we check out. I'd thought Cammie was doing that because she was bored or mad, but I guess she wasn't. She got that from him.

We go to the house last, and even though I try to keep an open mind and a cool head, I love it as soon as I see it. It's tiny and old and the yard is overgrown with vines and weeds, but I can already picture myself living in it. By the end of the tour, I'm ready to tell Mom and Kevin that the apartment jig is up, that I want this place to be mine for sure. And then Cammie points out the basketball hoop hanging above the rickety garage door.

"You and J can keep up your tradition," she says, looking back and grinning at me.

I almost start to cry. I haven't told Cammie or Hannah much about me and Jordan's plan for next year, other than that we're staying together. But it doesn't matter. They both know I'm scared it won't work out. Hannah has been giving me pep talks disguised as regular conversations, but Cammie has stayed quiet about the whole thing. Until now.

"You'll have to come up with him sometimes," I say, once I'm sure my voice is under control. "Play a game with us, for once."

She shakes her head, her expression more serious now. "Those games are for you two. But I'll watch."

✳

The night we get back from Lawrence I take Buffy over to Hannah's house. We go out to her backyard, where she has a fire going in her parents' chimenea, and Buffy curls at our feet while we settle into patio chairs with plenty of blankets to keep us warm.

"Okay," Hannah says, looking over at me. "You ready?"

"Ready," I say, and I toss the piece of paper with the rules into the fire.

We wait until the paper has disappeared into a curl of smoke before we start on the next part of tonight's project, and it doesn't take much longer than that before we have a new set of rules. Better ones this time. Ones that make my mother smile when I go home and show her. Ones that I feel okay posting above my desk in my bedroom, so I won't ever forget what they say.

the rules, revised

1. Always keep your eyes on the horizon, but don't forget to look at the here and now too. Forest and the trees and all that.

2. Get used to introducing yourself to strangers. It's going to happen a lot, and you never know who you'll meet. You could get lucky. (Of course, if said stranger looks like a creeper, throw this rule out the window and run.)

3. Protect your plate at all large meal gatherings, holidays and otherwise. If you don't, you might run into an Aunt Marin situation, and things will get awkward real fast.

4. Learn to tell the difference between when to depend on yourself, and when it's okay to ask for help.

5. Stop worrying so much. You'll thank me later.

6. Remember you love your mom. I know it's hard sometimes (sorry, Mom), but do it anyway.

7. It's okay to guard your heart, but don't hold it so close that you miss out.

acknowledgments

This book wouldn't exist without the help, feedback, and encouragement of a lot of wonderful people, and I feel so lucky that I get to thank them here.

First, thank you to my editor, Emily Settle. Your enthusiasm for this book has been clear from our first phone call, and I am so grateful for your insight and support as we worked to get it ready to share with the world. Thank you for loving Amber and her people (and Buffy!) as much as I do. Their story is so much stronger because of you.

Thank you to Jean Feiwel, Lauren Scobell, Perry Minella, Morgan Rath, and the rest of the team at Swoon Reads HQ for making my dream of being a published author come true. Thank you to everyone who read, rated, and reviewed *Rules We're Meant to Break* on the Swoon Reads site. Thank you to Kylie Byrd. And thank you also to Katie Klimowicz for designing such an amazing cover. I wanted to pet it from the moment I saw it, and I'm still not over the fact that now I get to!

Eternal squish hugs to the Swoon Squad. Thank you for welcoming me into the fold, for answering all of my random questions, and for being such supportive, awesome people. I am lucky to know each and every one of you. Special shoutouts to Karole Cozzo and Nikki Katz for sharing their wisdom; to Sandy Hall, the best mentor I could ask for, who read an early draft of this book *and* all my long, rambly emails; to Melinda Grace, who came to my rescue when I got stuck in the middle of edits; and to Prerna Pickett for sharing her words, for reading mine, and for all the chats about this debut journey.

Thank you to all the dedicated people involved with Pitch Wars, both now and way back in 2014, especially to Brenda Drake for creating such a wonderful contest and community for writers. Thank you also to Margo Berendsen and Rachel Lynn Solomon, and to the Pitch Wars 2014 ToT for their support and camaraderie. And extra-special thanks to Veronica Bartles, who selected me as her mentee and whose invaluable feedback helped shape this story into the version I originally uploaded to the Swoon Reads site.

Huge thanks to my first two readers ever: Krystal Marquis and Brittany Driskill. Krystal, this book would not be what it is today without your notes and comments on those early drafts. Thank you so much for helping me find the good bones amidst all the extra plot tangles and word vomit. Brittany, I will never forget the day you found out I was writing a book and said, "Well, I want to read it!" Thank you for reading as I wrote, for encouraging me to finish the story so you could find out how it ended, and for the last twenty years (!!!) of friendship. Here's to many more.

I've found that I am a better, happier writer when I have a day job that I love, so I also owe a giant thank you to my coworkers for their support and enthusiasm as I've gone on this publishing journey. Thank you all for celebrating with me the day I got "the call," for asking how the whole editing thing was going, and for only teasing me a little about how much chocolate I eat.

Love and thanks to my family for cheering me on in life and

in writing. Thanks to my dad for all those nights we spent at Borders, reading together in the cafe; to my mom for fueling my love of stories from an early age; to my brother for keeping me in the loop on what's hip and what's not (aka probably not saying the word *hip* in this context); and to my in-laws for always asking about my writing, even when the answers were super boring.

To my daughter: Thank you for bringing me joy every single day. I love you as big as the world, and night and day, and everything in between. And last, to my husband, Danny: Thank you for all the dinners and the dishes and the loads of laundry. Thank you for listening to me ramble about my characters way past our usual bedtime. Thank you for believing I could do this whole writing thing long before I did. I love you more than words can say. And I totally borrowed all of Jordan's best qualities from you.

Check out more books chosen for publication by readers like you.

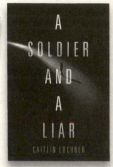

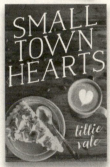
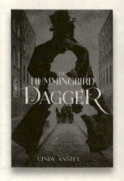

DID YOU KNOW...

READER
Swoon
READS
APPROVED

readers like you
helped to get this
book published?

Join our book-obsessed community and help us
discover awesome new writing talent.

1

Write it.

Share your original YA manuscript.

2

Read it.

Discover bright new bookish talent.

3

Share it.

Discuss, rate, and share your faves.

4

Love it.

Help us publish the books you love.

Share your own manuscript or dive between the pages
at **swoonreads.com** or by downloading the **Swoon Reads app.**